AT FIRST SIGHT

GLOBAL SECURITY UNLIMITED 1

SHARON MICHALOVE

COFFEE AND ECLAIR BOOKS

At First Sight (Global Security Unlimited 1) by Sharon Michalove

Published by Coffee and Eclair Books, Chicago, Illinois

sharonmichalove.com

Published in the United States of America

Editing by C. Marie

Developmental Editor Tex Thompson

Cover by Beetiful Book Covers

ISBN: 978-1-7369187-0-8

❀ Created with Vellum

Oxford, England 1993. An awkward American grad student runs into a gorgeous English undergrad with her bicycle. She's embarrassed. He's intrigued. They go their separate ways, but neither forgets.

Chicago, Illinois 2013. When Cress Taylor starts receiving anonymous threats, the successful novelist feels her world crashing down. Max Grant turns up at a book signing and wants to renew their fleeting acquaintance. Is the timing coincidental or suspicious? Should she fall into his arms or run like hell? Then the plagiarism accusations start.

A former spy now working for a global security company, Max Grant has always steered clear of relationships—until now. When he sees Cress in a TV interview, his curiosity ignites. Will the spark he felt twenty years ago burst into flame? Cress is a magnet he can't resist. As threats escalate to physical danger, Max feels driven to protect Cress. They must learn to work together if they want to stop her nemesis and find their happy ending.

In memory of Peter, who loved good music, foreign languages, and telling bad jokes.

EPIGRAPH

"Maybe love, at its essence, is being a mirror for another person—for the good parts and the bad. Perhaps love is simply finding the one person who sees you clearly, cares for you deeply, challenges you and supports you, and subsequently helps you see and be your true self. Love, I decided, is being a sidekick."

Penny Reid, *Capture: Elements of Chemistry*

It lies not in our power to love or hate,
For will in us is over-rul'd by fate.
When two are stript, long ere the course begin,
We wish that one should lose, the other win;
And one especially do we affect
Of two gold ingots, like in each respect:
The reason no man knows, let it suffice,

What we behold is censur'd by our eyes.
Where both deliberate, the love is slight:
Who ever lov'd, that lov'd not at first sight?

Christopher Marlowe, "Hero and Leander"

A NOTE ON SPELLING AND LANGUAGE

Just a word about spelling. Generally the book conforms to American usage. However, there are a few differences. For instance:

Whisky made in Scotland, Whiskey made everywhere else

Arse in Britain, Ass in the U.S.

Aeroplane in Britain, Airplane in the U.S.

And so on.

So the next time you visit the UK, wear a jumper, put your shopping in the boot, and leave your car in the carpark.

On the other hand, if you are lucky enough to live in the UK and you are visiting the States, wear a sweater, put your groceries in the trunk, and leave your car in the parking lot.

And for all of you, JL can give you some lessons on how to swear if you are French Canadian.

I hope you enjoy all the language variations throughout the book.

Chapter 1

Chicago, November 2013

CRESS

I STEP off the private elevator on the fortieth floor of One Financial Plaza in my new shoes. New shoes—ridiculous, bright-red, three-inch stilettos. What was I thinking? Oh yeah, Everest. Maybe the best restaurant in Chicago. One of the thirty or forty best in the U.S.

As I passed the store window, the shoes lured me in. My willpower collapsed like a condemned building. This is so not me. I've only had them a minute, and they're cheese graters for feet.

A quick roll of my ankle on the slick granite floor reminds me why I don't wear high heels. My arms splay and rotate like a windmill. The shopping bag that holds my serviceable flats and my small evening bag spins off my wrist. One shoe skids away. *Crap, crap, crap.*

The brown kraft-paper bag is a missile that hurtles toward a man on his way to the restaurant entrance. My mouth opens in soundless warning as it speeds toward an invisible bullseye.

Thunk. The bag bounces off his arm.

My evening clutch pops out, wide open. Damn that broken clasp. Change rings against hard wood and granite, spraying in all directions. I drop to my knees and crawl after the quarters and pennies. Out of the corner of my eye, I see him spin. A frown twists lush lips.

"You all right?" A foot in a brogue polished within an inch of its life rests a millimeter from my fingers as I reach for more coins. A shoe, a red shoe, is in his hand.

"Lost something?" He holds it out to me. His rich British accent sends a prickle down my spine. I tip my head up to give him a quick once-over.

A spark flashes through eyes that remind me of a walk on the beach in winter. A face bisected by a high-bridged aristocratic slash of a nose. My face tingles. The tips of my ears are warm. I grab the shoe, drop it on the floor, and hide my face in my hands.

"Fine. Sorry. I lost my balance and the bag escaped." My fingers muffle the sound.

He starts to bend down. His hand brushes my ear.

Zap. I scoot backward.

He straightens up and shakes his hand. "Pins and needles."

With effort, I wrench my focus back to the coins. My good luck charm, a Victorian black opal pendant I bought when my first book sold, slides back and forth against the sanded silk of my shabby chic little black dress. Streaks of fire reflect off the granite floor as it swings. I brush stray discs into the pile.

"Just trying to help."

"I can manage. Thanks, though."

A loud male voice calls out, "Hey, Max. Get in here."

"Half a mo'."

I wave him off. "Your friends want you."

"But…"

"I've got this."

"Sure?"

"Yeah. Go on."

He straightens, turns, walks into the restaurant.

I stare at his back in the perfect gray suit. The color matches his eyes.

The heap of change winks at me. I slip on my shoe and pick them up so no one else falls. Little traitors.

Purse and shoe box stuffed back into the shopping bag, I stagger through the wood-framed doorway.

The tables are all full. I have a word with the maître d' before he shows me to a center table where four people give me a standing ovation. Heat burns my cheeks. The other diners stare, some annoyed but more amused. In fact, complete strangers join in, clapping.

A group of men in elegant suits, ensconced at a round table positioned to enjoy the spectacular view, whistle loudly. My nose wrinkles. Over-aged frat boys.

With my unruly curls and my almost too-thin frame, all these people may wonder if I'm some D-list celeb. I look like a starved model, but the genes tell the story. I have the appetite of a hockey player after a game.

My best friend, Micki, leads the cheers. She is a statuesque platinum blonde, all curves, killing it in a red-sequined dress. My shoes would be perfect.

She glances toward my feet. "Nice shoes. New?"

"Yeah. Big mistake."

"About time you started to wear grown-up shoes."

We wear the same size. I'll wrap them up for Christmas. One pair of fancy shoes, light wear.

Her SO, Sam, is three inches shorter and resents it. My other best friend, Paul, is medium height with a monk's tonsure and average features that are transformed when he smiles. His wife, Ellie, is twenty years younger than the rest of us and short. I'm a giant next to her. She has long purple and pink hair with nails to match and a sharp, foxlike face.

The staff stare, wide-eyed, jaws dropped. I mouth an apology.

"Sit down already," Sam growls. He's dressed in an untucked plaid shirt and dark jeans. His gut hangs over his belt. I wonder how he even got in.

I slide into the chair pulled out by the table captain and check out the room. Enormous windows showcase the city. My best friend has done me proud.

I shoot a look at Sam.

"What? The only rule here is shirt and pants." A grin splits his face, and he pulls out an oversized clip-on bow tie. "Miche worried they might not let me in without a tie, so I brought this just in case."

He waves the red clown tie festooned with yellow, blue, and green polka dots in my face, clips the monstrosity to his shirt pocket like an obscene boutonnière, then runs his fingers through his sparse, straw-like hair.

"How many times do I have to tell you that a miche is a large loaf of bread?"

"You're tellin' me that's not a compliment? Bread is the staff of life." He smirks.

"Stop it." Micki raps his knuckles with her talons.

"Just teasin'." His fake drawl makes me cringe.

The rest of us sit down just as the sommelier comes over with a bottle of *Veuve Cliquot*, which she pours with a flourish.

Micki lifts her glass. "To Cress. Congratulations on being nominated for the most prestigious award a historical novelist can win."

"To Cress." They all lift their glasses and drink.

The server comes over. She seems slightly taken aback when she looks over our table, head slightly lowered, a glance from the corner of her eye. Her hand sweeps the air over the unopened menus. "Ready to order?"

Paul takes over. "We'll have the tasting menu with wine."

"All of you?" She picks up the menus, almost as if she wants to hide behind them.

"Yes." Paul gestures around the table. "All of us."

Sam's face twists. "Why not a bourbon tasting?"

"Wine. What a great idea." Micki squeezes Sam's hand so hard he winces.

"Okay." The woman scuttles away.

Ellie, Paul's wife, tosses her hair back and sniffs. "What got up her butt?"

"She looks familiar somehow." Micki stares after her. Paul nods.

Sam gives a dismissive wave. "Probably she's worked somewhere else we've eaten."

Micki turns and cranes her neck for another glimpse. "I eat here pretty often with clients, and I've never seen her here.

My spine tingles. The way she seemed to hide was weird.

"What is this award?" Ellie's eyes are bright with curiosity.

My apprehension drains away and excitement bubbles up.

I reach for my water glass. My hand hits the stem, and it keels over. Water gushes over the table. Sam gets the brunt of the deluge.

"Christ, Cress."

"Sorry." I put my hands over my mouth.

"You're fire engine red." Paul blots his shirt.

People hover around, mop up the table, hand napkins to Sam, and pour me fresh water.

Once everything is back to a kind of normal and Ellie stops giggling, I go back to my explanation. My hand snakes out for my glass. Micki taps my wrist then moves the glass closer to my bread plate.

"About ten years ago, the *Société des Romanciers Historique*, an international organization located in Paris, decided to start an award for the best historical novel of the year. Not sure why their year is September to September, but anyway…" My voice trails off. I rub my nose.

Ellie goggles. "Do you have to be so pretentious, Cress?"

I catch my tongue between my teeth before I can stick it out at her.

"They named the award for two famous historical novel-ists of nineteenth-century France."

Her eyes glaze over. Why did she bother to ask if she isn't interested?

"Go on, Cress." Paul rubs his hand over his bald spot.

"Anyway, it's named for Victor Hugo, who wrote *The Hunchback of Notre Dame*, and Alexandre Dumas *père,* who wrote *The Three Musketeers*."

"Why is he called a pear?" Ellie's face looks totally innocent.

Ellie's gaze wanders around the room, but like a homing pigeon, her attention goes back to the group at the window table, lingers on the wolf-whistlers. I glance over. Four handsome men in their forties lounge in the black armchairs and sip cocktails. I peek at the man who faces our table— the guy I hit with my bag. Almost black hair, glasses, a blue Oxford cloth shirt with the top button undone and a tie, loosened. Check him out again. Squint. Can't be sure, but it looks like Balliol. A striking oval face, high cheek-bones, and a chiseled, squared-off chin. Movie star good looks.

Micki checks him out. "Hey, he looks like David Tennant with glasses and dark hair."

"Who?" Ellie looks confused.

"Yeah, Dr. Who." Micki throws her a wicked grin.

"Uh…" If anything, Ellie looks more confused.

"Just some British sci-fi. Let it go," Paul advises her.

I pull my eyes away and clear my throat. "It's a really prestigious award, and I'm one of the five finalists for this year."

"But the pear."

"P-E-R-E. French for father. Now stop being silly." Paul's voice is impatient.

Ellie's cheeks pink. Micki chortles. Sam is glazed over with indifference.

"I'll be on *Morning at 7* Friday to talk about the book and the award." The words come out in a whoosh. I slump and push back the damp curl that clings to my cheek.

Our server hovers at a nearby table. I finish my hurried explanation, and she moves off. When she realizes we've noticed her, a flush rises on the back of her neck.

Sam raps lightly on the table to get our attention and starts an interminable story about an art exhibit where he will show his "found art" installations. I'm a little ticked but not really surprised that neither he nor Ellie wants to know about the book. Micki and Paul suffered through everything while I hid in my cave to pound out words, occasionally creeping out to whine.

On and off through course after course of delectable Alsatian specialties and far too much wine, the fishbowl sensation waxes and wanes. The middle-aged businessmen glance over on and off. Maybe they expect firecrackers next. I catch glimpses of our server, who hovers around the tables near us far more than she needs to. In the end, I shake off the discomfort and celebrate with my friends.

By the time the mignardises and petit fours arrive with coffee, I can hardly move. Our server has disappeared from the room, most of the tables are empty. Paul signals to the maître d'.

"We're ready for the check." He flourishes his black AmEx card.

"Your meal has already been paid for." He gestures toward me.

"What?" Paul frowns.

"My celebration, my treat."

Paul and Ellie offer to drive me home to the far north side, way past their own house in Old Town. A bus home doesn't seem like a great idea. Don't want to cram into Sam's truck either.

At home, I put the new shoes in the box. *Remember, Cress, wrap them up for Micki.* I pull the dress over my head and hang it in the closet. I don't set an alarm.

CRACK OF DAWN. My head throbs and my eyelashes glue my eyes closed. Dorothy and Thorfinn jump on my stomach. Double whammy.

"Fuck. Get off." I push them to the floor. Four green eyes glare at me. Dorothy hisses. Bad cat mom.

I stagger into the kitchen and pull a large glass out of the cabinet. A prairie oyster and a couple of ibuprofen are just the ticket with a big glass of ice water the chaser. Dig a bag of frozen peas out of the freezer then shuffle to the chair in the living room.

The pain recedes and my stomach settles. Micki shows up and suggests we go out for a hangover reviver before she drags my unwilling body downtown to pick out a suitable dress for my TV interview.

At Strings in Chinatown, I order spicy tonkatsu ramen to clear my still-fuzzy head. This is probably the third hangover I've ever had, and the worst.

"I may never drink again."

Micki rests her hand on my wrist. "You still have a pulse. This will pass, and you'll forget all about it until the next time."

"No next time." I pull my hand out of her grasp and hold up it up to stop her. "This is the worst morning of my life."

"Three hangovers in forty-five years is nothing. You'll drink again."

I drop my head into my hands. "No way. Never."

She giggles. "Your birthday is soon—we'll get you drinking again by then."

I pick up the check. My best friend offered to take the day off from her busy law office just to help me, so it's the least I can do.

Chapter 2

CRESS

I try not to swivel in the makeup chair as someone pulls out the scrunchy and fusses with my unruly hair.

"Lots of nice curl. I like the way the gray is coming in." The assistant runs a brush through. "Okay to leave your hair down?"

"Sure. If it looks halfway tamed, I don't care what you do with it."

She grins, sprays something, and scrunches to bring out the curl. Pins the hair back behind my ears. Then she turns me to look at the mirror. Wow. The curls cascade down past my shoulders. Shimmers of silver shine through the dark brown.

"Beautiful." The assistant stands, hands on hips, lips pursed.

The mirror shows me someone almost unrecognizable. I'll never make a fashion magazine cover, but I don't need to be ashamed of how I'll look on TV.

"Thank you so much. You're a miracle worker."

She waves away the compliment. "All part of the job."

"Can I take you home with me?"

She pats me on the shoulder and moves to the next guest.

In the green room, I perch on a plasticized faux-brown tweed chair meant to be impervious to spills. A harp sound tinkles from my bag, and I root around to fish out my phone. There's a new text message, probably Micki.

I bring up the message.

UNKNOWN: Bitch, be afraid. So the world will know you're a thief.

The phone drops to my lap, the message sending a chill down my spine. My fingers grip the arms of the chair. My logical mind scoffs. Afraid of what? My primitive brain ignites my sympathetic nervous system. Hormones flood through me, heart pounding, muscles twitching.

I count to five as I draw in a breath, hold it for five seconds, breathe out slowly. Over and over until my heart slows and my muscles relax.

By the time another assistant escorts me to the studio, I've convinced myself it's a misdirected message, or a prank. I fold forward, raise myself one vertebra at a time, reset my shoulders, and march down the hallway, following the sharp taps of her stilettos. She looks like a brunette office Barbie in a strawberry-pink plaid suit that reminds me of the Chanel knockoff Micki was mad for last season.

We skirt thick ropes of cables strewn over the concrete floor as we move toward the set. I bring my fingers to my mouth, then push them down. *No biting*, I tell myself.

I'm placed on an uncomfortable beige couch that tries to swallow me in its embrace. The stuffing is lumpy from wear. The wool fabric that scratches the backs of my knees makes me shift every few seconds. My eyes water, but I resist rubbing them. No raccoon eyes today.

I pull at the hem of the jewel-necked burgundy dress I bought after I recovered from yesterday's hangover. In fashionista mode, Micki went through my closet and informed me that I had nothing to wear.

She must have channeled her inner Zsa Zsa Gabor. "I will make you look gorgeous, dahlink." Why couldn't she just pull out some cute, long-forgotten dress? No such luck.

At Macy's, she dragged me from one department to another for the dress, jacket, tights, shoes. Hours of trying things on. I would have grabbed the first thing that looked okay, but Micki made me try on innumerable outfits before she assembled "the one." I drew the line at underwear. No one would see that.

The uniform is intended to give me a little confidence, but I feel like a fraud. Imposter syndrome. The heat of the studio makes me wish I could shed the jacket as sweat beads at my hairline. Before I can stop myself, I run my hands through my newly styled hair. Rub my nose, which I'm sure is now shiny and red.

Crap. Why bother to have the makeup and hair person fix me up when I'm a mess within minutes?

I slip the notecards out of my jacket pocket. Tiny crutches that fit in the palm of my hand, invisible to the viewers. They are my TV lucky charms. Hope I never have to look down at them.

The host comes in. "Hi, I'm Kimmie." Her gaze sweeps from my face down to the tips of my shoes. "I've always wanted an Apple Watch."

"Welcome back to *Morning at 7*." The voice-over booms out in the background. Fingers clenched, I focus on the interview.

"Good morning, Chicago. I'm your host, Kimmie St. John, sitting in for Lyle Gordon. Our Book Nook guest today is Dr. Cressida Taylor, author of *Queen of Nowhere*, a biography of—" I look up as she pauses, glances at the sheet in front of her, then clears her throat. "Caterina Cornaro." She stumbles over the Italian. "The Queen of Cyprus in the fifteenth century."

Kimmie is maybe twenty-five and blonde. Her fuchsia wrap dress gapes slightly as she leans forward, and I wonder if her producer suggested that she needs to show a little cleavage. She glares at me as if her verbal stumble is my fault. I give her a tiny smile.

Her lips twist as she takes a second to scan the teleprompter. Game face on, she plows forward. "The book, which came out in August, has been nominated for the…the Hugo-Dumas Award for Historical Fiction. Congratulations on the nomination, Dr. Taylor."

"Thanks." I paste on a bright smile. "You can call me Cress." I push an errant curl out of my face and hope the viewers can't hear the slight giggle in my voice.

"Okay, Cress."

She glances at the teleprompter. A prick of envy tickles my fingers as I clutch my secret cheat sheets.

"Could you tell us a little about the award?" She sounds edgy. Maybe she's new and this is her first biggish break.

I regather my cloak of confidence and tap the ragged nails of my unclenched hand against the arm of the couch.

"Sure, Kimmie. It's an international award named after Victor Hugo and Alexandre Dumas, two French historical novelists of the nineteenth century, established in Paris ten years ago. A nomination for the award is an honor, especially because the 1923 silent movie with Lon Chaney senior and the 1936 remake with Charles Laughton of Hugo's *Notre-Dame* were favorites when I was a kid."

Her jaw drops. Does she think I'm old enough to have seen them when they came out?

"That's *The Hunchback of Notre-Dame*? I thought it was a book." She emphasizes hunchback as if I am a dullard who doesn't know the correct title instead of the overeducated showoff who has to use the proper French title.

I roll my eyes, hoping against hope the home audience can't see behind my glasses.

Kimmie presses on. "I understand you attended Oxford University in the '90s."

She makes it sound like the Stone Age. I suppose twenty years might seem that way to someone who was barely alive then. I hope the target audience is a bit older. I clear my throat and launch into my potted bio.

"After I finished my master's at the University of Illinois, I was lucky enough to receive a Rotary scholarship. The opportunity to study at Somerville College from 1993 to 1997 was a real gift. To be at the same college that produced writers like Dorothy L. Sayers, Vera Brittain, A. S. Byatt, and Margaret Forster was amazing, and a DPhil in history provided the basis for my career."

Kimmie looks confused. "DPhil? I thought you had a PhD."

"Oxbridge speak. Doctor of Philosophy. Americans say PhD. Makes us sound more 'cultured' since American universities use the Latin version."

We're both fixed on the teleprompter. She swings her gaze to me and goes off script.

"Why did you decide to write historical novels rather than find a job at a college or university?"

Snark, snark.

I flinch. My instant reflex is to ask her why she chose fluff TV over something more serious. I don't.

"Getting an academic job isn't easy. I had some savings and always wanted to write, so I decided to try my luck."

"You say you are a medievalist, but your first novel is about polar exploration. How did that happen?"

NO, NO, NO. Move her to the Cornaro book. That's what I'm here for. I look her in the eye. My love of exploration history overrides my good sense.

"I was inspired by Beryl Bainbridge's *The Birthday Boys* about Scott's final expedition. I even got a fellowship from the National Science Foundation, so I was able to go to Antarctica for research."

"What sort of research can you do there? Check out the penguins?" She sounds dubious.

"The chance to visit places like Scott's Hut, McMurdo, and the Ross Ice Shelf. I learned to create descriptions that allow the reader to see the place."

I stop and chance a glimpse down at my lap. My fingers are twined so tight they're turning white. I loosen my grip. *Don't stare at the crumpled cards.*

Kimmie saves me. "Your current novel is about the Queen of Cyprus. Tell us about that."

I move my shoulders up and down to get the stiffness out, rein in my enthusiasm.

"Venice is one of my favorite cities, and the first time I was there I saw Gentile Bellini's painting of the Procession in St. Mark's Square in the Accademia Gallery. The canvas takes up an entire wall and was painted as part of a commission of nine paintings for the *Scuola Grande di San Giovanni Evangelista.* What captured my attention was a tiny figure of a woman who faces one of the doorways of the Basilica.

After I discovered who she was and her tragic story, I wanted to write about her."

Kimmie's lips tighten. Too much gush. The director gives a hand signal.

"Tell us something interesting about her in a sentence or two."

"Sure." Hand on my chest, I take a deep breath. *Remember to condense.* Fat chance. Words spill out.

"The Venetian government used Caterina as a puppet to control the sugar trade on Cyprus. After fifteen years, she was exiled to the Italian mainland." I come to a sudden halt as I run out of air.

"Well, your book sounds fascinating." Kimmie sounds sweeter than a mouthful of Skittles. "I wish we could chat more, but we're out of time. Congratulations on your book award nomination. Dr. Cressida Taylor will autograph *Queen of Nowhere* at Women and Children First in Andersonville tomorrow from five to seven PM."

The director motions that we are done; the lights come down. Relieved, I am guided back to the green room. I plop down on the couch, exhausted, my head in my hands. My mouth is dry with failure, and I scrabble in my bag for the tin of Altoids. The icy mint fails to soothe.

I rub my temples. I need this award, but I'm not sure I deserve it.

A small table filled with water bottles catches my eye. I grab one and manage to unscrew the stubborn cap. My hand shakes and I spill most of the bottle down the front of my dress. I wrestle with another, gulp the cold liquid. Two more bottles get shoved in my bag.

My stomach heaves at the thought of my close encounter of the less-than-friendly kind with plastic Kimmie. Water under the Michigan Avenue bridge now. Shaky from the adrenaline crash, my stomach roils. Need to sit down and have coffee before I collapse into a puddle.

Outside, I breathe in the cool November air. A film of despair lacquers my skin. The idea of a bus home to stand under the rain of a hot shower appeals. Maybe if I stand in the shower for an hour, the stickiness will disappear down the drain.

I jump off the pity-me wheel. Made it through the interview—a win.

~

THE SIREN SONG of caffeine sings sweetly in my ear. Coffee and pastry, breakfast of champions. I jog toward the seductive lure of black gold at Toni's Café and Patisserie. The revolving door deposits me at the sole empty café table.

Hang my coat over a chair back and make my way to the cashier. Plump for a large café au lait and add a croissant. They aren't my favorite—that would be eclairs—but I love them because the layers pull apart as I eat them. Easy on the stomach too. Chocolate and custard goodness will be my reward when I get some writing done.

I settle into the cafe chair and drink in the aromas of coffee, chocolate, and fresh-baked muffins. Eggs sizzle for breakfast sandwiches. The scent of a huge pot of onion soup wafts through the room. My mouth waters.

On a silver hanger stand, my order number sways on the small hook. A gleam on the metal winks at me as I set up my work area on the small, marble-topped round table. I dump my bag on the chair that holds my coat. I grab a small glass of water from the condiments table, a few napkins clutched underneath in my fist.

Just as I sit down to wait for my coffee, a woman comes

in from the Pittsfield Building lobby. She wears a wide-brimmed hat and a coat with the fur collar pulled up around her face. Odd since the day is relatively mild. She throws a few glances in my direction then looks down at her phone. I can't see her face clearly, but she seems familiar. Maybe a fellow bus rider.

I sip my water and gaze idly at the crowd. Dressed for a day at the office, colleagues share coffee and gossip. Lovers touch fingers as they reach for the same piece of toast. A guy in a pea coat is crouched over a keyboard. He raises his head suddenly. Catches my eye. Waves. A regular like me. Alone but not alone.

The harp trills. I grab my phone. Micki this time for sure. When the anonymous text message flashes on my screen, my fingers convulse and the phone clatters to the black-and-white-tiled floor. I can hardly bend over to pick it up without falling out of the chair. When I finally snag it, the message fills the screen.

UNKNOWN: I WILL make you pay.

What the hell? I should have just stomped the phone into pieces. My hand trembles as I throw it into my bag. Moisture collects on my neck and back. I hold my breath as if that will stop the tremors. The woman in the fur coat is gone—not that it means anything. She got her order and left. A waitress slides a large café au lait and a thick china plate with a croissant onto the table. I pick up the plate and offer it to the guy in the pea coat.

Chapter 3

MAX

"Hey, Max." My mate, JL Martin, yells over the noise of the treadmill. I shoot a glare at him. I'm in the zone with two more miles to go.

The sly grin on his face is too much. He knows better than to interrupt me when I'm running. I slam my fist on the control panel and grimace as pain runs up my arm.

No sotto voce response. I pitch my voice for maximum effect. "What the fuck?"

"Isn't that the woman we saw the other night at Everest?" He gestures toward the enormous TV that dominates the room.

Clay Brandon, former whiz kid and founder of our company, Global Security Unlimited, looks over. He owns the apartment building we're in, and the gym we're using. "Yeah, I think so."

We're in a large space on the roof of a high-rise east of

The Drake Hotel, right off Lake Shore Drive. Clay lives in one of the two penthouse spaces. He converted this part of the roof into a gym, outfitted with four treadmills, a couple of bikes, and weightlifting equipment. Three of the walls are glass, and one is masonry. The other part of the roof is dedicated to a garden area.

I look over at the huge screen that dominates the rear wall. Coincidences happen all the time, especially when you live in a big city, and when you go to a destination restaurant.

Two women sit on couches that face each other in a TV studio. A logo in the corner announces *Morning at 7*. One is a young blonde who tries not to look bored. The other, who looks like she's in her late thirties, pushes forward on the slanted sofa as she struggles to keep her feet on the floor. It is the woman from the restaurant. Her shoulder-length curls are tamed and pulled back from her face. A film of makeup makes her skin look like porcelain, although I can see a flush rise up her neck as she fidgets during the voice-over. Her eyes, magnified by large round wire-rimmed glass, flash green, then amber. Her eyes... I focus in. What I see stops me in my tracks.

"Bloody hell." I hit stop and the machine, set at six miles an hour, bounces me forward. My knee hits the control stand as it judders to a stop. *Crap, that hurt.* I massage my knee and grab the rough towel hanging from the rail, pull off my glasses, and mop the sweat that pours into my eyes. I rub the towel over my head to keep more from dripping off my soaked hair.

Once I can see again, I turn back to the screen. Those eyes pull me like magnets. A voice in my head shouts. *This can't be happening. It's her.* It can't be, but it is. After twenty bloody years. Why didn't I see that the other night? She doesn't look that different after all this time.

My colleagues stare as if I'm some mythical creature they've heard about but never seen. From their reaction, these words must not be just in my head.

I'm gob-smacked. If I'm right, she was the girl in my dreams, at least until the nightmares drove her out.

Clay walks over and hits my shoulder. "You're white as a sheet."

Twisting to face him, I release my death grip. "I'm fine."

As I turn back toward to screen, the sudden rotations make lights flash in my eyes. I grab for the rail to steady myself.

Clay moves between me and the screen. He gestures to the snack bar at other end of the room. "Let's sit down for a minute."

As I follow him over, JL trails after. "*Que se passé-t'il?*"

He's French-Canadian and likes to throw in French phrases just to aggravate Clay, whose second language is code.

"*Je ne suis pas sûr.*" The flash of her hazel eyes seems imprinted on my retinas.

Clay fills a cup with coffee and turns with a scowl. "Knock it off."

I grab a cup of tea, add milk and a little sugar, turn a vinyl chair to face the screen, and collapse into it. "That woman may be someone I was attracted to at university."

"The blonde? She's certainly looks good if she's your age. I'd put her at twenty-five, not forty." JL winks at me.

"Are you mad? She would have been a baby."

"*Une blague.*"

Clay glares again.

"A joke." He clarifies for Clay with a nonchalant lift of his shoulders. "But the other one looks good, too."

"She didn't register the other night? Why didn't you recognize her then?" Clay throws me a puzzled glance.

"I never really saw her. She was just part of that celebratory group."

We're all silent as the host mentions that her guest attended Oxford in the 1990s. Of course she did. I'm sure she's the girl with the bike, the one who sent me sprawling—and knocked me for a loop. It was 1993 and I was in my last year at Oxford. She looks older now, a sprinkle of gray in her hair, some fine lines around her eyes. As the interview unfolds, I am more and more certain.

"She knocked me down."

"Never pegged you for the love-at-first-sight type." Clay chuckles.

I can't help the hoot that erupts at the confusion on their faces. "My cousin, Guy, and I were on our way to the Randolph Hotel to meet our grandmother for tea when this girl ran her bike into me." I pause. I can't explain her effect on me.

They look at me as if tablets will come off the mountain.

"She knocked me down." My lips quirk. "With the bike."

Clay and JL smirk.

"I tried to introduce myself, but she was embarrassed and rushed off as soon as she could. She was a stunner. Her eyes…" I draw in a ragged breath. "Magnetic."

"Did you chase her down and ask her out?" JL's eyes sparkle with curiosity.

"We were late, and Guy dragged me off, complaining about careless, rude Americans. She wouldn't tell me her name." Thirsty, I grab a bottle of water from the bar. "All that term she was everywhere. At the Bodleian, the Covered Market, Carfax Tower. One afternoon, I saw her outside the

Radcliffe Camera and got up the nerve to approach her. This guy came over, took her arm, and they walked off.

"Over the years, a memory would pop up, especially when things went wrong. Wondered how my life might have been different if I'd gone for it." I rub the towel through my hair again. I smooth my hand over to push down all the little spikes. "I guess now I have a second try, if I want to chance my arm."

"Why didn't you try then, dumbass? Before you saw the boyfriend," JL prods.

"Because I was twenty and stupid. Thought I knew everything. I didn't see any way to have a career and a relationship —at least not a career as an MI6 operative. She was older and unlikely to be interested in me. Then life happens, and you realize you don't know anything."

"Other operatives in the services manage to have spouses and children."

"True, Clay. Lots of secrets, lots of divorces."

My attention shifts back to the screen. I ponder the shiver of fascination that coursed through me every time she crossed my path. A spasm hits my chest, makes me double over. I can't call Guy. We could have had a laugh over the way things have turned out. I mourn my cousin, my best friend, who died so young.

The tsunami of memories recedes, and I surface as the interviewer winds things up. "I wish we could chat more, but we're out of time. Congratulations on your book award nomination. Dr. Cressida Taylor will autograph *Queen of Nowhere* at Women and Children First in Andersonville tomorrow from five to seven PM."

"Where's Andersonville?"

"North." JL points.

"North." North is a pretty big place.

"Yeah. You drive north on Clark Street until you see the Swedish water tower. Why, you going to go?"

"Maybe. I'll have to see if I have anything on tomorrow." The directions sound rubbish, but if I decide to go, I'll figure it out.

"Kath likes that bookstore."

JL laughs. "I doubt a bookstore exists that your wife doesn't like."

"Just wait until you two have wives." He points toward the door. "Let's get cracking."

JL goes down to his flat, two floors below Clay's. I grab my stuff and use one of Clay's guest bathrooms to take a quick shower and change into my suit. When I come out, Clay is still in his workout gear.

"Want something?" Kath brandishes a spoon in my direction. "Oatmeal? That's what you Brits eat, right?"

"Most of the time we eat cold cereal."

"Like corn flakes?"

"Yes, corn flakes are very popular." I pick up the cup of tea she left on the counter and take two big gulps. "I really need to get to the office. I'll call Elephant and Castle and have them deliver something." The restaurant is just around the corner from our offices, and we order from them all the time.

When the lift hits the ground floor, I push out into the cool November morning, wave down a cab, and meditate on sparkling hazel eyes.

∼

THE BANK of elevators at the LaSalle Street entrance to the Rookery is just outside the atrium at the center of the building. The historic structure was designed by famed Chicago

School architects Burnham and Root in 1886, and the Light Court was remodeled by Frank Lloyd Wright in 1905. It's a popular venue for weddings and other events. As I wait for a car to arrive, I pace, my focus on the underside of the spiral staircase that starts on the second floor. It's a masterpiece of design, and I never tire of it.

Once in the lift, I push the button for our fifth-floor offices over and over until the doors finally close.

Still in my overcoat, I log into my workstation and drop into my chair. I drum my fingers. When the GSU home screen comes up, I tap my friend Google for all the intel. All these years wondering what happened to "the girl." I type Cressida Taylor into the search bar and hit enter. With such an unusual first name, I'm not confronted with millions of hits, and I locate her easily.

The first entry is a notice for her book award nomination; I click on it and quickly scan the page. The article praises the accuracy of her details and her writing's color and lyricism. The awards dinner is in Paris next April, and the winner receives a cash prize of €10,000.

A little nosing around gets me to her author web page. Plenty about her eight books, but very little biography. I assume she's not married as I read, "Cressida Taylor is a graduate of the University of Illinois at Urbana-Champaign and Somerville College at the University of Oxford. She loves gin, hockey, and classical music and lives in Chicago, Illinois, with her two cats, Dorothy and Thorfinn." A gin drinker, that's promising. And those cat names...where did they come from? Must be a story there.

One of the two photos on the site is her professional head-shot, which must be a few years old as there is no hint of gray in the deep brown curls that frame her narrow oval face. The hazel eyes that reeled me in twenty years ago are slightly hooded behind her glasses. The other picture is playful. She's on a sofa with her cats, posed like Egyptian deities.

My mind shifts as I speculate about the possibilities of other relationships, past and present. Her bio makes it look like she lives alone. Did she marry that guy who met her at the Radcliffe? Not out of the question even if she's single now. In a relationship? Likely, I think. After all, she must be in her mid-forties. My enthusiasm wanes as avenues open up that I don't want to travel.

And then, disconcertingly, I visualize a punt on the Cherwell with Guy. It was a warm spring day, daffs crowded on the bank. As I pole, I catch a glimpse of a girl on the towpath, arm in arm with another woman. Unruly curls blow in the breeze, her body hidden in baggy clothes—an Oxford Annie Hall.

Fingers intertwined behind my head in a stretch, I bend back in my chair. Back to the task. Born in Chicago in 1968. No other personal information. She's surprisingly private for a semi-public figure. Half an hour of searching and I'm not much further than I was when I watched her on the box. Time to stop, get back to the real work.

The major upgrade to our bank security software means meetings all day with the various computer analysis and information security teams. The clock on the screen tells me I have two hours to prepare. I lean over to grab the interoffice phone and ask my assistant to come in. French greetings echo when JL crashes down the hallway from his office in the WatchDog section of the building. He barges into my space and slams into the half-open door. The handle bounces against the wall.

"*Mon dieu.* Why are you still in your coat?"

"Got busy."

He snorts with laughter. "Checking out your woman

online." Arms folded across his chest, he narrows his eyes. "You look a little puny. Did you have your *petit-déjeuner, mon cher?*"

"Forgot." I glance at my watch. My stomach gurgles. "I have some free time. Let's go to Cochon Volant. *J'ai une faim de loup.*"

"Well, you certainly have a wolfish air this morning."

Jarvis Howard, our systems architect, calls through the open door that connects our space. "Food? Did you say food?" Then he pops through, pulling a ratty parka over an Oasis t-shirt and faded jeans. "Let's go."

As we walk out, JL claps me on the shoulder. "What's the plan for tomorrow?"

My stomach twists. This may be the worst decision of my life—or the best. "I'll go. In for a penny, in for a pound."

Chapter 4

MAX

My skin prickles. Cressida Taylor is a burr in my brain. I think of her as the Irene Adler to my Sherlock Holmes. Not that I'm much like Holmes, but she is THE WOMAN.

Excited? Terrified? Hopes raised or dashed. My emotions swoop like a roller coaster in a funhouse. My life isn't in danger, but my heart might be. I wiggle my jaw a few times then massage away the sudden pain that shoots through the joint.

Cress. A curl twisted around her finger, a nose rub, fiddling with her glasses. Jarvis called me out twice yesterday on my failure to focus. Daydreams, sneaky bursts of elation segueing into frustration that I can't bring my unruly mind to heel.

I roughly towel my hair while I obsess over how to present myself. After years as an MI6 operative, role-playing is second nature. I'm a series of façades, rarely revealing the real man behind the masks. Only my family is allowed to see under the surface, and even they don't know everything.

My need for secrecy made me an excellent operative, but real relationships were practically impossible. I'm not sure how he does it, but JL is the only outsider able to pry open the oyster.

In the end, I decide to be the cool guy, a reader with an edge, but not slide into hipster. I put on a blue Oxford shirt over a long-sleeved gray cashmere tee, black straight-leg jeans, and handmade boots. A leather jacket completes the ensemble.

I look over at the box of contact lenses then slip on my glasses. I should probably just give up and wear glasses all the time as the lenses become intolerable after the first hour. Probably a good thing I don't need to change my eye color anymore. I jerk my mind away from unwelcome memories that try to trickle in.

Polaris Slingshot autocycle or Porsche SUV? The sports cars are at the garage, and I seldom take them out this late in the year. Chicago winter weather doesn't really lend itself to high-performance sports cars. No ice on the roads today, so I plump for the cool vibe of the Polaris and the intimacy of a two-seater. Useful if she lets me drive her home.

Even though I've lived in Chicago for six years, most of my time is spent in the Loop, so I set the GPS. With a house in Gold Coast and offices in the financial district, my usual area is defined between Lincoln Park, where I play with a local rugby club in the oldies division, and the Rookery, where our offices are located.

When I can, I try to escape to Road America and similar venues around the U.S. I like to drive fast. Not a good bet in the city. The traffic can be a real pain in the arse. Never have made time to check out all the neighborhoods. Now I have the excuse to check out a new area.

As I drive to Andersonville, the GPS echoes JL's instructions to drive north on Clark Street. A Swedish flag painted on the water tower comes into view. Thought JL was joking. I creep down the block between Foster and Berwyn. Dante should have had an extra circle for parking hell.

It's Saturday and everyone is out to shop and eat. Street spaces are crammed. I drive around the block a gazillion times and, finally, someone pulls out. I slide into a space a couple of blocks down from the store, put money in the pay box, finger-comb my hair, and rush toward the large purple awning that summons me like a beacon. I check my watch. Perfect. There is only half an hour left in the signing.

Hands in the pockets of my Schott shearling leather jacket, I send a mental apology to my headmaster for breaking the no-hands-in-pockets rule. I was always being called out for it in school, but I've never broken the habit. Too old to stop now.

A tall blonde woman in a large-brimmed hat and long coat with a fur collar pushes past as I open the door.

I jostle through the crowd, glance around for an exit, and find a small door with an exit sticker and a panic bar. More people have shown up than I expected, and they hang like this is a social club. The woman who knocked into me earlier stands in a corner. After a short staring contest, she sashays over and grazes my arm as she sidles closer. She reminds me of one of the servers at Everest the other night.

"Hi, handsome." She gazes at me like she's a hawk and I'm a tasty rabbit. "A little tight, don't you think?" Her voice strains for a breathy, come-hither quality that makes me itch with irritation.

I back away to break the contact. "Yeah. I thought people would have their books signed and go."

Her mouth twists into a frown. "For some reason her books are very popular. Lots of people come to fangirl."

I note the bitter quality in that comment. "You're not an acolyte?"

"Hardly."

"Did you come for some other reason and the signing is an unwelcome surprise?"

"I saw her interview on Friday and came in to see what the fuss was about. I read the jacket copy and the first page. The book is trash. Why are you here?" She widens her eyes and bites her bottom lip. Her fingers reach out toward my arm. I pull back again.

I brandish my newly purchased copy of the book. "Christmas present for my sister. She'll appreciate that it was signed by the author."

"Your sister may wish you'd picked a different author. Dr. Taylor is in for a big surprise." Venom and satisfaction color her tone.

"What would that be?"

"Just look in the book section of tomorrow's newspaper."

We stand silent for a minute. Then, she holds out her hand. "I'm Tina."

"Max. You look familiar. Have we met before?"

"No." She backs away. "Nice to meet you, though."

"Don't you work at Everest?"

"No." Her voice scrapes like a knife being sharpened on a whetstone. "You must have me confused with someone else."

I file the lie as I watch her turn and push through the thinning crowd.

∽

CRESS

I GLANCE from the flyleaf of the book to the woman in front of me. She holds out her phone.

"Thanks so much. Can I get a picture with you?"

From the corner of my eye, I get a glimpse of a woman in a big hat and a coat with the fur collar turned up holding a book, not mine, who reminds me of the woman I saw in Toni's the other day. A prickle of unease runs down my spine. At least she won't turn up in the line. Just a coincidence. My phone is silent.

I focus on the woman in front of me. "Sure."

We need a staff member to take the picture. The woman in charge talks to an exceptionally tall man and gestures at the table. He goes to the register, presumably to buy a copy of the book, and she strolls over.

"What's up?"

"Could you take a picture of us? I'm crap at selfies. Short arms." I move out from behind the table while the woman drops her coat, the book, and her purse on a nearby couch and hands over her phone. We pose together for a couple of shots.

Crammed with bookshelves and tables, comfortable couches and chairs, Women and Children First is large, and its loyal clientele come for the books, the events, the cama-raderie. Today there are rows of folding chairs set up for the now-finished reading. Straight ahead is the children's book area with brightly painted shelves, books, toys, and games. The owners have been amazing promoters and supporters of women's writing since the original location opened in 1979. They moved to Andersonville in 1990, but the vibe is still welcoming and inclusive. I am always excited to have book signings here.

Back behind the table, I smile at several more women who are lined up to have books signed and chat. I love that people want to read my books. A bit surreal, though, that people want to meet me and talk about them. I send them out into the world as little emissaries. They are the performance. I am the backstage impresario. When the focus is on me, I'm always nervous that I'll do or say something stupid.

My throat is as parched as the Aral Sea. As I take a sip of water, the plastic cup slips out of my hand. Water spills all over the table and some of the display books.

"Fuck." I wince. "Sorry."

A staff member materializes with paper towels.

"I'll come in tomorrow and pay for the ruined copies," I promise.

Someone takes the book out of my shaking hands and produces a dry copy to sign. As soon as she leaves with her newly signed book, I breathe a sigh of relief and start to get up. Time to go.

"Excuse me." A deep British voice stops me mid-rise. The tall man I noticed earlier makes his way over to the table with a copy of the book open to the title page. I do a double take. Is this the same guy that was at Everest? Too many lookalikes today. Must be stress.

"Groucho Marx once said, 'Outside of a dog, a book is a man's best friend. Inside of a dog, it's too dark to read.'" He smiles and holds out his hand. "Hullo, I'm Max Grant."

Dark hair with threads of silver. Glasses with round, thin black frames magnifying silvery gray eyes. Runner's body. Movie star good looks.

I pick up a pen. "Do you want it personalized?"

"Yes, but not for me. It's for my sister, Margaret. Make it Meggy—with a y. She's a history buff."

"And you aren't? What a philistine." Where is this flirt coming from? I clear my throat. Roll my lips against my teeth. "Do you have anything in particular you want me to write?"

"Something cheeky? No, only if I was signing. Whatever you think would be appropriate. I suppose many readers want some personal message from the author, but I have no idea what that should be. Nothing fancy."

"Okay." I think for a minute, then pen something both trite and appropriate.

Dear Meggy,
From one history lover to another.
I hope you enjoy the book.
Cressida Taylor

I CLOSE the book and hand it back. He doesn't walk off. He stands there, staring at me. *What the...*

I squirm. "Is there something else?"

Crinkles form at the corners of his eyes.

"Saw your interview on television the other morning. I was at Oxford at the same time you were, and I think we actually met. So, I was very much looking forward to this event."

What? Oxford? An old friend of Kev's? Can't be—that was a lifetime ago. "Sorry, I don't remember."

"I remember a girl who looked like you, who..."

Just a pickup line. I scowl, hold up my hands, palms out

as if to push him away. "Stop. I don't appreciate this kind of come-on."

"No, seriously. I think you're the girl who knocked me over with her bike twenty years ago."

Now I'm at a loss for words. A red flush creeps up my neck. The room temperature zooms to at least one hundred degrees. I grab a handful of my promotional postcards and fan myself.

"The bicycle crash." The words drag out of me. "Oh God, how embarrassing. I've managed to bury that. Water under the bridge and all. That was you?"

"I thought the encounter was pretty memorable."

"If you hadn't said, I would never have recognized you."

"Do I look that different?"

"I don't know. I tried to blot the whole incident out of my mind." I don't tell him I used to see him around Oxford after that, but it was all look, don't touch. "A different place, different circumstances."

"When I saw your interview yesterday, I knew almost immediately. I guess the incident made more of an impression on me."

"I suppose so…"

His voice softens. "Come out for a coffee or something to eat. I'd love to catch up."

As if we knew each other well enough for a catch-up, when we never knew each other at all.

Micki, Paul, and Ellie crowd in.

Micki grabs me. "Finished at last. Thank the stars and planets. I'm starved."

"It's not much past seven, you idiot." I snicker. "How do you think it went? I saw all of you skulking in the corner."

"The reading was stellar, and you sold a lot of books."

"Certainly felt like it. My fingers are dead stumps." I stretch them.

"So many people. You ran over time," Ellie whines.

Chairs clatter in the background, a reminder that the store is closing.

"Past my optimal feeding time." Micki starts to dump pens into a box. Then she catches sight of the tall Englishman. "And who's this?" She looks him over.

"Hi, I'm Max Grant." Sticks out his hand.

"Weren't you at Everest the other night?" Paul purses his lips.

I was right. Max is the guy from Everest.

"We were celebrating," he adds.

Curious minds want to know what they were celebrating. A massive business deal? That the Bears won? A new baby? An engagement? He doesn't elaborate.

"He's an acquaintance from my Oxford days." I touch his forearm and wave some fingers of my other hand toward the threesome. "Max, these are my friends, Michelle Press, Paul Beam." A whisper-thin pause. "Paul's wife, Ellie."

"Nice to meet you, Max." Paul looks away in dismissal. "We thought we'd go to Hopleaf, Cress, unless you prefer Lady Gregory's."

"Hopleaf is good. I love their *moules et frites*." I'm relieved at the turn in the conversation. "Although the list of whiskys at Lady Gregory's is pretty impressive. I could use a drink."

"I thought…" Max snaps his mouth shut.

Ellie makes a face. "Can't you use English, Cress? Stop being so extra."

"Plenty of choices at Hopleaf, too." Paul shoots a glare at his wife.

Max smirks at her outrage. "*Vous ne parlez-pas Français,*

madame? C'est dommage." He makes a little Maurice Chevalier bow. Guess he's a smartass, too.

Ellie grimaces. "I know enough to understand that."

"Belgian beer at Hopleaf—yum." I give my lips a slow, ostentatious lick.

Micki's expression is gleeful. "All cleaned up. Let's scram."

"Off we go." Paul helps Ellie with her coat.

Then Ellie walks up to Max. "Who exactly are you?"

"I met Cress years ago at Oxford and took the book signing as an opportunity to renew the acquaintance."

"Oh, an old friend. Come with us then." Ellie invites him with what I can only call a mischievous quirk of her lips.

I stare in open-mouthed surprise.

"No reason for him not to come, unless he doesn't like the food." She grins and gives him a wink.

"Thank you for the invitation. I don't have any other plans and I'd love to catch up with you, Cress. Lead on." He takes my arm, and an electric sensation sparks from my elbow to my fingertips.

"Hopleaf is across and down the street." Paul frowns.

Ellie slips her elbow into Max's free arm and murmurs, "I noticed you and your group at Everest the other night. Four hunky guys in suits." She winks. "You can thank me later."

She releases him and pushes past with a toss of her pink and purple hair. The rat-a-tat of her heels lingers in my ears as she catches up to Paul.

Chapter 5

CRESS

When we left the bookstore, I was so startled by Ellie's comment, I let go of Max's arm.

As the group heads toward the bar, he seems to be hanging back. Eavesdropping?

I march arm in arm with Michelle, ignoring shadow man.

"I thought I recognized him from Everest. Do you think he's stalking me?"

Micki shakes her head. "Everest was probably a coincidence. Just a group of businessmen acting like adolescents."

"We were pretty silly too. That standing ovation..." I giggle.

"We acted like jerks twenty years younger. Inhibitions disappear after a few drinks." Max's voice comes out of the darkness.

Michelle stops and waves her arm in Max's direction.

"My guess is he saw you on TV, wondered what you are like now, and finds he wants to know you. Carpe diem and all that. Go with it. Who knows, maybe he's the one."

"Really, Micki, you're going there? After meeting this guy five minutes ago."

"*Coup de foudre*, baby, *coup de foudre.*" She starts singing, "*Voulez vous couchez avec moi, ce so*ir?"

"Stop it." I'm crying with laughter as Michelle shoves me through the door.

We all opt for the Belgian-style mussels and fries with aioli and heirloom tomato salads. I'm being super careful as I pour a bottle of English cider into a tall, slender glass.

"Trying to avoid it foaming up?" Max watches my trembling hand.

"Just trying not to spill it."

"Is that a problem?"

Glass and bottle safely on the table, I grimace. "Spill is my middle name."

He raises a brow.

"I spilled a glass of water all over a book at the signing. I can't be trusted with liquids around paper."

Michelle laughs. "You can't be trusted with liquids period. You've killed two keyboards and a laptop spilling coffee."

I'd been reaching for my glass, but my hand drops as if I've been burned.

Paul chimes in, "Even when you were a kid, you were always knocking glasses and cups over, when you weren't tripping over your feet."

"I'm a klutz. I admit it. There's no magic cure, so I stay away from people. And paper. And liquids of all kinds. Hell, I should probably live in a bubble, with a waterproof robot servant." I pick up my glass with exaggerated care and take a sip. Michelle takes it out of my hand and replaces it on the table.

"Do you spill stuff on your cats?" Ellie's tone is carefully neutral.

I flush. "Not so far. They're more likely to knock something over. But I do sometimes step on them, especially Dorothy. She's always weaving around my feet. You'd think they would learn not to lie down right in my path. When I step on their paws, the yowling is intense."

Ellie titters. "At least you can blame them instead of yourself."

Paul snorts.

Max sits across the table, chair tipped back, almost against the wall. Silver threads in his blue-black hair sparkle, and I want to run my hands through it. Too bad I don't see this going anywhere. A tiny Oxford connection from twenty years ago…we'd need more than that. There's a spark, but I don't have time, or the inclination.

Four orders of mussels arrive. Shared frites sit next to the shell bowl. Max devours mussels, greedy as he frees the succulent meat with his thumb and tips the shells into his mouth, tiny rivulets of juice running down his chin. I rub my neck, still sore from dinner at Everest. Teach me not to peep and look away at the same time.

Guzzling mollusks from their shells turns out to be erotic. Who knew? The way he throws back his head with noisy, unselfconscious slurps sends a shiver down my spine. I'm drawn by the soft moans. The sensual way his tongue flicks out to lick the drops from each shell. The clank of shells thrown casually into the bowl.

I can't tear my eyes away from his throat as he swallows.

He's putting on a show just for me. My desire to brush my arm against his is thwarted by our seating arrangement. Good thing. A touch, even an accidental one, would short-circuit my entire system. Water pools in my mouth. I wipe my lips over and over.

Micki nudges me with her elbow and hisses, "You're not eating."

I pry a shell apart and scoop a mussel out with my spoon.

"You look like you could eat him alive."

I choke when the mussel I just put in my mouth sticks in my throat. A hasty gulp of water dislodges it. I clear my throat. Acid bubbles up from my stomach.

I want to laugh, but my throat is too raw. I mime a blow-pipe shooting a poison dart into her heart.

She slaps my hand and hisses in my ear, "Eat your dinner and stop staring at him like you could swallow him whole."

Max slides another mussel into his mouth, swallows, runs his tongue over his lower lip. "So, Cress, what are you writing now?"

I jerk back. My project is too new, not ready for prime time. Only Micki, Paul, and my agent know about it. A sip of water gives me time to find the easy out. "Just getting started."

"But you know the subject, right?" he wheedles, and my heart gives a little jump.

He puts his elbows on the table and gives me a smile that feels like a hot chocolate cascade over vanilla ice cream.

A sudden prick of pain makes me check my cuticles. I stick a finger in my mouth to stop the bleeding.

Slurp. Two more mussels disappear. The shells clink against the shared slop bowl.

"Or are you taking a rest from writing?"

I glance around the table. Spoons and glasses are frozen in awkward poses. All conversation stops.

"Come on, Cress." Paul clinks his fork against his beer glass. "Spill."

"I do plenty of that already." I put down the glass I just picked up.

Ellie titters.

"Look, this is so new that I'm not even sure where it's going." Not true, but he doesn't need to know that.

Gaze lowered to the table, I realize there is still blood on my finger. I dip a corner of my napkin into my water glass and wipe it off. When I look up, everyone is focused on me and my finger. Silence is not my friend.

"It's about Moscow during the reign of Ivan the Terrible."

The words drop into a void. A little sigh. Just as I thought, no one knows who he is.

"Fascinating character." Max's deep voice breaks the dead air.

~

MAX

"DID THE SIGNING GO WELL?" I get the impression Ellie's looking for something to say rather than being interested in the answer.

Paul shakes an admonishing finger at his wife, then squints as he looks around the table. I guess he needs glasses. Pushing up my own, I wonder if he's vain. If so, why doesn't he wear contacts? I'm here on sufferance, so I don't ask.

The girls start to tease him. I learn that he's rumored to

make up in sexual prowess what he lacks in the looks department, and he reddens slightly. Ellie offers to supply more explicit details, but Cress and Michelle declare that they don't want to know.

"We've known him since we were eight," Michelle states emphatically. "He's like a brother. Thanks, but no thanks."

As the conversation fractures, Michelle turns to me. "Paul got divorced for the third time a couple of years ago. Several girlfriends, each younger than the last, and now it's Ellie. He has money and spends it. Probably why Ellie married him." She sounds both flip and a bit sad.

I turn my attention to Ellie. Pink and purple hair and a curvy figure with a foxlike face. She works in marketing at Lincoln Park Zoo. "Dorothy?" she asks Cress. "Isn't that an odd name for a cat?"

I'm surprised at the line of questioning. Unless Paul and Ellie had a quickie wedding and are newlyweds, shouldn't Ellie know this stuff?

"I don't think so." Cress sounds offended, and I can't help wondering if Ellie plans to poke at her all night. "As I've told you every time you ask, she's named for my favorite historical novelist, Dorothy Dunnett." She clunks a shell into the bowl and continues in an icy, lecturing voice. "I aspire, without much hope, to write as well as she did. And my other cat is named Thorfinn, for the earl of Orkney. Dunnett wrote a novel where she assumed he was the historical Macbeth. If he wasn't, he was a cousin. In any case, the willing suspension of disbelief is minimal." Cress leaned forward while lecturing Ellie. Now she readjusts in her chair, shoulders slumped. "Sorry, Max. Probably more than you want to know."

I guess she's referring to the relationships, not the information. "All fascinating." I turn to Paul. "Great place, this. Thanks for introducing me to it."

He grins, and I can see why he would be attractive to women. "Yeah, good food, nice atmosphere, no TV."

"So, you don't come often." I smirk.

Paul starts to answer, but Ellie breaks in. "We come too often."

"Too wild for an old lady like you, Ellie?" I'm more comfortable now, so I have no hesitation about winding her up.

Before she can respond, Paul breaks in. "Ellie likes loud music and wild dancing. In a word, clubbing. And we do some of that, but if we're out with Cress, well she likes quieter places where you can have a conversation." He looks down the table then beams at Cress and Michelle. Cress is waving her hands around, narrowly missing her cider glass. Michelle slides it out of the way.

"Ellie's so much younger, which makes it hard for her to put up with Cress and Michelle. They don't have that much in common, except me," Paul quips. "Micki, Cress, and I have known each other since third grade."

Ellie interrupts, "What do you do for a living, Max?"

Her question is reasonable, but I need to think about how much I'm willing to reveal. "I used to be James Bond." My tone is joking, even though the words are almost the truth.

She giggles.

"I head up CyberSec, the tech arm at Global Security Unlimited."

"Really?" Paul leans across the table. "Our bank uses your security software."

"Works well for you, I hope."

"We're looking forward to the new upgrade."

"Clay plans to roll it out in early April. We have a few neat new features to unveil."

"Like what?"

"Wish I could tell you but they're top secret, mate. Sorry."

Ellie looks a little glazed and re-channels the conversation. "You said you knew Cress at Oxford."

"Knew might be a bit overstated. She knocked me over with a bicycle."

"Ooh, details, please."

"And that was the beginning of a hot love affair." Paul sniggers. Then his eyes narrow and he glares at me. "I hope you're not that douche who dumped her."

I shake my head and laugh like a drain. Cress looks up from her tête-à-tête with Michelle. Another shot of electricity goes through me.

"God no. She politely apologized and rode away. I occasionally saw her around Oxford during that year, but I yearned from afar. Then I didn't see her again until she was interviewed on that morning program the other day."

Well, at least I now know what happened with the Oxford boyfriend. I'm relieved.

With the mussels decimated, I'm on my second beer. Brandy for Paul, coffee with Cointreau for Cress and Michelle. Ellie sips another Bailey's on the rocks and looks more than a little tipsy. Paul tells me a story about the bar.

"There's this TV show called *Bar Rescue*." I raise an eyebrow. "It's a reality TV thing where they come and renovate failing bars. The host was focusing on Chicago bars. He somehow thought Hopleaf needed rescuing and believed a renovation on the show would increase business. More exposure and that."

"Business looks pretty good. Is that because of the TV show?"

Paul laughs. "The owner said, thanks, but no thanks." He waves his hands around. "This place does just fine."

I put my glass down and tilt my chair back. "Was this a recent offer?"

"No, I think it was a couple of years ago. He said it would make the bar more generic, and he's not into generic. In fact, they expanded last year and put in a second bar and more seating. Not a remodel, though, an expansion since business is so good. People come here because they like the atmosphere. No sports TV, no gambling machines, just a great place for food and drinks. Why change it?"

I rock forward, knuckles against the table. "The mussels were as good as any I've had in Belgium. I'll definitely come back now that I know about it." I glance over at Cress. She and Michelle are chatting with Ellie, who is giggling and blushing.

Paul looks over at his wife. "Even though they said they weren't interested, I'm guessing they're talking about sex. Or maybe they're talking about you."

Ellie glances in my direction every few minutes, so maybe I am the topic. Cress frowns more than she laughs and seems a bit removed from the conversation swirling around her. When I look at her, she flushes and turns away.

The conversation segues from the bar to cars.

"What do you drive?" From his tone, Paul is repeating a question I missed.

A topic right up my alley. I pick up my beer and gulp some down. "I actually have a few cars—a Polaris Slingshot three-wheeled autocycle, a Porsche Cayenne Turbo, a Jaguar hybrid, a Lamborghini Aventador S, an Aston Martin

Vanquish S, a Bugatti Veyron, and a mint 1954 Mercury Monterey convertible."

"I thought my Corvette and Ferrari were pretty impressive. Which one did you drive tonight?"

"The Slingshot. That and the Porsche are the two I drive regularly, although the Slingshot isn't that practical in the cold weather, even with the optional cover. In the winter, the Porsche is the vehicle I drive most often."

"Motorcycles?" Christ, Paul is uncomfortably inquisitive.

Too many pictures. Scotland, my twenty-first birthday. Dad and I pose with his pristine vintage Ducati in the drive outside Grant House. Keys held up like a prize. And, twisted metal heaped in front of a bloodstained stone wall.

"I had a Ducati for a while."

"Wowsers. Why don't you still have it? Did you sell it?"

"I had a crash a few years ago." My voice is clipped.

Cress looks over, a question in her eyes. I focus on Paul but give her a sidelong glance. She answers some question from Ellie.

I rub my fingers through my hair. Short, thick hair like mine usually looks okay no matter what. "Anyway, no big deal. I have a two-car garage. The others are housed at the Collectors Car Garage. I take them out if I have a chance to drive at Road America or take a longish drive out of town. Maybe one day you could show me your fleet."

"I drive at Road America, too, but I have a house in the Old Town Triangle with a three-car garage, so I have my sports cars there along with the Audi I drive around town. I'd love to see your collection. Especially that '54 Monterey. We could meet at the Collectors Garage sometime. I'm thinking about getting another car, so I can investigate housing it there at the same time."

"No car for Ellie?"

"No, she hates Chicago traffic. It's Ubers all the way for her." Paul finishes his brandy, checks his watch. "Time to go."

Ellie gets up quickly but is a little unsteady. Her voice slurs. "Finally. I'm tired and we still have to walk Wally."

"Our Great Dane."

I stand. "Very nice to have met you."

I shake hands with both. Cress and Michelle wave.

"Byeeee," they trill like a flock of sparrows.

I scan the room: empty except for the three of us. I move over to Ellie's vacated chair, right next to Cress. I reach over to grab my beer.

Michelle flicks a glance at me and scoots closer to Cress' other side. "Are you still writing over at Toni's?"

Unreasonable jealousy washes over me. Who the hell is Tony? And why do I care? The thought that she's with someone unsettles me.

Cress responds, "Of course. Not too noisy, good coffee—and eclairs. How can you go wrong?"

The unexpected pain in my chest disappears and my hands unclench. A location, not a boyfriend.

"And so convenient, right, just off Michigan Avenue."

"Yeah, I can take the bus almost door to door. And I have lots of coffee and something to eat, so taking up a table all day is okay."

"Something to eat," Michelle mimics. "You mean you stuff your face with eclairs."

A dreamy look steals over Cress' face. "I love eclairs," she exclaims.

I put my arm over the back of her chair and ask Cress about her book.

"I don't want to talk your ear off." She glances at her watch. "Past my bedtime."

I grin. "Meet me for dinner one night this week. I'll ply you with drinks and you can enthrall me with tidbits about your writing."

"That sounds like fun." She sounds a little uncertain.

Michelle, having checked her phone, yawns pointedly. "Time is moving on. We should move. Sam just texted me. He just got back from the gallery opening and wonders where I am."

Cress scowls.

Picking up on Michelle's declaration, I ask, "Do you live far from here?"

"Not too far. We'll take the bus. Micki and I live two stops apart."

I frown, regretting that I chose to drive the Slingshot. Obviously, my planning was off base. I had expected to spend time with Cress, not Cress and her friends. I can't take both Cress and Michelle in the two-seater. They're a package deal tonight.

"Sorry I can't offer you a ride, but my car is a two-seater." Still, I want to keep in touch. "I've had a really great evening and I'd love to see you again, Cress. I am serious about dinner. Can I have your number?" God, the desperation in my voice.

Cress roots in her bag then hands over a card. "I don't answer calls from unknown numbers, but I respond to texts and voicemail." She's been fiddling with her phone and now looks around for our waiter. "Micki, we need to pay, and I don't want to miss the bus."

They push back their chairs and put on their coats, looking anxious when the waiter remains invisible.

"Don't worry about the bill. I foisted myself on you, so let me treat. It's my apology," I tell them.

"Oh." Cress looks nonplussed. "You don't have to do that."

"No problem. Just consider this my shout."

"Well, thanks. We appreciate it." She waves her hand to include Michelle.

"Night." Michelle wiggles her fingers, and they rush out the door.

They run across the street and scramble up the stair and into the newly arrived bus as I drop back into my chair, finish the beer, and order a double shot of Balvenie, straight up. I sip my drink, turning the card over and over.

My phone rests face down on the table. The picture gallery icon leads to a curated collection of horrors.

Guy stands with his back to the river. His thick golden hair gleams in the sun. Dressed in an ice-cream-pink suit, Christchurch tie wrapped around the brim of his boater like a ribbon, he's a dead ringer for Anthony Andrews in *Brideshead Revisited*. On stage, decked out in his tux, he leans against a grand piano. The score of "Dreams of the Cherwell" is held up like a trophy. Propped up in a hospital bed in striped pajamas. He's bald, hollow-eyed. A death's head at thirty.

I swipe quickly, and Guy's photos give way to dreams of Turkey. Fairy chimneys in Cappadocia, vistas from a hot air balloon while we sip champagne in the chill of an early morning, telling stories from the mosaics at the Chora Museum in Istanbul. Zehra in a sundress, lounging on the hood of a Jeep. Red hair flows down past her shoulders. A stolen kiss outside the Blue Mosque, caught by her brother Yavuz, our unwanted chaperon. Slow revolutions by whirling dervishes in Konya. The nightmare of an alleyway reduced to rubble in the Fatih district.

I slip off my glasses and grope for the drops that live in

the pocket of every jacket. Tremors make it hard to hold the lid open. Third time's the charm, and liquid drips into the corners of my eyes. Blink. Blink. Blot. Shove the glasses back on. Wipe my face with a napkin. Sip my whisky.

The fire from Cress' hazel eyes burns pools in the mirror of my mind, and I capsize into the depths. Maybe I don't deserve her, but I want her. The card fits neatly into a slot in my billfold. I savor the last dregs in my glass and melt into the darkness.

Chapter 6

CRESS

I crunch through an amalgam of sand, gravel, dead leaves, and ice pellets on the pier between Pratt and Farwell. The waves are so high I can't make it past the curve. I've never noticed the warning signal, flashing red from the top of the rusty metal tower, at the end of the pier.

The water laps at my shoes as I turn back toward the beach. I shove my hands into my heavy coat to warm up my blue fingers. As usual, I think my hat and gloves are in my pockets. Nope. The tips of my ears and my hands are numb.

I lean against the painted wall to admire the hanging clouds that swirl slate, ash, and pearl into bizarre peaks. Another bad night. I'm groggy and grumpy.

I'm motionless on the icy shore, and my emotions are in shreds. I gave him my number. Agreed to go out with him. What was I thinking?

As I trudge through the detritus piled up on the path, my

thoughts swing between daydreams about spending time getting to know him and wanting to stay as far away as I can. I didn't actually commit to seeing him again, did I? Urgh. I know I will regret the impulse.

As I turn away from the lake, memories rise up, as raw as they were twenty years ago. My watch chimes, warning me that I need to catch the bus. Thirty minutes of walking at Loyola Beach then sitting on the gaily painted wall, looking out at the lake, has resolved nothing, and now I need to be thawed out. I take a last look as angry waves, whipped by the wind, roll into the shore. Then I traipse home, knock the sand off my shoes, change out of my sweats into a favorite Blue Fish tunic over jeans, and catch the bus to Big Jones for a southern-style brunch with Micki.

Pawing through my bag for my Ventra card, I see a note pushed down into the pen pocket. I'm tempted to pull it out but, in the end, I decide I'll wait until I get to the restaurant. It could just be an old receipt, but somehow this random slip of paper seems more ominous.

I retrace my steps to Andersonville, scene of last night's encounter, and try to frame what I'll tell Micki. Maybe nothing if I can come up with an alternative conversation. Perhaps encourage her to relate some amusing courtroom anecdotes. Get my mind off Max, at least for a while. I do not want to gush or lament.

The yellow building sports accents in what I can only describe as a greeny blue. Rectangular tables face the bar and open kitchen, and I'm escorted back to one of the tiny rooms off the main space. Micki is ensconced on one of the mismatched chairs, sipping café au lait. As I'm taking off my puffy coat, she gazes at me speculatively.

"He's hot."

I feign confusion. "Who?"

Staring at me, she snaps. "Don't play the innocent with me. You know exactly who I mean, and you must admit he's hot. And interested in you."

I lean my elbows on the table. "You mean the guy from my past who suddenly popped up out of nowhere? Who stuck to us like a barnacle last night? Okay, I admit he's hot, but so what? Looks aren't everything. Really, they aren't anything. Look at Kev." We're both silent. Kev looked good, but inside he was rotten.

"I want to know what he's after. I don't doubt his Oxford story. Unlikely he would know about it if he wasn't the victim. But why seek me out twenty years later? Even seeing me on TV shouldn't make any difference. It's more likely the story you tell your pals over a beer. And frankly, all I remember from the accident was mortification. I thought he and the guy with him were arrogant snobs. I was happy to escape."

"He remembers you after all this time, but you don't remember a guy who looks like a black-haired David Tennant." She sighs dreamily. "That should have made some impression."

"David Tennant?" I shake my head, remembering Elie's response at Everest and playing dumb.

"You know, Doctor Who."

"Max is tall enough, but he definitely doesn't look like Tom Baker." I shoot her a side-eye.

Her voice is all not-this-stupid-conversation-again. "Not the old Doctor Who, the revived, hip series. Get your head out of the Middle Ages. There have been a bunch of Doctors since Tom Baker."

"Okaaaay." I give her a concerned look. "They haven't gotten rid of the blue police box to update the Tardis, have they?"

She laughs and shakes her head.

I pause, rub my arms. "You know I hardly ever watch TV."

"Except for hockey."

"Yeah, except for that."

"And you didn't recognize this guy?"

"I'd only been at Oxford for a week, I was late for a first meeting with my tutor, and I was constantly getting lost. I remember that he was very tall and seemed very la-di-dah. He was with another, slightly shorter blond guy who was sneery and called me a bitch. They were two upper-class English fools, and I was my usual clumsy self."

"Why did you give him your number?"

"I don't know. If he calls, I can block him."

Micki looks at me cross-eyed, a trick that always makes me chortle. Then she switches mood. "Hey, let's not worry about it right now. Here's our food."

I remember the scrap of paper in my bag. "I found this this morning, pushed into the pen pocket, but then I forgot about it." I pull it out, unrolling and smoothing out the scrunched-up piece of paper. My breathing grows ragged as I scan it, then I hand it to Micki. She reads it out.

Watch yourself bitch. You won't know what hits you.

"Wow. Do you think this is connected to the text messages?"

I can't talk. A sip of water makes me choke. Micki gets up to pound on my back.

"Stop." I drop my head into my hands.

"Must have been someone at the bookstore."

My suspicions roar back. "Oh my God, do you think it was Max?"

Micki's eyes widen. "Maybe…nah."

I push my plate aside. "I don't think I can eat."

"Want to pack up the food and go back to your place?"

Easy to take the shrimp and grits and the cornbread, but Micki's buckwheat and banana pancakes swim in a pool of syrup and melted butter.

"No, your pancakes will be cold and icky. Impossible to reheat."

"Your call."

I stand up, move into the larger room, and flag down the waiter. "Hi, can you pack up my meal?"

"Sure. Your friend's meal too?"

"No, she'll eat it here." I need to get my mind off this new message. And off Max. Small talk, the weather, movie gossip, hockey. "You're still with Sam?"

"Of course I am."

"He's not good for you." I want to shake her. Micki is the most clearheaded person I know—except about Sam.

"Come on. He's a tease, just kidding around."

"Relentless lawyer jokes and telling you that you need to lose weight. Only wanting to see you once a week then complaining if you make plans with anyone else. He's gaslighting you."

Fork halfway to her mouth, Micki's face crumples.

Crap. My heart drops to my stomach. "Sorry. I didn't mean to get so upset."

"Everyone makes lawyer jokes. Even Shakespeare." She forces a laugh. "Sam's an artist, so he needs his artistic space. And he travels a lot. It works for us, so stop riding me about him. It's not like we're getting married tomorrow or anything. Anyway, I'll be seeing a lot more of him. He's given up his apartment and moved in."

"What? Are you joking?" I'm grasping the edges of the chair seat so hard my hands hurt.

"No. He can't afford to keep both his studio and the apartment. Besides, he thinks we need to move our relationship up a notch. End of the discussion."

I want to tell her she's crazy, that this is the next move in his mind-control game and I'm worried. But I have to stop now, or I'll drive a stake into the heart of our friendship, which would play right into Sam's hands. Instead, I take a big breath.

"Besides the profile in the *Tribune*, I found out when I got home last night that I'm getting a big write-up in *The New York Times* next week, because of the award nomination."

Micki screams, then jumps up and hugs me. "That's so great. This will keep you on the bestseller list for months."

"I'm dreading the reaction to it."

She looks at me in surprise. "Why?"

"Dad." The word hangs there, as welcome as Poe's Raven.

BACK AT MY PLACE, Micki makes herself at home by the fire, pulling a thick stack of papers out of the brief bag she hauls everywhere. She grabs one out of my collection of oversized art books to use as a writing surface and uncaps her fountain pen; green ink flows across the paper. When you work for one of the top Chicago law firms, ridiculous hours come with the job. Just a typical Sunday afternoon.

Thorfinn sits on the table next to her, swatting at her pen as she moves it across the page. Micki is all about fine pens and elegant notebooks. She prints on heavy bond. Her collection of fountain pens is jaw-dropping. Even though I appreciate all the finer points of stationery, for my own work I go as paperless as possible.

If I print something out, I use cheap copy paper, reuse the back sides, and correct with Pilot pens I buy by the boxload. While she makes notations in elegant cursive, I'm doing Google searches rather than actual writing, muttering under my breath.

"Damn." I'm exasperated, forcibly keeping myself from throwing the iPad across the room.

"No juicy stories from your work in progress today?" Micki frowns.

"Not writing at the moment, and I have plenty of historical material. I've been looking up Max Grant."

"Because you're afraid or because you're interested?"

"Have we reverted to our kindergarten selves? Not afraid and not interested." I'm lying to her, and to myself, at least about the second point. "I'm curious, so I'm checking out this guy to see whether I need to worry about him. Not that I'm finding much."

"He's a void? How annoying."

"I'm not joking around. Someone threatened me then this guy from my past shows up. Shouldn't I be a little cautious? Especially after the note." I close the cover on the iPad and tap my fingers against it.

"Of course you should. But I don't think he's the source of the threats."

"Oh?"

"Somehow he just doesn't fit for me as your stalker."

"Why not?"

She taps her fountain pen against the papers on the table. "He's too visible."

"True."

"And what would be his motivation?"

"No idea. Revenge for the bike incident?"

"Yeah, right." Micki convulses with laughter.

"He's not completely invisible on the web, but he might as well be. Here's what I found." I start to read.

"This is from six years ago. 'Global Security Unlimited has hired cybersecurity expert Max Grant as their new Chief Information Security Officer. A graduate of Oxford University, Grant's extensive experience in programming, computer security issues, and administration will take GSU to a new level.'"

I pause. *Hmmm.* "Some stuff about racing cars. Nothing else."

"You knew he went to Oxford. Did you know his field was computers?"

"He mentioned it last night when Ellie asked him about his job."

"That's right. I forgot. I think I was more interested in his looks than what he does for a living." She snickers. "Maybe you should be too."

"His digital footprint could be all over the dark web. I haven't thought about him for years. Last night I remembered that I used to see him around Oxford that first year, at the pub, in the Bodleian, in front of the Radcliffe Camera, punting on the Cherwell once or twice. He gave off a very *Brideshead* vibe. The 2008 film with Matthew Goode comes to mind."

Micki grins. "Not the miniseries with Jeremy Irons?"

"Okay, that works too."

"Remember how you would sneak over to my house to watch *Masterpiece Theater*? Such a thrill when we were thirteen."

My face stretches in delight. "Paul refused to join us.

Thought watching British miniseries wasn't good for his nascent macho teenage image."

"You've been thinking about him. You might as well admit he's gotten to you."

"I didn't think he ever noticed me at Oxford, and I thought he was in a relationship with the guy he was with when I knocked him down." I pause again. "There was Kev."

"That douche."

"It took me a long time to understand that. And he's the reason I know you need to be careful with Sam."

She glares, giving me an adder flick with her tongue.

"Anyway, nothing else about Max. No other hits at all. The man could almost be a ghost."

"Just because he doesn't have much online presence doesn't make him a serial killer."

"Come on, he's a computer guy. He should have a huge internet presence."

"I'd guess the opposite. He probably knows all the dangers of having a lot about himself online, knows how to erase himself. Maybe you can winkle out more if you spend time with him."

My neck grows hot. I don't want to admit that the idea excites me. "I think, maybe, I kind of sort of agreed to go out with him. But who knows, he probably won't call anyway." The thought makes me surprisingly sad.

I struggle up from the couch, dislodging Dorothy, who's been grabbing at my arm while I type. She gives me the stink eye and flounces off, tail in the air. "Making some tea now." I am so done with this conversation.

"Ooh, can we have Marco Polo blend? I looooove that."

"With your current attitude, you don't deserve my *Mariage Frères* tea."

"Now you're being mean. You should treat me better.

After all, I'm one of your only friends. So come on, make the good stuff."

Filling the ancient Russell Hobbes electric kettle I brought home from Oxford after I took my degree, I frown at her wheedling tone. "Okay!" I yell, trying to be heard over the running water. "But only because I was planning to make Marco Polo anyway."

Everything is quiet as I carry on making the tea. Papers rustle. Micki is back to work.

"Oh my God." It's the shriek heard round the world.

A cup slips from my hand as I run out of the kitchen. Tea puddles as the china hits the floor, but I skirt the mess. "What's wrong?" I search the room for signs of a break-in or an enormous spider. No, it's much worse.

Micki holds up a newspaper page. I scan the enormous headline that takes up the whole front page of the Sunday book section.

Plagiarism???? Book Award Nominee Taylor Accused

Shrimp and grits spew out. When the cats come over to investigate, I get my ass in gear to clean up all the mess. Micki hands me a roll of paper towels and a sponge then starts to pick up the broken bits of the cup.

"You look as white as a piece of printer paper. I'll clean this up. You get over to the toilet before you barf again."

"Nothing in my stomach." I just want to hide in the closet and never come out.

"Bet there is. Scoot."

By the time I make it to the bathroom, another rising tide overwhelms me. What a waste of good food. Half an hour later, cold and clammy, I wipe my face and re-emerge to a perfectly clean floor, drowsing cats, and the scratch of Micki's pen.

"Bad memories?"

My head bobs up and down like a buoy in choppy water. "Remember when I was accused of cheating on my term paper junior year? Kind of the same thing."

"Wasn't that Tina's gang?"

"When wasn't it Tina's gang? Holding me down and writing slurs down my arms in fifth grade."

"The puke-green blob that slithered out of your locker in junior high? You spent an hour in the girls' bathroom."

I gag as if I just opened the door, but there's nothing else in my stomach. "So gross. I never liked Jell-O before that, but I can't even look at it now."

Micki hugs me, stroking my hair. "Paul and me, we're here for you."

I choke. Tears and snot drip down my face and soak Micki's silk t-shirt. She doesn't pull away.

Micki and Paul. We came together at eight, school misfits. The only ones to stick around when everyone else left. We're the Three Musketeers. One for all and all for one. What would I do without my found family?

Chapter 7

MAX

A whisper in the dark. A hand on my arm. "Max, where are you? I'm scared. I don't want to die."

I lurch out of sleep. Sweat pours down my face. I grab the towel that sits on the table next to the bed for just this scenario. I only make it as far as the armchair near the arched windows that look out on the garden area before collapsing.

This nightmare guts me, and yet I never heard those words in real life. I wasn't with Guy at the end. My brother Ian told me he was at peace and his last words were, "Tell Max to forgive himself."

Ten years on, this fictive cry haunts my dreams. Bile floods my mouth as I recall the rejection of my request to take leave. Guy may have forgiven me, but I haven't forgiven MI6, or myself.

A few minutes later, I crawl back into bed and start the relaxation exercises the therapist taught me, but when I close my eyes, flames rise up and the eye-watering pong of burning gasoline gags me. Sounds of explosions and gunfire rend the air.

I roll to the floor and crawl to the loo. Twenty minutes later, I'm collapsed on the cold floor, muscles aching from the extended episode of vomiting, wondering if I'll ever get up or just lie here until I starve to death.

Groaning, I push against the toilet and totter to my feet. I run my hand against the wall to steady myself and guide me back to the bed, but I don't plan to sleep.

Instead, I switch on the lamp, grab my glasses, and push my feet into slippers before shuffling down the stairs. I grasp the handrail as darkness surrounds me, even though my watch tells me it's already half past seven.

My phone is on the kitchen counter. Three missed calls, the screen scolds me.

I select voicemail and hit the first message. "Where are you, asshole?" Clay's grumbling baritone fills the room. "You're half an hour late. We're going without you."

"*Câlice.*" JL is nothing if not succinct. "Why didn't you call? Are you dead? Has your ghost answered? If you don't call back in the next ten minutes, I am coming over. And if you are still alive, you won't be for long."

"Hey, Max. Barons have a scrum at eleven. Hope to see ya." Senior rugby at eleven sounds just the ticket. I feel every one of my forty years today, maybe even a few borrowed from Dad.

No point in worrying about the first two. I'll apologize in the morning. I pour hot water over a tea bag and let it steep. Builder's tea. No refined leaves for me this morning.

I think over my Sunday plans. Sanctioned violence always helps assuage the residue of anger and guilt that lingers after nightmares. With plenty of beer after—perfect.

I anticipated having good dreams after seeing Cress. I have achieved my first objective, beginning the process of reconnecting. I didn't expect that stirring up the past would bring unexpected consequences. I haven't had an episode in months, so I thought I'd gotten past this. Evidently not.

Now that I'm awake, if not fully functional, my mind wanders to thoughts of Cress. I was enchanted by the care she took in drinking her cider, concentrating on putting the glass down without knocking it over. There was the way she pursed her lips to hold back the sarcasm when she talked with Ellie. Her ebullient enthusiasm leaked out in the few chances she had to talk about her cats, or food, or books.

The way she licked her fingers while eating cannoli makes my pulse hammer. An ache streams through me as I picture the times she shut down while conversation eddied around her. I was surprised at her vulnerability. I guess being a successful author doesn't have to make you a diva.

After another gulp of tea, I rush upstairs to put on my gear, but my bell goes. The video camera shows JL pacing in front of the door. I press the release and hear footsteps in the foyer.

"Max, you *con*, where are you?"

"In the kitchen."

"*Ostie. Saint ciboire. Tabernak.*" He pulls off his hat and gloves and throws them on the counter.

"Feel better?"

He looks me up and down. "Better than you. Spend the night on the floor near the toilet?"

"Hardly. Just a bad night's sleep."

"Nightmares? I thought you were done with those."

"I was wrong." My tea mug sits on the counter, the bag still stewing away. I slurp some down. "Sorry I didn't call. I overslept." The kitchen clock confirms I more than overslept.

"Clay was pissed off. I told him you probably had a sex hangover."

"I wish."

"No luck then? I'm sorry."

I fish the card out of my billfold. "I have her number and a lukewarm promise of a date."

"You're out of practice, *mon ami*." He slips an espresso capsule into my coffeemaker and rummages for a mug. "So, what is your plan for today?"

"Rugby."

"A little violence never hurts."

"It's an oldies game. Want to come?"

"I don't play."

"Cheer on the sidelines and stay out of the scrum."

He looks uncertain.

"We usually have shots on the regular."

"Whisky?"

"Only the finest single malts." I brandish the bottle I have ready as my offering.

"Let's go."

I look down at myself and crack up. "At least let me put on some kit."

"You mean a tight shirt and little shorts."

"Yeah, that."

As we pull into one of the spaces near the tennis courts, teammates spill out of other cars along with blokes from a couple of other clubs. We're all older players, so we usually have just a few scheduled games each year. Informal scrums are common because we all love to play. Today, we have more than enough to play a sevens match.

"Hey, guys, this is my mate, JL. He's just a Canadian onlooker."

"We'll still let you share the whiskey." Our captain shakes his hand.

"*Parfait.*" JL is all smiles.

We play a semi-rough game with breaks for shots of whisky. JL goes home, but I hang with my teammates. Plenty of pints at Kincade's make us forget the bruises. I'm physically exhausted and past thought of anything but rehashing the game.

There is something to be said for hanging out with a bunch of guys who are just sports buddies. The inconsequential chatter keeps your mind off other things, and these chaps don't ask inconvenient questions.

No personal shit allowed. No nightmares. Once I'm home, I make a cuppa and sit in a cold bath for ten minutes. Fingers crossed that will help keep the aches and pains manageable.

THE COLD BATH isn't enough. I wake up stiff and sore after I tossed and turned all night, no comfortable position for my battered body. The skin over my ribs is tender and multicolored.

My knee hurts, and I have one hell of a hangover from the nips of scotch during the game and the many pints after. Limping, I manage to drag myself to work and slump over my desk, hardly able to keep my eyes open.

A drumming noise sets itself up in my head. JL is hitting his fist over and over against the doorframe, trying to get my attention.

"Where the fuck were you this morning, *ostie de colon*?

You could have told me yesterday that you were skipping again." He growls. "We only waited five minutes this morning."

"Oh, the run." I groan and look up blearily at my colleague, who scowls like a belligerent middleweight boxer trying to intimidate an opponent. "Damn, I thought I messaged last night."

"Thought being the operative word." He looks me up and down. I sip my now-cold tea. "You look like something worse than what the cat dragged in."

"Too bad you didn't go with us for drinks. Then we'd be matched set."

JL frowns. "I had to be somewhere else. I told you."

"Couldn't have run today anyway." I get up and limp over to the window. Staring down at the street somehow seems like the logical reaction.

"I wondered when we left the field."

I catch my breath as a spike of pain stabs my temple. "After you left, we went to the pub to drown our sorrows and lament the sad fact that we don't play like the All Blacks. We're all old guys, at least in terms of rugby." JL looks at me. "What? We are not in the flower of our youth."

"I get that. Who are the All Blacks?"

I'm open-mouthed with astonishment. Everyone knows the All Blacks, even if they don't follow rugby. "The New Zealand rugby team. Brilliant players. Their pregame haka is awesome."

I push my thumbs against the back of my neck, trying to relieve the headache. "Word on the street is they may come to Chicago next year. If they do, we'll go, and you can see how superior rugby is to football."

JL shakes his head. "I'll take you to see the Whitecaps play the Fire. That's football. Good luck with that hangover."

In the office next to mine, Jarvis must have heard us. "Fuck that soccer stuff. Bears and Packers, guys. That's football." We laugh.

JL closes the door with a loud bang. Chuckles echo as he moves down the hallway.

After the Monday lunch meeting with Jarvis and Eric, our operations manager, I spend the rest of the day trying to work on the final paperwork for the contract we got last week and a pending project presentation for a potential client at the end of the week.

The regular ingestion of ibuprofen helps keep the pain at bay, but my thoughts keep drifting to Cress. I google Toni's. Rather than call her, I plan to drop by for a tête-à-tête tomorrow. I've already decided to take her to Navy Pier for the Winter Wonderfest as our first real date.

Loud voices filter in from the hallway. People are leaving. I settle back in my chair for another hour or so—nothing to rush home for.

A loud rapping on my frosted glass door makes me look up. Looking at my watch, I'm surprised that several hours have passed.

JL and Jarvis stand silhouetted in the doorway.

Jarvis shoots me a quizzical glance. "Max, why are you still here? We thought you'd be long gone."

"Why are you still here?" I stand up and move in front of my desk.

"I've been down in JL's office, shooting the breeze, and lost track of time. Just walked down to grab my coat." Jarvis smirks.

"Get your coat on, Max," JL growls. "We're going for a drink at Elephant and Castle."

I shake my head. "Thanks, but I'm—" They move in on either side and grab my arms. "Hey, let me go." I struggle, but not very hard. The thought hits me that having friends who look out for you may be a good thing. Except for my family, no one looks out for me but me.

"You need to unwind. We'll watch some sports and *mange un peu.*" JL licks his lips in anticipation. "I'm definitely up for poutine."

"Fine." I give them the basilisk stare. No reason to let on that I appreciate their concern.

I'll have one drink, go home, and figure out a time to check out this Toni's Cafe tomorrow. If I'm lucky, Cress will be there, writing. If not, I do have her number. I'm smiling as we walk out into the cold evening.

Chapter 8

CRESS

A quick peek around the room before I stick my finger in my mouth. No point wasting delicious custard if I can get away with it unseen. I stare at the jumble of letters on my screen. I'm on my third eclair.

I look at the lineup of little plates. When I got here this morning, I ordered five, hoping for a sugar high. Instead, I trudge through deep, loose sand. The grit rubs me raw. Every time I metaphorically empty my shoes, they fill right back up.

Much as I want to slough it off, ignoring my fifteen minutes of shame is not an option. My award nomination might be in jeopardy. I welcomed the higher visibility to solidify my standing, but now I'm a target.

If the committee decides to remove me, any acceptance I've garnered will be tarnished, if not trashed. I have a call in to Cal to discuss damage control. Maybe he can get the publicist to write a press release to refute the allegations.

No point worrying about the award, though, if my books are no longer in print. These assertions, even though they're fabricated, could cause my publisher to break my contract and withdraw my books for damage to their reputation.

I don't have to be guilty. The accusations alone could be enough. My livelihood could be destroyed.

I slap at my neck as if wasps are buzzing around. *Stop thinking about it!* I'm shouting in my head—or was it out loud? Oh my God. I can't tell what's real and what is just in my head.

I look around, my breath caught in my throat. No one is staring at me. Safe. I try to refocus on sixteenth-century Moscow.

I usually pull up a picture to put me in the mood for writing. It helps move my focus back to the past. When I was writing the Caterina Cornaro book, I had the Gentile Bellini painting of the Procession in Piazza San Marco as my background screen.

For this book, I usually look at a wood cut of a sixteenth-century map of Moscow, but today I need something with a little more oomph. I give up on the meaningless jumble of black marks and pull up a scowling portrait of Ivan the Terrible, but it morphs into Max.

I reach out and touch it as it shifts back to Ivan. Saturday night is still on my mind, but I don't have time to moon over a handsome face. The picture flickers back and forth between the two images.

Being a successful writer is a dream come true. I won a short story contest when I was ten, and that lit the fire. My writing identity is everything. I might be a failure at life, but I'm a success in my career. My achievements make up for my lack of family, my inability to sustain meaningful relationships, the personal rejection that follows me like Eeyore's little black cloud.

And Max. What do I do about this man who causes me to shiver every time I think about him? How much of my reaction is fear and how much is attraction? My emotional life is locked in a large chest freezer. I threw the key away when Kev walked out. Seventeen years later, I haven't replaced it. Cold is better than rejection.

Paul and Micki have tried to set me up more than once, but the few dates I've agreed to haven't worked out. Finding common ground never happens. I'm too serious, too boring, and not inclined to sit around at bars, which are evidently the chosen environment of these bankers, brokers, lawyers, and car salesmen.

Even the one hockey date didn't work out. The guy seemed to think I was a hockey novice and spent the evening explaining every play—wrong most of the time. What should, in theory, have been the ideal date was the most irritating. And then these guys all acted like I owed them. After that, I told them to stop trying to fix me up.

I touch my screen, and custard and chocolate smear everywhere. I've picked up the eclair and squeezed the hell out of it. Dammit, I need to get a grip. Cleaning up is tricky.

First, I put an empty plate in front of me and pour on some water to rinse the residue from my fingers, napkins piling up in a soggy hill. Then I pull wipes out of my bag to remove the residue. I turn off my screen and start cleaning it with another wipe.

The first passes only make the screen worse, but eventually I can turn the iPad back on. Ivan stares stonily at me before changing, like a kaleidoscope, into Max.

I can't believe I'm thinking about possibilities with Max. If I never see him again, I can craft him into a new memory, a better one than the Oxford fiasco. If he shows up, I'm not sure if I'll tell him to leave me alone or melt all over him like hot fudge.

My fears about trust and abandonment, my ridiculous lack of self-worth, my anger at being used by people who should have loved me are the ice wall that protects me. I force myself to work. Ivan glowers, not some smooth, sexy Englishman.

I peer at the words on the screen. Moscow is even more cold and uncouth than usual. Ivan the Terrible is being, well, terrible. My English merchants have become "weary, flat, stale and unprofitable" to quote Hamlet. I've been suffering from long-term jet lag since I got back from my research trip to Moscow.

The threats, and the encounters with Max, intensify everything a million percent. I hardly slept again last night.

When I did fall asleep, my dreams oscillated between twisted bicycle frames and swirling black newspaper headlines screaming *Liar, Thief, Cheat*, like something out of an old movie. When I woke, pillows were thrown across the room. The duvet was rucked, half off the bed.

I start to pack up my stuff when Micki's ringtone stops the spinning wheel.

"Hey, beautiful. Did you have delicious dreams last night?" Micki sounds way too cheerful for a Monday morning.

"Hah."

"What, no tall, dark, and handsome in your subconscious?"

"Oh, he was there." I can't suppress my irritation. "When I wasn't dreaming about my writing career going down the toilet, I was reliving the bike accident over and over, hearing Max and his friend laughing at me."

"Crap." Then she giggles. "Sorry, I couldn't resist. Have you heard from your agent?"

"No, I called him after you left, but he was probably out doing fun Sunday stuff. Since he hasn't responded, maybe he thinks watching and waiting is the best way to go. Or he's getting ready to dump me as a client." Tears slide down my nose. "I can't believe anyone would think I stole someone else's work."

"People will believe anything. I remember the first time you published an academic article and the editor insisted on checking every quote. You sent that huge envelope with copies of all the research, and all the t's were crossed and all the i's were dotted."

"Yeah, well, I'm sure the people who care will think no smoke without fire." My voice catches.

"Fuck. This is bad. I'd hang out with you, but I'm in court for the rest of the day. We need a few cocktails to cheer us up."

"Cocktails? It's only ten AM."

"The sun is over the yardarm somewhere, as the English like to say."

"Not over my yardarm." I sniffle. This is turning into an unwanted pity party.

"Think about getting together this evening. Got to go. Recess is over."

A hand appears, proffering a dry, clean napkin separate from the pile of wet, pastry-streaked garbage to wipe my eyes.

"Is that a friend of yours?" The waitress points toward the back entrance to the cafe. She's cleaning off the empty plates and café au lait cup, the repository for the mess.

I look up, but all I can make out is a shadow wearing a big hat, turning away.

A shiver runs down my spine. I take a deep breath. "I don't think so." I still the nervous movements of my hands. "Why?"

"She's been staring at you for half an hour."

I ponder Ivan's portrait, take a deep breath, and turn to my chapter.

Max

ELEVENSES. A favorite from my school days not usually indulged in these days, it's a family tradition I mostly honor in the breach. Whenever we were home for hols, Mum would call us all to the tea table for a slice of Madeira cake and a cuppa. Warmth runs down my spine as I think of hanging out with my sibs, comparing the cars we covet and the flights we want to try.

Some days I wonder why I don't just go home. I could work from our London office. Long weekends in the Highlands salmon fishing. Tempting, but a pipe dream. I chose Chicago, or Chicago chose me. A little flutter comes alive in my chest. Maybe there will be another reason, too. The possibility might be waiting for me at Toni's Café along with tea and a bikkie.

Cress. Fingers crossed she spends the whole day writing at this place. Christ, it's cold. I jog to warm up. The secondary benefit is that the sudden anxiety pouring through me may burn out by the time I arrive.

I race down Washington, then slow as I see the awning. After my heart rate comes down, I stroll past the plate glass windows several times, stopping as if to admire the Thanksgiving decor. I cast sidelong glances to see if I can locate her without having to go in. This is a trickier maneuver than I expected.

The sun's glare on the windows makes it difficult to see anything, and the large pumpkin and pilgrim decorations block a lot of the interior. On my fourth pass, I finally catch a glimpse of her biting into an eclair, oblivious of anything around her.

I push through the revolving door and step inside, slipping off my now-fogged glasses in time to see disaster strike. Cress is suddenly a mess of exploded pastry, chocolate, and custard running down her chest.

I start to grab a fistful of napkins and rush to her aid. Bad idea. I skirt her table and walk to the register in the back to order a cup of tea and some shortbread while I keep my eye on her as she blots at her shirt.

I have to crane my neck around a tall woman wearing a large hat who is standing in front of me, chuckling. Hmmm, she looks familiar. With her face obscured, I can't be certain, but I think it's the woman from the bookshop.

"God, what a slob."

"I feel sorry for the poor woman."

She spins on her spike heels.

I chance my arm. "Any luck at the bookshop?"

"Oh, hi. Bookstore, right? Last Saturday?"

She glances back and forth between me and the cashier. How can she stand so still on those toothpick heels? No shifting, no teetering. Not even a stance meant to balance her weight. I sigh. Note to self, ask Diana on next family Skype call.

"I found a great biography of Catherine the Great. Definitely a step up from the trash that woman writes." She flaps a hand over at Cress.

"You're next," the woman at the register calls out.

"A large black coffee to go." She turns back to me. "I don't know if you remember. Tina." She holds out a hand. I shove mine in my pockets.

"Max." I squint, trying to make out her features, but her collar obscures her chin, and the hat casts a shadow over her face. If she's hiding, why are we having this conversation?

Not acknowledging my snub, she adjusts the brim of the hat as if that was her intention all along. "I remember." She gives a coy giggle. "I'm a writer. I'm writing a historical novel about Catherine the Great. That's why I bought the biography. Research."

"Have you published much?"

"No. I have a few things being considered by publishers, but nothing out yet." Somehow, she manages to lower her face farther into her collar.

"Your coffee is ready." The cashier sounds impatient.

Tina grabs the cup. "Gotta go. See you around."

"Yeah, sure."

She minces off, hips swaying provocatively. I may not have seen her face, but I'll know her again. Funny. Mannerisms can ID a person just as fast as facial recognition.

I move up to the counter. "A cup of English Breakfast tea and two pieces of shortbread." She rings me up. I turn toward the table where Cress throws wet, sticky napkins on a plate. Then she crams her iPad, books, and papers into a huge courier bag.

I grab the number the cashier slides toward me and reach her table just as she throws the bag over her shoulder. There's isn't a second chair, but I put my order number down anyway.

I clear my throat, and she jumps, eyes wide. I burst out

with a joke. "There are three guys on a boat, and they have four cigarettes but nothing to light them with—what do they do?"

Cress gapes.

I rush to the punchline. "They throw one cigarette overboard, and the boat becomes a cigarette lighter."

I hope for a smile and maybe even an unwilling laugh. Instead, she scowls.

"Not funny?"

"What are you doing here?" The flush that spreads up to her cheeks is adorable.

I reach out and touch her arm. "Don't go. I was looking for somewhere to have a midmorning snack and saw you in the window. This looked like a good place, so I thought I'd stop in, grab something to eat. And here you are, so I thought I'd take the opportunity to chat." I give her a reassuring look as the lie rolls smoothly out.

Cress studies me carefully. Is she willing to buy it? She is silent for a long moment, looking me up and down, and I hope she is appreciating my runner's body and my well-tailored suit. Perhaps I've distracted her from dwelling on her own appearance: no makeup, hair mussed, baggy sweatshirt covered in pastry detritus. None of that bothers me.

Her face continues to flush, a slight tremor in her voice. "I'm leaving. Working at home is the best option today. This" —she points to the mess everywhere—"is my second eclair disaster this morning. A message from the writing gods that I shouldn't be out in public."

"At least stay while I drink my tea. Please."

Her gaze narrows. "No way. I've had a shit morning." She gestures to her splattered shirt.

"Nobody cares what you look like."

She laughs bitterly. "I care. I need a shower and clean clothes."

Desperate, I lean over the table, willing her with my eyes. "I read part of your book last night…"

Cress interrupts, her tone snarky. "I thought the book was for your sister."

"It is. I bought it for Christmas. In my family, we all read the books we give each other as gifts. No one is surprised if they look slightly used. Anyway, I like history, and your writing impressed me." I lean toward her.

Cress' posture softens slightly, and she pushes her bag to the floor, sitting down with a thump. My stomach uncoils. Sweat dries on my back. My jacket hides any wet spots. I seize an empty chair as a customer gets up and straddle it, my arms resting on the back, my chin resting on my arms.

"What most appeals to you about the story?" She waves her hands and manages to knock over my steaming cup of tea, splashing me liberally. "Shit. I'm sorry, so so so sorry."

I jump up to avoid the worst of the spill. Two staff members rush over, one with a towel, the other with a mop. I grab at the towel. The woman holds on.

"For the table." She gestures toward the mess.

I grab some napkins and start to mop myself off.

"I told you the universe is telling me to leave." Cress looks me over, assessing the damage. "Aren't we a pair." She falls about, gesturing at our mutual disarray, and I join in. "Are you okay? No burns. I hope I didn't ruin your suit. I wasn't trying to attack you. Or your tea." Cress' chair rocks back, crashes to the floor as she stands.

"Not a bicycle at least."

"I'll go now." Cress' voice squeezes. She backs up, hits the fallen chair with her foot, and tumbles to the floor. "I'm fine."

She rights the chair, picks up her coat, and struggles into it. I'm paralyzed as she picks up her bag and walks off, weaving around the tables of gapers. I can't take my eyes off her as, head down, she slams into another customer.

"Hey," he yells. "Watch where you're going."

"Damn it to hell. Sorry, sorry. I didn't see you."

His fists unclench and his face softens. "It's okay. No one got hurt."

"Please sit down for a minute." I touch her arm, and she lets me steer her back to the table. "I'll have to be careful around you, catastrophe girl."

"Yeah, clumsiness is my superpower." She pastes on a watery smile. "Sorry to have soaked your suit." Cress focuses on the large tea stain on my white shirt and the splashes down my light gray trousers. "Let me pay for the cleaning. And a new shirt."

"It's okay. I have another."

∼

CRESS

BACK IN THE CHAIR, I zero in on the big question.

"Look, I don't buy the line that you've remembered me all these years. What do you really want?"

"Maybe if we learn more about each other, we could be friends." From the predatory light in his eyes, being friends is not his goal.

I look at my watch. There won't be another bus for twenty minutes. "Fine. Let's do that." I eye him warily. "Are you in Chicago for business?"

"No, I live here. I work for a security company headquartered here."

"Security? Like bodyguards or the guys who monitor people in and out of corporate buildings?"

"We do that, but I specialize in cybersecurity."

"Really. Can you catch hackers?"

"Sometimes. Have you been hacked?"

"I don't think so, but I did get a threatening text message. Probably some crank who goes after authors. I got a threatening note too, after the book signing, but I wonder if both are from the same person..." I pull at my hair and chew on a curl.

"Have you spoken to the police? If you haven't, you should."

"They're looking into it as stalking."

"I'm glad you reported it. Electronic harassment is a crime." The words come out in a staccato burst. "The hacking I deal with is more about compromised security systems, but if you need personal security, just let me know. The other side of our business takes care of that."

I shake my head no. "Thanks, but I'm not at that point." I fish around for another question. "Do you like living here?"

"Yeah, I do. Chicago is probably in the top five of my favorite cities."

"So, you've traveled a lot?"

"Yes. I still have a place in London, but I've lived in Bonn, Prague, Cairo, Budapest, Istanbul, and other places. And Oxford."

"I haven't been back to Oxford since I finished my doctorate in 1996."

He nods but doesn't say anything.

"Did you grow up in Oxford?"

"No, I mostly grew up in London."

"Mostly?" I regard him curiously.

"My family is Scottish. We have houses in London and the Highlands. I went to public school, so I lived away in term time from when I was eight."

"Such a crucial year," I murmur.

"Why?"

"For me, everything changed. Sounds like it did for you too."

"My brother was already there, although since he's five years older, we didn't have much to do with each other." He sips his tea. "Why did life change for you at eight?"

"My mom died," I tell him, willing emotion out of my voice.

"I'm sorry."

I hastily change the subject. "If I went back to Oxford, I'd want to visit the Headington Shark."

"I didn't take you for such a frivolous person." He grins as I flush.

"Excuse me? Don't you know the point behind the sculpture?" I give him my Medusa look, but he doesn't turn to stone.

"Come on, you think there's a point to a slightly ridiculous sculpture of a shark crashing through a roof? I always thought it was a joke."

My lips twist into something resembling a snarl. "Well, you're wrong. The shark is a political statement. The house owner said, and I quote, 'The shark was to express someone feeling totally impotent and ripping a hole in their roof out of a sense of impotence and anger and desperation. The point was to say something about CND, nuclear power, Chernobyl, and Nagasaki.' I recognize that sense of outrage. I often want to rip something apart, even if in my case the personal overrides the political."

"I guess I shouldn't be so judgmental." He spreads his hands out in surrender. "Anyway, Oxford. When I decided to change jobs, I went back to take a DPhil in cybersecurity, but I've not been back since I came to work in Chicago six years ago."

He takes another sip of what must be lukewarm tea and grimaces.

"My brothers and sisters all live in London, except the eldest. Ian's in the diplomatic service, so he moves around. My parents live in the ancestral home, Grant House, near Grantown and visit London a few times a year."

I giggle. "Your family, the Grant family, lives in Grant House, near Grantown? So you own that part of the highlands?"

Max gives me a look, like I've lost my mind. He pushes back his chair and grabs his cup. "Be right back."

I watch him chat with the cashier, money changes hands, and he comes back to the table.

He turns the chair around and straddles the seat; his arms are folded and rest on the top. "Sadly, I get back too little, but when I do go, I try to pick a time when the racing is on at Goodwood, so I can go with my dad. No time for dreaming spires these days."

"Goodwood," I exclaim, a pleasurable warmth in my chest.

"You know it?"

"I love racing."

"Me too." Then he frowns. "Paul told me you aren't interested in cars, so I'm surprised you like racing."

"I don't."

"But you just said you loved racing." He looks perplexed.

I grin at his confusion. "I do love racing—horse racing. I have no interest in cars." I twist my face into a look of disgust. "Horses. *Black Beauty, Misty of Chincoteague.* I wanted to be Elizabeth Taylor in *National Velvet.*" I'm bouncing with excitement. "Ascot, the Derby, Goodwood. I watch the Triple Crown, too." I fan myself. "I've always wanted an invitation to the Royal Enclosure. The hats, the dresses, and everything. A chance to meet the Queen."

"I've met the Queen."

"Did you get knighted?"

He roars with laughter that goes on and on. When the paroxysm passes, he wipes his eyes. "Not likely. And she's very gracious."

I frown. "Back to Goodwood then. You go for the racing, but not the horses?"

"For me, Goodwood isn't horse racing. I go there for the cars." Exasperation colors every syllable. "There's a big event every summer, the Goodwood Festival of Speed."

He grabs my hand. Heat runs up my arm, and I try to pull away. He holds on tighter.

"Crushing my fingers," I gasp.

He drops it like a hot potato. "Sorry. Do you need ice or something?"

I wave my fingers to show him they still work. "Go on."

He smooths his hair and straightens his collar. "I have a few race cars myself. I'll take you up to Road America some time if you like."

My fizz flattens. This is much trickier than I expected. "I'm not interested in cars."

As the server comes over with his new cup of tea, he deflects. "Another coffee?"

"Nice of you to offer, but my first priority is to clean up." I gesture at the encrusted shirt peeking out from under my parka. I'm sweating. "There's a bus in a few minutes." I clutch my bag, in flight mode.

"I'll walk you out." He stands up and pulls on his over-coat. "Before you go, let's set our date. I thought we might go to Navy Pier for the Winter Wonderfest tomorrow night. Would that work?"

I freeze.

"Seriously, I'm not a creepy stalker, and I'd like to see you again."

"Why?"

"You're different."

I give a bitter laugh. "Yeah, I've heard that before."

"I want to see if I can change your mind about me. I like a challenge."

I pull out my phone. "On Wednesdays, I tutor in a literacy group from four to six at Harold Washington Library."

"Fine. I'll collect you at the main entrance about quarter past. "Do you skate?"

"Yes. Not all that well, but I can sort of manage. My balance isn't great." I think of my weak ankles and tendency to fall.

His mouth breaks into a big smile. "I'll hold you up." Then his phone starts ringing and he holds up a finger. "Yes?"

An agitated babble comes out of his speaker.

"I'll be there in a few minutes." He takes my hand, and we walk out.

When I get to the bus stop island, I turn and watch as his elegant backside moves down the street.

I notice a woman with a big hat and high fur collar standing in the doorway of the Pittsfield Building. I wonder if she's watching me.

My bus comes and I forget about her.

Chapter 9

CRESS

Home. I change into fleecy sweats and heavy socks and settle down to work with another cup of coffee. I need to salvage something from this shit show of a day, even if just clean clothes.

My thoughts pull back to Max. At Oxford, he was hot but too young for a serious twenty-five-year-old. That didn't stop me from noticing the ripple of his back muscles, the way his legs braced, and the flex of his biceps when he was punting. Now he's filled out. I imagine sculpted muscle rippling under his shirt, defined quads and calves. A runner's body for sure.

I could drown in the hidden depths of those soft gray eyes.

I wonder if his easy manner may be more façade than reality.

My phone rings. It's not a special ringtone like Micki's or

Paul's, so I grab it off the table. When I see the caller ID, I choke and decline. Dad. I knew he would come out of the woodwork once the award was announced, like a hound scenting prey.

He dumped us when I was eight, and the next time I heard from him was on my twenty-first birthday—the day I received control of the trust fund. I've blocked him in the past, but he just gets another number. Contacts list is my early warning system.

Cut out the toxic people. But what do you do when they come back over and over? *The Man Who Came to Dinner* amplified by *Groundhog Day*. My father is as selfish as Sheridan Whiteside, but not as charming.

Everyone wants something from me, or they leave. Or both. My parents, grandparents, my brother Tom, asshat Kev. I ignore the anomaly that my two best friends are still here after multiple decades.

I haven't had a relationship since Kev dumped me in my last year at Oxford. A few dates, one-offs. As soon as someone wants to get close, I back away. Until Max. What does he want? And why now? And why I am not running away?

I rebuild my ice wall, slab by slab. I'll take safety over warmth every time. Dad is persistent. After the fifth call, I turn off the phone, grab a throw, and curl up on the couch.

Buzz.

Wasps? They swarm around the rim of my cocktail glass as I share a drink on the beach with Micki. I disentangle my hand from the warm alpaca covering me and flap away the nuisance.

Bzz. Buzzzzzzz. Buzzzzzz. Bzzzzzzzzzzz.

The fog clears. The door buzzer, not an insect invasion. I sit up, roll my neck, and slip my glasses on. "Hold on."

Yowls join the incessant buzz.

The room is dark. I trip over the edge of the rug as I stumble to the wall speaker. "Who is it?" I cough as I push the listen button.

"Open the fucking door." Micki's voice bellows through the speaker.

I push the button until the door downstairs clicks open. Turn on all the lamps and close the blinds against the darkness. I need brightness tonight.

The sharp rap against my heavy wooden door alerts me that Micki has made the short climb to the elevated first floor. I pull it open, and she almost falls into the room, her fist still raised. "Hey, Cress, what the hell? You're not answering your phone."

I yawn and rub my fingers against my lips. "My dad called a few times, so I turned it off. Then I took a little nap for…" I check my watch. "Shit, a five-hour nap is so not good." I collapse into the armchair. "What a waste of a day."

"I'm here to make it better. Change into something not sweats. We're going to gorge on dumplings at Furama."

"It's late. I want to write a little more then chill with the cats, and the Hawks are on at eight."

"Unlimited dim sum. *Shumai, har gow*, pork buns."

I start to suggest we order out and eat in front of the television, but she's still talking.

"Sorry, I missed the end of that."

"And Sam, I said." Her voice is artificially bright, high, and tight. "He's meeting us there. Soon."

Sam's ringtone, Tim McGraw's "It's Your Love," breaks the sudden silence.

"Hey. Yeah. We'll be there soon. Just get a table."

I don't want to go out with Sam, not even for Micki. I want to talk about Max. Can't do that if Sam is there. I grind my teeth. "Just go without me. Or tell him something came up and we'll hang here."

"I can't ditch him. Not tonight. Not after I told him we could go."

Guilt. So much guilt.

"Sam will insist on sesame chicken and fried rice. Please save me from cliché Chinese food." She leafs through my book on John Singer Sargent watercolors.

I walk into the bedroom to change. "Okay." I hate the grudging note in my voice. "But you have to let me order. And Sam can't talk. He's got to be under the cone of silence."

"Oh goodie."

I re-emerge a few seconds later in a decent sweater and jeans.

"I'll make sure Sam eats but doesn't talk." She puts the book down and grabs her coat. "To the L."

As we rush out of the station at Argyle, I'm hit by the stench of urine, beer, and gasoline. I'm in such a hurry not to linger under the viaduct that I slip in the wet entryway and barely keep myself upright, scraping my palm against the brick wall. Micki, knowing I will just pull her over if she tries to help, backs up.

Once I'm steady, I hold my breath as we walk the block to the restaurant. By the time we run up the stairs to the highly decorated second-floor foyer, I'm puffing. Sam spots us as we exit.

"What took you so long?" His fake drawl drips acid.

"Had to wake Cress up. She was napping." Micki gives him an apologetic kiss on the cheek. "Thought you were going to get us a table."

The hostess comes up. "Three?" At Micki's nod, she picks up three menus, some dim sum sheets, and a few pencils. Sam's eyes follow every move of her backside. Micki fiddles with her phone.

Micki leaves the ordering up to me. She'll eat anything. Sam never wants anything I order, so I'm not surprised when he shakes his head in negation at every dish I propose.

"I want sweet and sour chicken, an egg roll, and fried rice." Sam hands his menu to the waitress with a smug grin.

She picks up the dim sum menu, checks the order. "Anything else? Hot tea?"

"Probably another round of dim sum. Tea would be great," I reply.

"I have a new joke."

No, no, no. Sam's lawyer jokes are so demeaning. I close my hands around the edge of the table, anchored so I can't run away.

"What's the difference between a lawyer and a prostitute?" Micki and I trade glances. "Too hard for you?" His lips twist with a nasty edge. "A prostitute will stop screwing you when you're dead." His guffaw booms out over the restaurant.

Heads swivel. My fists clench. His verbal abuse is destroying Micki. How can she stay with this asshole? He cuts her down at every turn. The "jokes" turn my stomach. I bite my lip and grab a dumpling with my chopsticks.

Micki silently pleads with me to say nothing and just leave it.

Sam talks all through his sweet and sour chicken while Micki and I share a pan-fried noodle dish and a large variety of dim sum options.

"Too many carbs and not enough protein. Gunna make you fatter. You ain't naturally thin like Cress." Micki winces as Sam grouses.

I know part of my prejudice against Sam is because he puts on a patently fake redneck persona, even though he is from Lake Forest. A not-very-successful folk artist, he tells people he is from Alabama.

His uniform is overalls with a ratty t-shirt and a frayed flannel shirt, work boots, and a red and black ball cap with a Budweiser logo. When he forgets himself, he sounds like any other North Shore rich kid. Still, I could overlook all that if he stopped his denigrating comments about Micki.

The table is littered with marked-up dim sum forms, piles of small plates, and smears of sauce and chili oil. Sam pulls Micki in close and murmurs something into her ear. She giggles.

"So, what are you two lovebirds planning now?" Even Sam is tolerable in my current dumpling coma.

"Drinks and dancing," Sam and Micki answer together. Her face shines with happiness.

I wrap my arms around her. "I love you, Micki."

"I love you more, Cress." She squeezes me.

"Impossible. The ocean couldn't contain the love I have for you." I let her go and give them a little wave.

She grins. "How are you going to get home? We could drop you off before we head to the club."

"No, don't worry. I'll just call an Uber. Have fun you two."

They float away, arms around each other. Laughter drifts back from some shared secret.

A brief twist of pain in my chest reminds me of Max. I shake it off and wrench my mind to a more attainable goal. The hockey game calls.

If the driver is quick, I might be home in time for the third period. I pull out my phone and see the text.

UNKNOWN: Die bitch

I swallow down the bile that rises in my throat. I think about calling Max. Then I throw the phone back into my purse.

Chapter 10

MAX

I roll through the revolving door. After last night's adventure in ice skating, I'm ready for more Cress. The cashier sees me across the room and waves then mimes pouring tea. Awash from a day's worth of English Breakfast, I shake my head no.

She turns to the next customer in line. Funny—it's Tina, the woman with the big hat and the fur collar. Guess she's a regular too. My neck prickles for no good reason.

Last night I met Cress at the Harold Washington Library after her tutoring session, and we went to Navy Pier for the Winter Wonderfest. Cress still doesn't trust me enough to meet anywhere but public places.

We had a great time walking around and doing a little skating. She wasn't kidding about her balance, so I was able to take advantage by holding her around the waist as we glided around the rink, surrounded by twinkling lights and Christmas decorations.

She tried to ask me more about my life before Chicago, but I deflected. I want to earn her trust, but I can't give up my secrets. People died and I couldn't save them. If she knew the real me, she'd run.

I survey her workspace and raise my eyebrows. Every evening one of the counter people calls out that the cafe is closing. Cress crams her iPad, books, and scrappy notes into a jumble so she can leave before she's thrown out.

Tonight, the table is clear except for a small glass of water. Her bulging brief bag peeks out from under the parka draped over the back of a chair. She squints at her phone.

"Cress. Fancy meeting you here."

She jumps and clutches at her throat.

"Sorry, didn't mean to scare you."

Her breathing slows. "Oh my God. Didn't hear you come up." She holds up a hand, fingers crossed. "I hoped you'd show up before closing."

"Were you worried?"

She raises a shoulder. "We didn't have a date."

"Then why were you hoping I'd show up?" My insides warm up as her cheeks redden.

"Because I want to abduct you." She grabs my wrists and pretends to cuff me.

"Got me, officer. I'll come quietly."

When I gaze into her eyes, a kaleidoscope of gold, amber, and green flashes. Heat rises through my chest and neck. The same electricity that surged through me at Oxford is pulsing a thousand times hotter.

Regret chokes me. I was so stupid all those years ago, when I might have deserved her.

"Where are we going?"

"Just down the street. I want to take you to one of my favorite places."

"And it's just down the street?"

My mind shuffles through the possibilities. Millennium Park is across the street. You can see the Christmas tree from here, so that can't be it. Skating? There's a rink in front of the Park Grill, but no, we did that at Navy Pier.

I've got it: a secret concert at the Pritzker Pavilion, the two of us so cold we're oblivious to the music. A two-person huddle to keep warm. We would press against each other. Deep kisses to keep our teeth from chattering. Other parts of me warm up. I push against her. She frowns.

"Sorry, I was just thinking of possibilities."

She drops my wrists like hot potatoes and shrugs on her parka. "Like what?"

"A secret outdoor concert." Ridiculous said out loud.

"Nice try, but no cigar." She twirls an imaginary cheroot, slings her bag over her shoulder, and moves toward the revolving door. "We're going to the Art Institute." Then she pushes out into the cold, dark night.

I rush to catch up. "Never been there."

"Too busy? Or maybe…"

"Maybe what?"

"Maybe this was a bad idea." Instead of walking down to Michigan Avenue, she moves toward the bus stop.

"No. Why?"

"You've never been. In six years."

"So? Now you get the chance to introduce me to one of the great art museums of the world." I take her arm and turn her back toward the corner. "When I was growing up in London, I loved museums."

"No lie? What museums did you go to?"

"National Gallery, Victoria and Albert, Museum of London, Wallace Collection, Madame Tussaud's. Lots of places."

"Not the National Portrait Gallery? That's my favorite."

The cold pierces my woolen overcoat. I tighten the scarf round my neck and pull out gloves. I glance over and see her hood's up.

"The tips of your ears are bright red. Do you have a hat?"

"Of course not. Stupid really."

Little gusts of icy air puff from her mouth.

"Wasn't thinking." I put my ungloved hands around my ears. Fat lot of good that does.

Cress unwinds a scarf from around her neck. I shake my head as she holds it out to me.

"I have another one. Wrap this around your head and stuff your hands into your pockets."

"I'll look like—"

"Fuck your looks. If you lose an ear, you'll ruin your looks. Unless you're jonesing to be Van Gogh."

She takes my arm, leans in for support. We manage a slo-mo walk-run for the three blocks to the gleaming Beaux-Arts building ahead.

A queue snakes along the pavement outside. I stop, scanning for the tail, but Cress grabs my hand and pulls me to a clear space on the steps at the far right of the entrance.

"Wait, what are you doing? We need to go to the back of the queue." I'm a proper stick-up-the-arse Brit about queuing.

She laughs and points to the door. *Members Entrance* is clearly visible. She waves a card in my face. "Member. No waiting in line or buying tickets."

We're through the door. To the left, people wait to buy tickets. To the right is a long counter. A center aisle is clear.

She points. "Coat check. Let's dump our stuff. I have a packed program planned for you."

A big hat brim catches my attention, but Cress pulls me away before I can manage a shufti.

"Cress, stop. I think I saw someone I know."

She swirls around. "Who?"

I scan the crowd but no hat. Maybe it was my imagination. "Don't see anyone now. Sorry."

Once the preliminaries are done and Cress' card is scanned, we walk into the magnificent hallway.

"The museum's evening hours are on Thursday. Very popular with working stiffs stuck in offices all day."

I notice a sign for an exhibit of paintings by Artemisia Gentileschi. I viewed some of her paintings in the National Gallery, and I'm curious to see what's in this exhibit. Before I can point it out, Cress herds me to a staircase going down.

We get to the bottom, and I step in front of her to get her attention. "Will we have time to see the Gentileschi exhibit?"

"Sure. You're interested in women painters?"

"She's interesting and controversial. I love a good controversy."

"First stop is the Thorne Rooms. Decorated for the holidays."

"Fine." I have no idea what these Thorne rooms are, but I'm willing to go along.

"When I was about twelve, Micki's mom introduced us to the Art Institute. She chose a hot day in the middle of summer. I remember the heat reflecting in waves off the sidewalk when we got off the bus.

I'd never been to a museum. My grandparents had empty walls, painted white. A few cheap prints Micki's parents had in their living room were the only art I'd ever seen."

We're standing outside a space labeled Thorne Miniature Rooms. I glimpse a maze-like space with deep green walls. Small apertures have wooden surrounds that frame them like paintings.

"The museum is too big to see in a few hours, or even a

day. Micki's mom knew what would keep two twelve-year-olds interested. The Thorne Rooms, lunch in the garden, and the Impressionists were our three stops.

I'm ashamed to say my favorite thing was the air conditioning. All we had at home were some stand fans. No cooling dips in the lake. I never learned to swim."

She's looking into the room, not at me. I touch her cheek then turn her face toward mine.

"I can't imagine a Chicago summer without air conditioning."

"You get used to it when you have no choice."

I move closer. Eucalyptus, camphor, and menthol tickle my nose. Eau de Vicks overlays her usual scent of orange and ginger.

"Are you having trouble breathing?" I look at her with concern.

"Nonallergic rhinitis. I use a lot of Vick's in the winter." She sniffs.

I try to lighten the mood. "A truck loaded with Vicks overturned on the highway."

Her lips compress.

"Amazingly, there was no congestion for eight hours."

She coughs.

"Was that a laugh?"

"You wish."

I do wish. Just once I want to crack that hard shell and feast on the tenderness of her soul.

Another slight cough. "Air conditioning rocks. Once I found out I could get in for free, I haunted the place all summer. Saved the money I got from pulling weeds so I could afford the bus. I wasn't home, I was happy, and I learned a lot about art."

She manages a shaky smile as a few tears trail to her

mouth. I touch my lips to hers, and the taste of salt fills my mouth. Cress melts into my embrace for a second before she pulls away. Shoulders hunched, she walks through the entryway.

A 180-degree turn makes a lighthearted trip to her favorite place into a 40-car pileup on the M1.

Cress tells me one of her secrets. Rips open a painful memory. My heart is torn and bleeding but also amazed. This woman built a life out of the rubble of a childhood filled with neglect.

I want to protect her, wrap her in cotton wool. Stupid. She doesn't need that.

She needs someone she can trust. Someone without secrets, who lets her know she matters. Someone who stays.

I could have been that man twenty years ago. Now I need another way to build her trust.

Chapter 11

MAX

I'm a coward. I should have told Cress about Istanbul when we were at the Art Institute, but I couldn't. She'll never trust me if I don't, but she'll be disgusted with me if I do. Taking that risk is beyond me, so I bottled it.

I'm not surprised she decided to go home. Giving up is not in the cards, so today I'm meeting Paul for lunch. Now, more than ever, I need to have her friends on my side.

Since Paul's bank is on LaSalle, just down from my office, lunch at The Berghoff was an obvious choice. Just down the street for each of us.

Paul seems delighted with the prospect of debating cars, tracks, and Formula One drivers. I'm hoping to turn the conversation to Cress, but this is my way in. I'm on a teeter-totter, rising to dizzying highs then plunging to devastating lows.

I'm desperate for tips on ways to win her affections.

Wowing her with elegant meals and trying to learn about hockey hasn't gotten me too far. I know what she wants is openness, but I still can't do that.

My first thought was to try to pump Michelle for information, but I could tell from her repeated side-eye that she isn't going to give me anything except mixed messages. On the one hand, she appears to be encouraging Cress to spend time with me. On the other, she is fiercely protective of her friend.

A lightbulb goes off. I have something in common with Paul—two things since Paul is a banker and my company provides security software to banks. Paul's bank is a client, but I don't want to talk about security software or banking, and I would guess Paul doesn't either. A shared obsession with cars provides a much better entrée.

"This is a great place," Paul enthuses. "It's a real slice of Chicago history. Herman Berghoff opened it in 1898 to sell his beer, which was a hit at the 1893 World's Fair. During Prohibition, he changed to a restaurant, specializing in German food. When Prohibition ended, they were the first place to receive a liquor license in the city.

For decades, the bar was for men only. Then Gloria Steinem showed up in 1969 and demanded to be served. That opened the bar to women."

He picks up his menu and taps it on the table. "If you haven't eaten here before, I suggest either the sauerbraten or the sausages with a side of creamed spinach. The spinach is one of Cress' favorites. Along with the potato pancakes."

I've been many times, but his suggestions are fine. I have the sauerbraten, and he plumps for the sausages. We both add potato pancakes with applesauce and sour cream.

Once our orders are in, we sample their Pfungstädter Urbock Winter beer and spend some time discussing the Sports Car Club of America since we are both members. I also mention belonging to the British Car Union in Chicago and the British Racing and Sports Car Club in the UK.

"Do you work on your cars?"

"Not anymore, but I did when I was younger—cars and aeroplanes."

"Your dad owns planes?" Paul's eyes gleam.

"He used to have six or seven. When he had to stop flying, he sold off most of them. He collects cars and kept a couple of World War I planes, a Sopwith Pup and a Bristol M1. My younger brother Frank has tried for years to buy the Pup. Dad loves tinkering with engines, so I used to help him when I was home from school."

"Too bad your dad can't still fly."

"He takes his planes up for short flights. Otherwise, no. He won't even take commercial flights. When he sits for too long, his back goes out of whack."

"Do you fly?"

"I've a bit of training for small planes and helicopters, so I probably could in a pinch. But flying was never my passion."

"Why did you stop working on cars?"

"I loved being the greasy mechanic when I was a kid, but I don't have time anymore. And I'd rather drive, and play rugby, when I have the leisure." I think back to how those skills have been useful in some of my covers over the years and shudder slightly. My Turkish cover was as a mechanic. "What about you?"

"I like working on cars, too. My dad and I rebuilt a couple when I was in high school. I even thought about becoming a mechanic, but my folk's arguments about B-school won me over eventually."

Promised snow descends, and huge flakes swirl against the windows. Just as well that I took the L this morning.

Slushy, icy streets aren't my favorite, even though the Porsche is a champ in this weather.

"Do you watch racing much?" Paul recaptures my attention.

"TV, mostly. I was able to go to the *Circuit de Catalunya* in May because I was working on a project in Spain and the *Autodromo Nazionale Monza* in September when I had meetings in Italy. Watching Vettel and Weber race for Infiniti Red Bull was exciting.

I would have liked to have gone to the British Grand Prix with my dad, but I couldn't take the time. Silverstone is a favorite, but I haven't been in a few years. "Weber made his retirement announcement there this year." I shake my head regretfully. "How about you?"

"I'm strictly U.S. I go to Daytona and Indy. I was disappointed that the Grand Prix of America didn't work out. I would have been willing to go to Jersey, and Ellie could have had a few days in New York—probably breaking the bank."

I look at him questioningly. "Does she gamble?" I think of the film *The Man Who Broke the Bank at Monte Carlo*.

"Gambling? Nah. Shopping. She loves fashion, jewelry, that shit. With what I spend on cars, I can't say no." He throws out a wry grin. "Maybe we'll see something else in the future."

"F1 isn't so popular here, I'm afraid, but you might look into the Goodwood Festival of Speed. Ellie might enjoy a shopping trip to England."

He shakes his head. "Never heard of it, but I'll check it out." He pauses, drawing lines on the water that dripped on the table when our server filled them. "So, the cars you own —what made you choose the Porsche SUV? It's not a sexy car."

"I needed an SUV, and the specs on the Cayenne Transsyberia were perfect. It drives like a sports car, but with the practicality I need." The Cayenne is good, but I hanker after something a little sportier, more compact, more fun to drive. The rumor that the Macan will come with PDK transmission is the icing on the cake. "I'm looking to upgrade next year, maybe trade it in for the Macan Turbo when it goes into production." I pause. "The sports cars are the sexy choices."

"Which one is your favorite?"

I think for a moment. "Hard to choose. The Bugatti Veyron is the fastest."

"And I'll bet that one is the priciest."

Paul is the perfect lunch companion. If he wasn't a banker, I'd schedule a weekly date. "I think the Aston Martin Vanquish S Ultimate edition might be my favorite at the moment. Only 50 were made."

"Isn't that a James Bond car?"

"The prototype V12 was. It does 0 to 60 in 4.8 seconds."

"And the top speed?"

"I did manage 200 mph once on the track."

Paul's eyes gleam. "Must have cost a bomb."

"I got a good deal. It retailed for $260,000, but I got it for 221."

"Did you get a good deal on the Bugatti too?"

I give him a sharky grin and manage an East End gangster voice. "If you want a car like that, you have to be willing to pay the price."

"Tell the truth, I'm envious of your '54 Monterey."

"We'll make a date and take her out for a spin when the weather is better. In the meantime, I do have pictures." I pull them up on my phone and we ooh and aah for a bit while I point out salient features.

"I would have loved the experimental model, but it was never put into production. But the 161 hp, 120 kW, overhead valve Ford Y-block V8 was new that year, and I love a convertible."

"Sweet. Really looking forward to that ride."

"What about your cars, Paul?"

"The Audi R8 Spyder is great for running around, and I have a fabulous Bang and Olufsen sound system. The 5.2-liter V-10 engine with 525 hp and 391 lb-ft of torque give it plenty of power. I'm looking to add a 2013 Challenger SRT8 to my collection."

"What do you like about it?"

Paul rubs the top of his head. "It's a great take on the 1970 Challenger. I like American muscle cars, and this is a terrific example." He gives the table a triumphant smack. "And it goes from 0 to 60 in 4.2 seconds, so a bit faster than your Aston Martin. Top speed about 180 on the track, plenty fast for me."

"Manual or automatic?"

"Both are available, but I prefer manual."

"If you're thinking of it primarily for the track, I'd recommend storing it at the Collectors Car Garage. They'll take care of everything for you. Unless you're still a tinkerer."

Paul holds up his hands in negation. "Not anymore. I'll check that out. I do like to go to Road America when I have the time. Are you thinking about adding to your collection?"

"My dad saw the Spyker B6 Venator Spyder at Syon Park in September and loved it. Definitely a possibility. They're handcrafted and all carbon fiber. Production won't start until late next year, so no rush."

We've finished our meal and moved on to coffee for him and tea for me. Now that I have Paul in a relaxed frame of mind, I shift gears. "I need some advice."

Paul sits up. "On cars?"

"In a way." I pause, thinking over how to put this. Finally,

I ask, "Which of my cars do you think would appeal most to Cress?"

Paul does a double take. "Cress?" He snickers. "She's not into cars."

"I know that. I want to tempt her into it, though. If I wanted to take her for a drive, which one would impress her?"

"Just ride on the bus or the L with her. She'll be more impressed that you were willing to take public transportation."

I frown. I may have to rethink this.

"Her father spent a lot of her mom's family money on cars and gambling before he dumped them. Her brother, Tom, is just the same. That's why she despises anything to do with driving. In fact, you should probably be careful about talking about your car collection around her. It's kind of a flashpoint."

"I want to change her mind, not hide my passions. My goal is to win her heart."

"With cars? Good luck with that." Paul laughs.

"Any other ideas?"

"Creamed spinach and potato pancakes."

"You're pulling my leg."

"Nope, she's a connoisseur. Ask her where to get the best creamed spinach."

"That will impress her?"

"No, but she'll be happy you asked." He puts his elbows on table, rests his chin against his fists. "Don't try to impress her. She's more interested in ideas than in things. Be open, have lots of conversations, tell her you're there for her, show her some affection. Be nice to her cats. Cress hasn't had much of that in her life. She'll respond." Paul pauses, then smiles. "And take her to some hockey games."

Chapter 12

CRESS

At Toni's on Friday afternoon, my phone starts going off with innumerable text messages. *Shit.* I have a deadline I won't meet if I stop now. I scrabble for it, intending to turn it off, but what I see on the screen stops me.

Message after message from Micki scrolls past with variations of "Call me." The subscription service that monitors social media mentions is going crazy. I usually have just a couple of notifications a week to cope with.

Not what I need when the words are pouring out. I vow to call Michelle when I come to a logical stopping point. Nothing can be that important. If one or the other of my two surviving family members died, the news could wait.

Just as I go to silence my phone, "Michelle" by the Beatles sounds. I am tempted to send the call to voicemail again, but after all the texts, I accept the call. "Hey, Micki, I'm swamped. Can't it wait?"

"Noooo." Her hiss raises goose bumps on my arms.

"What's going on? My phone shows fifty plus notifications."

"Do you remember that bitch Tina Monroe?"

"Yeah. What about her? The last time I saw her was at a book signing a few years ago. We had words." I bite the tip of my index finger to keep from adding more. "Is she dead or something?"

"I wish she were." The edge in Micki's voice could slice through an overdone steak. "You're probably going to want to kill her."

"Look, I'm past all that school shit. Life's too short—"

"This is not about school, not about the past. Tina went on *Trash TV* today and told everyone you plagiarized your novels. I bet she planted the newspaper story, too."

"What? Why? And who's everyone? This makes no sense." I go still.

"I can meet you at Remington's in a few minutes for a drink. You can tell me all about your close encounter with the Divine Tina."

I get a call waiting beep. It's Max. "See you in a few, Micki."

By the time I switch over, he's hung up. I curse under my breath. Then I see the voicemail message.

"Cress. Call me."

I hit the button to call back.

"Cress?"

"Yeah, hi. What's up?"

"Did you see the story on *Trash TV*?"

"I heard about it."

"Do you want to talk?"

"I'm on my way to Remington's to meet Micki. Can you meet me up there?"

"Right. Sure. About six?"

"Fine. Bye."

I set the phone to silent and put it in my bag. Can't process anything. By the time I pack up and walk down the block, Micki is seated at a corner table away from the bar. A few voices murmur in the distance.

When I sneak a look around the room, only a couple of guys sit at the bar. This is the quiet time between lunch and after-work drinks.

Our table sports a big pitcher and two cocktail glasses. I point and laugh. "Did you order as you walked in the door?"

"It's Negroni time." She waves her glass at me then glares at the few drops that have spilled onto the table.

My shoulders drop from my ears to their normal position. Ruby red liquid sparkles in the glasses. The bitter orange scent of Campari makes my mouth water.

I focus on her new nail color. "What's this one?"

"Sinfully Sweet, just like me." She takes a long swallow and narrows her eyes. "Tina? Two years ago?"

I fold like a broken umbrella.

"I was doing a book signing at the Barnes and Noble in Gold Coast. It was for *Lost in the Mist*."

"I remember that signing. You had a huge turnout."

My first best seller. The line was out the door and down the street. "There was a woman with about six copies, and she wanted them all personalized. Plus she wanted a selfie with me.

The next woman in line muttered curses, under her breath but loud enough to catch my attention. I scurried back behind the table and smiled. She scowled at me, slammed a copy down on the table. Pens flew everywhere."

I fiddle with my phone. The waterfall of messages has dwindled to a trickle.

"Then she said, 'Bet you recognize me. Bet you saw me in line, and you've been shitting yourself over the memories.' I was speechless."

Drink forgotten, Micki leans forward, hands flat against the table.

"I stared at her for a few seconds, but nothing registered until she said, 'Tina Monroe.' That was a shocker." The Negroni calls to me.

"After twenty-five years, well, I couldn't see it, but if she was Tina Monroe, what was she doing there? Finally, I told her I wouldn't have recognized her, but I certainly remembered who she was."

"Bitch." Micki scowls.

"She gave me a poisonous look then said I hadn't changed at all. She'd recognized my name on the window display, thought she'd say, 'Hello, congratulations,' or 'Maybe we could get together, reminisce.'"

"Interesting way to congratulate you."

"Yeah. Anyway, I grabbed the book and scribbled on the fly leaf, 'Tina, thanks for buying my book. Hope you enjoy it. Cress Taylor, DPhil.' Then I handed it back and motioned the next person to come up.

"She pasted on a fake smile. Called me a drab little geek. Then I gave in to my base instincts. I taunted her. 'I have a doctorate. And six best-selling novels.' Then I asked her if she had won any beauty contests lately."

"Oooh. That was cold."

"And now you have an enemy."

I swivel toward the voice—Max's voice. I check my watch. He must have dropped everything and rushed over.

"She already hated me. I don't know why she's taken so long to retaliate."

Double response. "Award nomination."

Max and Micki high-five.

"Sit down and have a Negroni." Micki gestures toward the half-full pitcher.

"Maybe for a second." Max unbuttons his coat but doesn't take it off.

I chug my drink.

"Going out to dinner?" The corners of Micki's mouth turn down.

Max slips off his coat and smiles at me. "We can have dinner here. Okay with you, Cress?"

AFTER A DINNER of French onion soup and lamb chops, I start thinking about catching the bus. The stop is a few blocks away. "This was lovely," I tell Max. "I'm grateful for the respite."

He polishes off the last of his steak frites. "Pudding?"

"No, I'm stuffed."

"That means something else where I come from."

I snort. "I didn't say get stuffed, you idiot."

"Coffee or a liqueur?"

"I'm tired. I want to go home and cuddle with my cats."

"Ah, Dorothy and Thorfinn."

"Yes. I'm sure they're wondering where I am. They need to be fed."

"Come on then. Let's fetch my car and I'll drive you home. You too, Micki."

"Thanks, but I need to put in a little more time at the office."

"We'll walk you down."

"That's silly, Max. My office is practically across the street." She grabs her coat. "Thanks for dinner. It's on me next time." With a quick final wave, she vanishes into the winter darkness.

"Cress, I would like to see you home. We'll Uber to my place and pick up the car." His phone is out, and I'm too tired to argue.

My coat on and my bag over my shoulder, I slip my arm through his.

He turns me slightly so he can look in my eyes. "Ah, here's our chariot. I'll tell you jokes and stories. That will cheer you up." He hands me into the silver car. "Now for the joke of the day."

"I'd rather be waterboarded."

"You'll love this one."

I sneer. He chuckles.

"My friend asked me if I wanted to hear a really good Batman impression, so I said go on then. He shouted, 'NOT THE KRYPTONITE!' and I said, 'That's Superman...' 'Thanks, man,' he replied. 'I've been practicing it a lot.'"

My shudder is all for show. I press my hand against my stomach and grimace. "No more jokes, please, I'm nauseated already."

"No promises. Telling jokes is in my genes. Just wait until you meet my dad."

"Meet your dad?" My heart lifts then comes down with a thump. I can't believe whatever this is will last long enough for meeting the parents. I start to sniffle.

"Are you all right? Are you upset, or is it allergies?"

"Yeah, allergic to your jokes." I wipe my face with the handkerchief he hands me.

"And I thought it was from the banks of flowers that bloom in a normal Chicago winter."

I try to suppress my desire to chuckle.

"I hear that snigger." His voice burbles with suppressed laughter.

"No snigger, laugh, or guffaw."

The Uber pulls up to the corner, and Max pulls me over to the only house on the street with an entrance to an underground garage. Warmth hits my face as we walk in.

"You heat your garage?" I ask.

"Yeah. Chicago winters are cold, and I like my cars to start."

The Polaris Slingshot looks kind of like a space-age insect, but the Range Rover SUV is impressive. "I don't think I've ever seen cars like this except on TV."

"You obviously don't travel in the right circles. I take it you drive a Bug or a Smart Car."

"I never learned to drive."

"Everyone in America learns to drive." His gob-smacked expression is adorable.

"Not me."

The corners of Max's mouth turn down. "You must be unique, an anomaly. You are foregoing one of the great joys in life. Why did you never learn?"

"It's long story." I suppress a yawn. "I've told you enough of them for one day. Maybe some other time."

Max gets me settled in the soft leather and turns on the seat heaters before pulling out of the garage as I tell him, "I live in Rogers Park."

"I thought you lived in Chicago."

"I do."

"Well, I have no idea where that is. Out in the wilderness somewhere, I would guess. By a park." He smirks. "Give me the address and I'll set the GPS."

"It's straight north."

"Funny, that's what my mate said about the bookshop.

Just go north." He purses his lips. "I live and work down here. I don't go to many other places in the city." Max sounds a little defensive.

"Well, I take public transportation, so I don't always pay attention, but my bus takes the route you want, so take the Outer Drive."

We're both silent for a while. An itch of discomfort nags between my shoulder blades.

"Could we have some music?"

He shifts, uncomfortable for some reason. "Sure. Just say the station clearly and the radio will tune to it."

"WFMT."

The radio comes on with Vaughan Williams' "The Lark Ascending." Warmth fills me as at the soaring notes of a solo violin play the opening.

"This is nice. What is it?"

"I thought any Englishman would be familiar with Vaughan Williams." God, when did I become such a snob?

"I doubt the whole population of the British Isles listens to classical music."

Now I feel like shit. "Sorry. I guess that was pretty judgmental."

Max speeds down the Drive like he's on the Indy 500 Speedway. Now I know what people mean when they say they are white knuckled. I restrain myself from grabbing something as I try not to panic.

We're coming to the end of the Drive. "Stay right. You want Sheridan Road, not Hollywood."

Max negotiates the curve, his mouth bowed in a wicked smile. "What does Tarzan say when he sees a herd of elephants in the distance?"

"Not again." I moan and roll my eyes.

He gives me a sideways glance.

"Fine. What?"

"Look, a herd of elephants in the distance."

I don't bite.

This does not dampen his enthusiasm as he tries again. "What does Tarzan say when he sees a herd of elephants with sunglasses?"

I shake my head.

"Nothing. He doesn't recognize them."

My shoulders shake.

"You're laughing."

"In your dreams." I am laughing inside, but damned if I'll admit it.

"Right. I don't listen to music, and you don't have a sense of humor. I guess we're both weird."

"I do have a sense of humor. You just tell bad jokes. But I will cop to the weirdness."

He huffs. "My jokes are excellent. If you do have a sense of humor, we need to excavate it."

The resulting silence is painful.

"Where do I go now?" Max sounds grumpy.

"Just keep going on Sheridan. It will curve around when it runs into Devon, so keep to the right. And I should warn you, parking is a bitch in my neighborhood."

At my building, Max grabs a parking space around the corner. "I'm usually lucky with parking." He gives a satisfied smirk.

MAX

TWO FURRY HEADS try to push out as the door swings open.

"Dorothy, Thorfinn, back," Cress chides. She grabs my hand and pulls me in. The door shuts before the cats can squeeze out.

I strip off my coat and gloves and hand them to Cress. As she walks into another room, I call after her. "It's bloody freezing in here." I shove my hands into my pocket.

She reappears through French doors. "It's perfect. I have the radiators off. I don't like overheated rooms."

I blow on my hands. "Can you turn them back on before I turn into an ice cube?"

"I had no idea you were such a tender plant. Isn't central heating anathema in Britain? Don't you sleep in unheated rooms with the windows open?"

I ignore her and prowl around her small space. Rooms with high ceilings, crown molding, and narrow-planked, honey-hued hardwood floors. The latter are covered with a collection of Turkish and Afghani rugs. Their deep colors mirror the walls and the various furniture coverings. Her jumble of English cottage style and Venetian decadence is cozy.

A woven basket, heaped with balls of wool, sits next to the armchair. I touch it with my toe. "Is this for show?"

"I knit." She roots in the basket and pulls out a small bundle. As the toothpick-thin needles stretch out, a tube of bright colors appears.

"What is it?"

"A sock. I knit socks. One of these days, if I decide I like you, I might knit you a pair."

"In those colors?" Purple, navy, yellow, and black intermingle. I'm torn between laughter and desire. Those socks— ridiculous as they are, I covet them. Handmade socks, knit by

Cress Taylor. My mouth dries with want for this badge of love.

"Do you think these colors are too feminine? Paul didn't. When I offered to make him socks, he picked these colors himself."

"For Paul? How did he earn the prize of handmade socks?"

"He's my friend, one of my best friends, so why wouldn't I make socks for him? And he loves my socks. Anyway, if I ever decide to make socks for you, I'll just use solid colors." She stuffs the socks back into the basket. "What do you think of my place?"

I can't resist the smart remark. "It's like a tiny doll-house. I haven't seen so much chintz in years. Are you trying for overblown Victorian or a failed attempt at twee cottage?"

"Excuse me. Are you dissing my decor?" Arms folded, she glares, but I see the small smile too.

"No, just wondering what the look is. At least you haven't put faux wooden beams on the ceiling."

"Fuck you. I don't think hand-knit socks are in your future."

I walk though inviting French doors, and I'm in her bedroom. Modern and Renaissance art are juxtaposed on the beige walls. My eye is drawn to her bed, covered with a gray duvet and matched shams. *Don't go there, Max.* I back up and bump into Cress, posted like a sentry at the door.

"If you took out the bedside tables, you could have a bigger bed." Bugger. I feel like Basil Fawlty as the remark slips out.

"It's a queen. I don't need a bigger bed."

"Perhaps not now, but you never know. Mine's a California king." I give her a wink.

"Well, you're a giant and I'm just a tiny morsel." She herds me back through the doors to the living room.

I collapse in the armchair next to the fireplace, my legs stretched out, fingers running over the balls of wool. The soft fibers caress my fingers. "These must be a temptation to the cats."

She laughs. "Only if they are in motion. They're not toylike at rest. Just don't knock them on the floor."

She taps a forefinger against her teeth. "Do you want something to drink? I can make tea, or you could have a night cap. I have several single malts."

"A dram of whisky would go perfectly with a chat. We should watch the television replay so you can see what you're up against, and you can tell me why this Tina woman is attacking you."

The TV show is cringingly awful. Cress knits, her gaze cycling between the screen and the rapidly growing sock. Fortunately, the segment is less than ten minutes. She stares at the screen Tina as she reels out her accusations.

At one point, the knitting drops into her lap. My chest hurts as I watch her swipe her eyes. Why is this news? *Trash TV* is like tabloid magazines. I can't imagine anyone finds this garbage believable.

The remote is on the table next to me. I switch it off as silent tears roll down Cress' face and drip off her chin. I reach over and wipe at them with my fingers.

"No jokes suitable to this occasion."

"No." Her voice sparks like a knife grinder. "My career is being sucked into a cesspool."

She's perched on the sofa, muscles bunched. I pull her close, stroke her back. "I have been seeing this woman every-where—the book signing, the cafe. Do you know her? I think she's stalking you."

"No one will believe this. She's no one, a person I went to school with. No credentials, no credibility." Her lopsided grin is unconvincing.

"You know how the media works. We have a 24-hour news cycle desperate for some salacious story. Right now, you're it. Doesn't matter that she appeared out of nowhere to accuse you."

I stroke the back of her hand. "No one cares if the story is true. No one even cares how important you might be or not be. Something to jaw over is everything, and Tina Monroe can enjoy her fifteen minutes of fame."

As my words shred her bravado, she gulps. Then, with a glare at the screen, she straightens her back.

"All lies." The phone rings. She glances at the screen. "My agent. Maybe I should let it go to voicemail?" Her body shakes as if a tidal wave is running through her.

I take the phone out of her hands and accept the call.

"Hey, what are you doing?" Her voice is two octaves higher.

"Hello? Are you calling for Cress Taylor?" I brush my hair back. "I'm a friend. As you know, she's had a shock." My tone is dry. Then I turn to Cress and hold out the phone. "Do you want to speak to your agent?"

"I don't know. Maybe." The uncertainty in her voice guts me.

Her hand reaches out to mine like a snail coming out of its shell and takes the phone, pressing the speaker button so I can hear.

"How bad is it, Cal?" Eyes wide, Cress drops to the floor. The normally low tone of her voice rises. "She must have sent me the texts and left the note at the signing. Now what?"

"Damage control, dear." Cal's emollient tone spreads like cream.

"Dear?" I raise a brow.

She waves me off, then taps the mute button. "My agent is 80 years old and a courtly Bostonian. He's known me since he sold my first book. Of course I'm his dear." She unmutes the phone.

"You're not alone."

"No. My friend Max is here."

"Your friend...never mind, you can tell me about that some other time."

"Right. The plan?"

"We need to get your side out there—quickly. I've already heard from your publishers, and they are not pleased. The publicist arranged for you to go on TV and confront this Tina. I'll text you the details."

"What? No."

I grab her in a hug.

"Can't you put out a statement?" Her face presses against the phone. The phone presses into my chest. Her words are inaudible.

"What? Did you say something? I can't understand you."

She pulls away. "Sorry, Cal. I said, can't you put out a statement?"

"I did that when the newspaper article came out, a Band-Aid. Your reputation is hemorrhaging. I know this will be unpleasant, but you'll live through it."

"Fine." She ends the call and throws the phone on the couch, then clings to me as if I can pull her from the avalanche.

Chapter 13

MAX

I grab the hot dog JL shoves under my nose with one hand, typing with the other, brushing stray poppy seeds from the keys. I've developed a yen for Chicago-style steamed dogs.

The combination of the soft poppyseed bun, Vienna hot dog, tomato, chopped onion, celery salt, sport peppers, mustard, and fluorescent-green relish is perfect if a bit messy. I have chips on the side with malt vinegar.

No chance to walk over to Toni's, so I text Cress late in the day and propose dinner. After we watched Tina's *Trash TV* appearance last night, I tried to be her safe harbor, but by the time I left, she was starting to retreat.

ME: Dinner? I'll pick you up at 6.

CRESS: Worked from home today. Couldn't face going out. Migraine. 😩

ME: 😳 I'll bring dinner.

Damn Tina Monroe. My fingers twitch.

CRESS: You don't need to check on me.

ME: I want to feed you, unless you're nauseated.

CRESS: I took ginger. Pain is manageable but I'm tired.

ME: I'll rub your back.

CRESS: *writing bubbles*

ME: I'll be there soon.

A few minutes pass. I try to focus on my screen, but my eyes keep moving back to the messages open on my phone. A ding and I grab the device.

CRESS: FINE

~

I'M A SHERPA, loaded down with bags of Chinese food.

Cress, face tinged with green, gags. "Not sure this is a good idea. The smell is overwhelming."

"I thought you said you feel better."

"Better than when the migraine was at its height. Not a hundred percent better."

"This is the good stuff—pork belly buns, pot stickers, spring rolls, crab Rangoon, fire duck, sliced lamb with ginger and scallions, green beans with fresh garlic, three-mushroom pan-fried noodles, and eggplant with garlic sauce."

Cress runs out, and I hear her vomit.

"Sorry. I'll put this in the fridge for another time."

Now she's back in the darkened room, on the sofa, with a cold pack on the back of her neck and a warm cloth over her eyes.

"Did you invite an army of your friends?" Her voice is leaden with exhaustion.

"No."

"You ordered enough food for ten people." She struggles to pull free of the cocoon of blankets.

"Just wanted to give you some choices. You never know what you might fancy." I move over to the sofa and kneel on the floor. Like the rest of the dollhouse furniture, the sofa isn't wide enough for me to sit next her while she's lying down.

"You should eat, Max."

"I'll fix some tea and toast."

We nibble toast, and I swill tea as Cress sips water.

"Feel better?" I ask.

"A bit. I needed something bland."

My thumb caresses her fingers, and she laces them through mine. I relax. My fear that she put her walls back up melts like the snow flurries tumbling lazily past the windows.

"Tell me why you don't drive," I ask.

Cress frowns. "It's not very interesting."

"Oh, go on. Try me."

"The easy answer is that I grew up in the city with plenty of public transportation, so I've never needed to learn."

"What if you need to leave the city?"

"Bus or train."

"What if you want to go somewhere that doesn't have bus or train service?"

Her tongue peeps out from between her teeth. "I'd pick another location."

"But what if you need to go there?"

"I'd take a bus or train as close as I could and take a cab or an Uber. If I was visiting someone, they could pick me up."

"You have all the answers." I push a curl away from her face.

"Of course I do. I'm a forty-five-year-old Oxford DPhil." She pauses, then continues sotto voce. "Almost forty-six."

I file that information. "There must be some reason why you never learnt in the first place."

She stretches her arms above her head. "My mom was a terrible driver. We were in frequent fender-benders, and she'd clip parked cars, that kind of thing."

Her voice fades as she takes the plates into the kitchen.

When she gets back with another glass of water, I pull her down next to me.

"Mom did have a baby harness and seatbelts were mandatory a few years after I was born, but the protections weren't great. I guess we were lucky to just be shaken up. Anyway, the fact that no car would have been pristine after a few days meant Dad made her drive a beater."

Her bottom lips catches between her teeth. "He loved fast and expensive and changed sports cars every few months, even though we could never afford it. They argued constantly about the expensive cars, the fact that she always had to drive the kids, and the accidents."

"You could have taken lessons to be a good driver and settled for a moderately priced car." For some reason I am being stubborn about this.

"If I don't want to drive, that's my choice. I don't need your judgmental attitude."

I hold up my hands in apology. "The first time I saw you, I felt a deep pull immediately."

"Hard to believe." Her voice is soft.

"Guy and I were trying to disentangle you from your bicycle, and your eyes drew me in right away. I'd never felt an instant attraction like that before, and truthfully, I haven't since. It burned like constant electric shocks. I've always wondered if we could have had something then. I was devastated when you rode away."

Cress pulls away and perches on the edge of the armchair.

"What are you talking about? You acted like a jerk, with your cut-glass accent and your condescending manner."

She glares at me. "And I didn't ride off—the chain was messed up. You sauntered off, laughing. I was already late, and I had to push the bike to my tutor's room, looking like something the cat dragged in."

My face and neck heat. "I can't believe our memories are so different. What made you think I was such a jerk?"

Putting her finger under her nose, she tilts her head up and throws out a really bad imitation of my accent. "Your bicycle is too big for you." She makes air quotes. I fail at a keeping a straight face.

After a minute, I get myself under control. "Well, it was."

"Not a comment calculated to touch my heart."

The temperature in the room drops a good twenty degrees. This is sliding sideways into a pit of shame. Not good. Time to apologize for my former self.

"Sorry. I was twenty years old, was educated at a public school, and the guys I hung out with were my rugby team, also twenty-year-old males. Not a lot of polish there. What would you expect?"

We sit in silence to let the tension settle.

"Do you travel to do research for your books?"

Her muscles relax. "I like to see the places I'm writing about. For example, I spent a lot of time in Venice and Cyprus for Caterina Cornaro. For my new book, I went to Moscow to see the Kremlin and St. Basil's Cathedral. Pictures are all well and good, but seeing places, feeling the air, experiencing the smells gives an immediacy to the setting."

"Do most novelists do that?"

"I'm very lucky. I had an inheritance from my mother, and my grandparents left me a trust fund. Not all authors can afford to travel. That's why the internet's so useful. You can travel the world without leaving your desk. Google Earth is a game changer."

I turn my gaze from her to the cats, who are chasing each other round and round the furniture.

"Have you had a lot of relationships?"

The suddenness of the question knocks me sideways. I continue to watch the cats as Zehra comes to mind. No words come out.

A flush runs from her neck to her cheeks. "Sorry. I didn't mean to pry. Well, I guess I did mean to. I've been told I can be a bit blunt."

I cross my ankle over my knee. "Relationships? Are you asking if I've dated a lot?"

"No, relationships. With someone long-term. Live with someone."

"Not really." I fiddle with my mug. Does my month with Zehra count? "One-night stands. A few second or third dates. One woman I spent a bit more time with when I was in Turkey." *Shit.* I've already said too much. *Evade. Evade.* "My main relationship is work." I look away.

When I look back, I see her stare at me in disbelief.

"Seriously? I can't believe that. Women must swarm you."

My shoulders bunch. "What about you? Why haven't you married and had a gaggle of children?"

"Not in the cards."

I want to ask why, but her face closes up, the corners of her lips turned down—a big no trespassing sign.

I coax her back to the sofa and essay a gentle kiss. She doesn't push me away.

"Is this okay?" I ask as I press my cheek against her hair.

CRESS

"I think I should tell you some other things about me."

"Okay."

I bite my lip. "I told you that when I was eight, my mom died. We had an apartment in Uptown."

This is so hard. I just hope the payoff is that I get a revelation in return. Glasses—I grab them from the end table. I need to see Max in focus.

"My dad left my brother and me with my grandparents. They lived in Evanston. I started a new school and was surrounded by new people. School was the one thing I was good at but being a smart-aleck showoff isn't a great way to make friends."

"Tell me about it." Max's smile is complicit.

"Micki and Paul befriended me. Tina lived across the street. She was in my face, every day. Impossible to escape. She was part of the popular set, pretty.

Even at eight, she was always the center of attention. Her group made fun of me, my glasses, that I was thin. The know-it-all who hung out with the uncool kids."

"A know-it-all—who would have guessed?" I'm sucked into the glint in his eyes as they turn dark.

"Micki was smart too and had no filter. Being pudgy and small for his age but not willing to be the class clown put a bullseye on Paul's back. We were the Three Musketeers, misfits all."

Max reaches out to play with the curls that have escaped from my messy bun. He licks his lips, the big bad wolf ready to devour Little Red Riding Hood.

"By high school I was the butt of all the jokes, and the

girl gang spread rumors. I was accused of cheating on tests and plagiarizing papers. That made me unpopular with the teachers, who were always monitoring me to see if the accusations were true. No smoke without fire, right?"

"Ah, you've had accusations before."

"There was never any evidence because I never did anything wrong. It's the same now. If people excavate my writing to look for plagiarism, let them. Nothing to unearth. It blew over then and I'd like to think it will again. It's not like I'm famous, and the prize I'm nominated for is for historical fiction. Maybe if it was a Pulitzer, that would be more reason for people to be interested."

"Times have changed with 24-hour news cycles and the internet. People latch on to untruths all the time, and as they spread, people believe them. This is not going away any time soon."

"You're probably right." I wipe my eyes. Tina is my bad penny. When she turns up, my life crashes. "My grandparents disapproved of my mom marrying my dad. They treated us as if we were tainted. I don't remember ever getting hugs or kisses or even praise when I did something good."

He unwinds the curl from around his finger and brushes my hair back. Then he kisses my temple, puts his nose against my neck, and breathes in. "I love how you smell like oranges and ginger."

Er-h'r'm. I touch my fist to my lips. Heat spreads through me. "I couldn't wait to leave for college. The Musketeers stuck together and went to the University of Illinois. Being smart paid off when I got a Rotary scholarship to go to Oxford."

Max rubs his thumb over my hand, and my flush deepens, my face on fire.

"When I was at Oxford, I was attacked and robbed." My

words spill out like vomit. I rub my lips with the back of my hand.

His jaw drops in shock. "Wha-a-a…"

"Please let me finish. Then you can talk."

He nods.

"I was pretty battered. Kev, the guy I was living with, insisted I move on. But I couldn't." A catch in my throat stops me. Kev was another entitled jerk.

I bite my lip to hold back the sob that wants to tear out of my throat. "I was devastated. Closeness is hard for me. You are the first person outside my charmed circle that I've told about my time at Oxford."

"Was he your first?"

I want to snap shut like a tapped mussel shell. Instead, I loosen my shoulders, unclench my fists.

"He was my first, and my only." My voice is as sharp as vinaigrette. Then I drop my face into my hands.

Max gently moves my fingers and brushes away the tears gathering on my lashes.

"What did you do after you were attacked?"

"I went for counseling. After I healed, I took self-defense classes."

"So, I need to watch out?"

"I'm not a ninja. I can do a few things to escape, but I can't exactly beat someone up."

"That's a relief. Although maybe a few refresher classes might not be a bad idea, in case you can't run fast enough." His eyes darken more. Now they are almost black. "No boyfriends after Kev?"

"I finished my DPhil and started writing books. Like you, my relationship was with work. That seemed to be enough."

"And now?"

"Not sure. You push me in directions I don't want to go."

"Why?"

"Why, what?"

"Why don't you want to try a new path?"

I drop my gaze and squirm away. "I've been hurt too many times. My mom died. My dad, my brother, Kev the jerk —they all left. My grandparents...well, enough said there. I trusted too easily and was betrayed over and over. I thought I was in love and was thrown away like some used rag." I rub at my lips. "I'm afraid you'll open me up, knock down my carefully constructed walls, then you'll move on, and I'll be trash again."

He puts his arms around me. The hug he gives me is fierce. "We'll go as slowly as you need. I'm in no rush. And I'm not going anywhere." He leans in for another kiss. My lips burn. "Let's cuddle on the couch." Max stretches out and pulls me on top of him.

I relax a little at his words. *Drip, drip, drip.* The ice walls around my heart melt a bit.

I settle into his arms, press my nose into his neck. So warm and comfortable, I could stay here forever. After an hour of tentative exploration, we have given up on the couch. Pillows are strewn across the floor.

My back rests against Max's chest, his arms around my waist. I moan softly. This is dangerous territory. My body reacts as he adjusts himself.

Tug-of-war rages between my mind and my body. The well-known butterfly sensation flutters through me while my mind replays Kev's insults. I need to tell him that sex is not on the menu tonight.

"*Tesoro mia, la mia stellina, cara mia. Potrei guardarti tutto il giorno.*"

I twist a curl of hair around my finger. "Sounds beautiful, but my Italian's not that good."

"My treasure, my little star, my dear. I could look at you all day."

I lick his bottom lip. His answering kiss brands my mouth.

"Nice. You could kiss for England."

"Scotland." He kisses me again. And again.

Being called his treasure, his little star, is a real turn-on. I respond with a few French endearments while I rub my nose against his neck, breathing in the scents of juniper, cedar, wood sage, and sea salt. A mix of the forest and the ocean, with an undertone of gin. One of my favorite drinks. My guy smells like my favorite fragrance. Wait. Is Max my guy? I'm so confused. Not a decision for now. "You smell so good."

"Yeah?"

"What is it?"

"The brand is Jo Malone. It's British. My sisters bought me two different ones, because you're supposed to combine them. Anyway, one is Black Cedarwood and Juniper, and the other—"

I laugh lightly and stroke his neck.

"My sisters got it because Wood Sage and Sea Salt is one of Prince William's favorites. They hated the cologne I used before."

"And that was…"

He grins. "Number 89 from Floris."

"Floris? That posh place on Jermyn Street?"

"You know it?"

"Kev got his cologne there. He took me once when we went to London at Christmas."

"Hmmm. Good thing I don't go there anymore. If I saw him, I'd punch him in the nose."

I chuckle. "Doubtful. You don't even know what he looks like."

"I could find out." He points to his chest. "Computer guy."

I laugh then press my nose in again. "Why that cologne?"

"It was the one Ian Fleming used."

"So, you did want to be James Bond."

"Of course. The cars, the girls, high adventure in exotic places. And the toys. I loved the scenes with Q. Not that being a spy is anything like that. Definitely more Le Carré than Fleming." A harsh edge seeps into his voice.

Okay, guess there's a sore spot there. I shift back to the cologne. "Why didn't your sisters like it?"

"They thought it wasn't masculine enough. The combination of orange, bergamot, and lavender offended them."

I'm blissed out, more relaxed than I've been maybe ever. Even massages don't make me relax like this. My muscles are almost liquid, as if I've been drugged. Max runs his fingers through my hair. His nose caresses my collarbone. We kiss until our lips are so swollen we need a break.

We continue to cuddle as I propose we watch a movie. I want to watch *Andrei Rublev*, a film about the medieval Russian icon painter by Andrei Tarkovsky made in 1966. I happen to have the DVD.

Max wants to watch *Rush*, some race car movie. After some friendly arguing back and forth, we compromise on *The Wolf of Wall Street*. The movie attracts and repels at the same time, but we can't pull ourselves away.

"I don't like Leonardo DiCaprio." A twinge in my back makes me moan when I lever myself off the couch, where I've been pressed against Max. "How could we keep watching?"

"Because Scorsese is a brilliant filmmaker." Max stretches his arms up before jackknifing into a forward fold, his palms flat on the floor. He slowly comes up then repeats the movement several more times.

"That's better. Try that for your back, Cress. My back is bad too. One of the curses of being tall."

"Mine is incipient arthritis. I wouldn't know about tall." I eye him uncertainly. Does he do yoga? He's constantly surprising.

"My couch would be more comfortable." His face brightens slowly, like the end of an eclipse.

"Maybe next time."

I barely register a vague roar from outside and Max strides to the window, raising the blind.

"Cress." His voice is a distant murmur. "A gaggle of reporters and photographers. Come see." He leads me over to the window. "Look." He's behind me, pressed against my back. Strong hands dig into my shoulders.

"What the hell..." A full-scale invasion storms the sidewalk.

"They watch television. Tina Monroe's fifteen minutes. I'm afraid the fallout will extend that time for you."

I sigh. "The publicity will be bad, even if nothing is proved."

"Don't publishers love scandal?"

"The short answer is no. Especially this sort of thing." My eyes cross with exhaustion. I don't want to talk about this, but Max is persistent.

"Aren't you innocent until proven guilty?"

"This isn't a court of law. This is the court of public opinion, so much more unforgiving. Unfavorable publicity can be used as a reason to terminate an author's contract, even if there is no proof that the author did anything wrong. By keeping up the pressure and continuing to spread and amplify the lies, Tina hopes to create enough scandal to pressure my publisher to terminate my contract, pull my books, and perhaps keep any other publisher from taking me on."

"That's absurd. Have your publishers contacted you? Threatened you?"

"You heard Cal last night. They aren't happy." I force a smile. Then the light on my phone catches my eye. The blood drains from my face. There are dozens of text messages and hundreds of emails.

Max takes the phone out of my hand, turns it off, and sets it on the mantel. "Leave it for now. You can deal with it tomorrow."

Tomorrow. I push the thought away. "You'll have to go out the back."

"What?" Max looks like I've slapped him.

"That way you can avoid all that mess. Here's your coat." I push it into his arms and turn toward the door.

"Don't you want me to stay with you? I thought you wanted the closeness."

My emotions are a runaway elevator. "I need to be by myself for a while. Can't process what's happening." This is a huge mistake, but I can't stop myself from pushing him away. I'm bereft even as I insist that he leaves.

Max stubbornly shakes his head. "I should stay."

The more he protests, the more I want him to go. "You want to protect me." I scoff. "I don't need your protection."

"No, I-I-I want to comfort you."

Comfort sounds nice, but I don't trust myself around him.

"Just go, Max. Comfort isn't what I need."

"What do you need?" His fingers graze my cheek.

"Time. I just need some time to be alone."

"You're not fucking Greta Garbo." Then he's gone.

Chapter 14

CRESS

Max hasn't been gone five minutes before regret swamps me. *Stupid, stupid, stupid.* So off balance I'm ready to throw away the only man ever to treat me with consideration. If I were flexible enough, I'd kick myself in the ass.

His fingers still whisper against my skin where they brushed my cheek. I forced him to leave, even though I wanted him to stay. I knew I was making a mistake as soon as the words started spilling out in an unstoppable spate. The panic I felt at seeing the reporters and photographers camped out in front of the building overwhelmed every other thought.

Everything is so confused, jumbled, and I'm struggling to make sense of it all—Max, Tina, reporters, photographers. I can't figure out what I could have done to deserve this. A quiet life with a few friends with shared interests, a satisfying career, and cats is all I've ever wanted.

Well, my life isn't quiet now.

Maybe Max has a Cyrano complex. Relief floods through me when I peek out the window and see an empty street. The paparazzi have vanished into the darkness, but so has Max.

No cavalier stands under my window, hopeful for a glimpse of his lady love. Why would he when I ordered him out? I yank down the blind in disgust at my behavior and my unrealistic expectations.

Damn, Micki and Sam are at a gallery opening. Won't be back for hours. Saying sorry won't be enough to make this right. She'd suggest I bake something yummy and surprise him with breakfast. Not a bad idea. A strenuous session in the kitchen would be a great way to work off my nervous energy.

A quick run through the memory bank of old standbys dredges up a few winners. Soda bread with walnuts and figs spread with goat cheese is always good. Max would love my lemon-blackberry coffee cake with a dollop of *crème fraîche*.

More work but worth it are chocolate-hazelnut croissants, warm from the oven, golden brown and crunchy. I'd have to bring them ready to bake then keep him in bed till they were done. Not sure I'm quite ready for that.

I start toward the kitchen to check for ingredients, sure my freezer contains puff pastry. Dried figs are always in the pantry along with walnuts. *Hmmm.* A figgy baklava is a tempting thought. I stop dead in the hall.

This is not the right course. Food's a recurring theme in our hesitant courtship but showing up with baked goods is too easy. I need something different to fix this debacle, something that's all about him. Knock-his-socks-off special.

I make a circuit, living room to study through the bathroom into the hall through the bedroom, back to the living room. Over and over, faster and faster, until I'm dizzy. I'm the Pied Piper leading Dorothy and Thorfinn. They trail after me under the mistaken impression that I will give them treats.

What does Max love? Languages, James Bond movies, terrible jokes, exceptional single malts. If we were in Vienna, the Third Man Museum might work. But we're not in Vienna and there's nothing like that in Chicago.

Then it hits me. Something to do with cars would be perfect. Not that I know anything about cars, though Paul told me about Max's fleet.

Ask him to take me for a drive? That's lame, and not exactly an apology. Must be some better idea. I check my watch. Only ten o'clock. I'm sure Paul and Ellie are still up. Just hope they opted for a quiet night in rather than clubbing. "Siri, call Paul."

Four rings. My finger hovers over the cancel button. I don't want to leave a voicemail. Just as I give up, the ringing stops. "Hello?"

"Paul? It's Cress. Did I wake you up?"

"Nah…well…probably. Ellie's out with the Zoo group. Thought I'd catch a movie. *The Car* is on, classic seventies horror, so I thought I'd watch that, but I must've dozed off. You'd think a *Jaws*-type movie with a car standing in for a shark would keep me awake. Middle age is such a downer."

"Speaking of cars, I need your help."

He chuckles. "Never thought I'd hear that from you. What you need?"

After our chat, I have a plan and fall into bed.

Too early for light to seep in around the blinds, but I feel chipper after a good night's sleep. First order of business, check my email and see if my reservation was accepted. Yes. A limo will pick me up at ten AM.

I paw through my meager wardrobe for suitable attire.

Sweats, jeans, and my one dress. Not the stuff dreams are made of.

I push down the acid bubbling up from my stomach, call Micki, and whine. "Nothing to wear."

"What, wear where?" Micki's befuddled response makes me realize it's 6:30 on a Saturday morning.

In the background, Sam's opinion is unrestrained. "What the fuck? It's the effing middle of the night."

When Micki turns up at my door, she has a shopping bag over each arm.

"Whatcha got?"

"Sixties duds straight from the Michelle Press collection. There are choices. You can be a hippie, a Bond girl—"

"Twiggy. Twiggy with long, curly hair."

"So, the not-Twiggy Twiggy."

An hour later, she gives me a critical final check. "You look righteous." She pushes hair out of her eyes and motions me toward the full-length mirror.

"Girl, you are rocking not-Twiggy. She would have killed for your hair. When Max sees you, he won't know what hit him."

As the limousine pulls up to the curb, I check my look one last time: a sleeveless A-line minidress in color blocks of lime, orange, white, and yellow; orange stockings; flat white go-go boots. So not practical for December.

My makeup is matte with pale lips. Micki went wild with my eyes—heavy on the mascara and eyeliner with sky blue eye shadow on the lids and brushed just under the eye.

She offered to try a Twiggy pixie cut, brandishing her scissors while she chased me around the room like the Mad Barber of Fleet Street.

Then she produced a flatiron. My hair is too curly for the sleek Emma Peel look I covet, but it is straighter. It hangs loosely around my shoulders. I'm the very definition of sixties mod.

The chauffeur opens the door. I want to burrow into the butter-soft leather seat and tell him to take me home, even though I am home. I giggle.

The temptation to say "Home, James, must be suppressed. I will go through with this. I step to the sidewalk. The dress clings to my thighs, but my parka is so long that I can't reach under to fix it.

Deep breath, Cress. Take the risk. Go for it

We zoom to Gold Coast. Max's house looms ahead. I am so not ready, but when the car pulls to the curb, I let the driver hand me out,

Halfway up the walk, I turn. The Rolls-Royce Ghost, black with a silver hood, winks in the pale December sun. I take a step back, straighten my shoulders, and climb the steps.

Why didn't I call first? Max may have gone out for a run, breakfast with friends, a rugby match. Hope he likes surprises more than I do.

I uncurl a fist slowly, finger outstretched, reach for the doorbell. The chime sounds like the bells of the orthodox churches I heard when I visited Moscow.

A disembodied voice emanates from the speaker. "Hallo?"

"It's Cress. Can I talk to you?"

"Half a mo'."

Max stands in the doorway, sleepy-eyed, hair tousled, in low-slung plaid flannel sleep pants. He's shirtless, barefoot. I drink in his lightly muscled arms and smooth pecs. He scratches his chest. Blinks.

"Cress. What are you…"? He trails off, his attention caught by the vision of car-ness at the curb. "Why is a Silver Ghost sat in front of my house?"

"May I come in?"

"Uh, sure." He pulls the door wide so I can sidle past him.

"I didn't expect you. Just got up. Need tea." He points to the living room. "Go sit down. I'll be back."

By the time he pads back in, my stomach is in knots. "I want to apologize for last night."

He brings the mug to his lips. I want to be the mug.

"I panicked."

He sips more tea. *Urrgggh.* This is so hard.

"I don't know how to make this right…"

Max holds up a hand to stop me. "Cress. Don't."

Crap. Massive fail. He doesn't want an apology. I grope for my parka and stumble up from the chair. "I'm so sorry, so sorry."

He reaches out a long arm and grasps my wrist as I try to run from the room. "You don't need to apologize. I understand." Hot kisses rain down on my face and neck as he rocks me in his arms. "I pushed too hard last night."

He pulls me in tighter. "Thought I could fix everything. That's my *modus operandi*." He points to his chest; his gorgeous, bare chest. "Knight in shining armor, me."

His words are balm to my soul. Max is an inexhaustible well of forgiveness. What did I ever do to deserve him? What will I do if the well runs dry?

My puffy silver-gray parka slips off and puddles on the floor, a glinting liquid mercury lake, like Max's eyes. I pull my gaze away.

He bends down for my coat. I rush to grab it and our hands touch. A blue spark of static electricity crackles between us. I pull my hand back and stick my finger in my mouth.

Max throws the coat on the end table. "I planned to come over later so we could talk everything out, make a plan."

My shoulders stop hovering around my ears as my muscles relax. Oh, frabjous day. I have a plan. Now I have to convince him to go along with it. "If you get dressed, I have a plan."

"Oh you do, do you? My plan wouldn't involve clothes."

I wave away his innuendo. "My plan is a cunning plan."

"Well played, Baldrick. Must be quite a plan with that Roller out there. By the by, how did you escape from the paps?"

"I had the chauffeur meet me in the alley. He zoomed out like a getaway driver. Zero to whatever in whatever." Adrenaline races through me at the memory, and I grin like a loon. "It was ace."

Max's gaze runs up and down my body. "I like your sixties gear. Especially the boots. What's it in aid of?"

"Part of the plan."

"Time-travel fashion?"

"What do you think of spending the day at the Klairmont Kollection?"

His brow furrows. "Maybe? What is it?"

"A car museum. Three hundred cars for your delectation. Classic cars, famous cars, all sorts of cars." I gesture at my outfit. "Classic clothes, classic cars."

"So, a Bond girl without the bikini? Pity, that."

"Twiggy, actually. She had several famous cars in the '60s, including a 1967 gold Toyota and a 1969 Lamborghini, lime-green with orange and white stripes. It was just sold last year at auction in Australia."

"Look at you, telling me about classic cars. That's so hot."

Hot—that's what I am right now looking at shirtless Max. I wish this was go-as-you-are, but I don't think they would appreciate a half-naked man showing up, no matter how glorious his body happens to be. "Get dressed."

"I will be ready in the flashiest of flashes."

How can you not love a man who quotes Rowan Atkinson in *Love Actually?*

Hours and 300 cars later, we stand in the parking lot, waiting for the Rolls to, well, roll up. Max stops a couple to take our picture under the signs that proclaim Imperial Car Sales and Klairmont Kollection flanked by wall art—wooden cut-outs of four enormous classic race cars.

We face each other. Max cups his hand to my chin, presses his lips to mine. The go-go boots pinch. My feet are on fire, but the result is worth the pain.

The man hands the phone to Max. "Great picture, huh?"

"Amazing. Just amazing." They shake hands.

"Thank you for this special day." Max beams at me.

My heart chimes like his Russian doorbell. Who knew a car museum could bring so much joy. My cunning plan is a success. Blackadder, Baldrick loves you.

MAX

I walk in from the kitchen, wiping my hands with a towel. Cress offered to clean up after dinner since I cooked, but I didn't want her to see how much of a mess I'd made.

"Dishes are done. The kitchen is clean." I pause. "It might be time to hire a housekeeper. Let someone else cook and clean. We could while away the time feeding each other grapes."

Cress looks up from *The New York Times* crossword puzzle, her pen still hovering over the page. Even though we've been together for hours, cooking, eating, talking, my breath still catches every time I look at her.

Today was magic. I don't care if it was out of guilt. The day was a gift. I wish I deserved it.

We wandered around the car museum for hours. The breadth of the collection left me gob-smacked. Who knew a treasure like that existed on the west side of Chicago?

And Cress…Cress found it, arranged everything including a ride in one of the most luxurious limos in the world. If she wasn't actually hanging on every word out of my mouth, she did a good job of faking it.

She's gazing at me now. I can't help wondering what she sees.

"Tell me what you see when you look at me."

"What do mean?"

"It's not a trick question. I want to see myself through your eyes."

A deer-in-headlights look turns her eyes dark in the lamplight.

"Please. I don't want you to be uncomfortable, but I'm desperate to know. Then, if you want, I'll do the same."

"I see a tall, lithe man, legs slightly apart, twisting a towel with long narrow fingers. The pushed-up sleeves of his cobalt blue shirt emphasize smooth, muscular forearms dusted with a sprinkling of dark hair. But his Cheshire Cat grin, rather than his buff body, sends the tingles down my spine."

She pauses, runs her gaze up and down my body, then focuses on my eyes. Clears her throat.

"His gray, elongated eyes can be placid like a gray mist but turn steely or stormy without warning. Right now, they hold an intense focus as if I am the only thing he sees. He can turn me to liquid or set me off like a firework. My skin fizzes when he touches me." She stops, looks at the floor.

I cup her chin in my hand and raise her head.

"Sounds like a writer's description of a character. Is that what you wanted?" Her voice sounds ragged.

"Am I hot?"

"So hot." She wraps her arms across her body as she trembles slightly. Then I grab her and pull her arms around me.

Twenty minutes later we come up for air. Cress' phone is plugged in, a playlist always at the ready. I usually try to tune it out, but the current piece catches my attention. "What's that music? It sounds faintly familiar."

"It's the John Dunbar theme from *Dances with Wolves*."

I shake my head. "Not sure why it sounds familiar. Maybe I've heard it as *Tafelmusik*."

Cress looks at me, surprised I mentioned a musical term, and in German no less.

"My cousin Guy loved peppering his conversation with music-y jargon."

Her eyes are wide with disbelief. "It's a film with Kevin Costner from 1990. John Barry won an Oscar for the music."

"Nope. Never saw it." Another pause. "Strange name for a film."

She can't help sliding into lecture mode. "It's about a Civil War soldier who goes to the western frontier and develops a relationship with the Lakota Sioux. He also befriends a wolf. When the Lakota see him playing with the wolf, they give Dunbar the name Dances with Wolves. Hence the title."

She examines my expression. "Sure you aren't familiar with it? It was very popular. Your Balliol chums didn't drag you to see it?"

I raise a brow. "My main 'chum' was Guy. We didn't go

to many films, certainly not American westerns. Perhaps an art film or two if the music was important."

"The music was important in this movie." Her voice rises at least an octave. "John Barry is a big deal composer. He wrote the music for some of the Bond movies, like *Goldfinger*, and the scores for *The Lion in Winter* and *Out of Africa*, among others."

Her voice peters out as I wince at her tone. "He won two Oscars for *Born Free*, score and best song."

"Never heard of him." I know I sound dismissive. I love cranking her up this way. "I didn't go to James Bond films for the music."

"You've never heard *Goldfinger*? You don't know Shirley Bassey? What did you go for—the Bond girls?"

"No." I grin. "Well, not only for that. They were about secret agents. By the time I was ten or so, I knew I would be a spy. Sean Connery, a Scot. Gadgets, cars, glamour. Q was my hero."

In my mind's eye I envision a parade of supercool sports cars. "The Bentley Mark IV in *From Russia with Love*, the Aston Martin DBS from *On Her Majesty's Secret Service*, the Lotus Esprit from *The Spy Who Loved Me*…"

Cress frowns and put her fingers to my lips. "Of course, it would be the cars. How could I have forgotten?"

"Your sarcasm is wasted on me. And yes, even I have heard *Goldfinger*." I hum a few notes, and her eyes widen in surprise. "One of the most iconic of the Bond cars, the Aston Martin DB5, was in that one. But that doesn't mean I can identify the composer, or even the singer. It's just a tune."

"You must have lived under a rock."

I try to look offended, but the beginnings of a smile start to poke through.

"Culturally deprived," Cress mutters dismissively, turning

back to the crossword puzzle.

"Culturally depraved, you say. I like the sound of that."

My suggestive gaze ignites her, the tips of her ears glowing bright red. She rubs her stomach as if trying to soothe some upset.

I wad up the tea towel, throw it on the console table. "I have something to tell you."

Cress freezes.

"I want to tell you a story."

Her posture softens. "Perhaps a wee dram to go with it?"

"I have several excellent single malts." I pull out a couple of bottles and wiggle them at her. "The Oban? Or would you prefer the Aberlour?"

"I like them both. Whichever you want."

I take out two Glencairn whisky glasses, pour two fingers into one and a little less into the other. She chooses the short measure then curls up against the arm of the sofa and twirls her glass.

I'm silent as seconds tick by. Finally, I clear my throat as I work up the nerve to start. "You don't like that I keep secrets."

"You're just realizing that?"

"I have a hard time parting with details about my life." I sip at the whisky, coughing as my swallow goes down the wrong way. Once I stop sputtering, I go on. "As you know, I went to public school…"

Another longish silence. I stare at the amber liquid in my glass. *Get on with it, Max, now you've started.*

I drag my gaze back to her. "Right, well…" I pause, thinking of the best way to put this unpleasantness. "Public school boys are known to indulge in a spot of bullying and hazing. Worse if you look weak or have secrets. I roomed with a boy I knew from London."

I hesitate. "His dad was an embezzler, but when his parents got divorced, his mum went back to her maiden name. He kept it close to his vest. I think three of us in our house knew, just because we knew him before. Anyway, it got out."

A twinge of guilt assaults me, even though I wasn't the weasel.

"The boys made his life a misery, especially when it turned out the head boy's father had been one of the victims. But he couldn't bring himself to tell his mother what was going on, or the housemaster or anyone. I told him to go home, but he thought he could tough it out."

Even though she's no stranger to bullying culture, Cress looks horrified. "Max, other people must have seen. How could everyone let it happen?"

I shrug with a pretended nonchalance. "It's what school was like. Generation after generation of students and masters. Everyone accepted it. And in this case, sins of the father…"

"Even you?" She sounds outraged.

"No. He was a mate. I had a tender conscience and a sense of justice with no knack for self-preservation. I tried to stop it. The pack turned against me. I was tougher than he ever was, so I hoped that would help get them to leave him alone."

I shudder remembering the de-pantsing, head dunked in the loo, being force-fed disgusting messes. "Just gave them two targets."

"What happened?"

"I came in from rugby practice and found him hanging from a ceiling beam late one afternoon."

"Oh my God. What did you do?"

"I froze. Allan Mason, another boy in the house, fetched the housemaster and the prefect. We were all interviewed by the police, but I never talked about the bullying that led to it. Turned out the authorities had no trouble finding out. The boys who were responsible were sent down for the rest of term. Just a slap on the wrist."

"They went on to have successful careers?" Her mouth twists.

"Of course. Only to be expected."

Cress takes off her glasses and rubs the lenses against the hem of her shirt. "Did you have therapy?"

"Not then. That experience taught me a lesson. I learned that life is safer when you don't trust anyone and keep your secrets close. Spies are good at that. Perfect career choice." This conversation is over.

"Okay, I told you one of my secrets. I never talk about this shit. So, can we watch a film, or do I take you home?"

Cress gets up and stretches. "How about the Marx Brothers? We could use a little slapstick. I think *Duck Soup* is available from Amazon or Apple."

"Funny, I thought you were going to suggest *Dances with Wolves*."

Cress' phone buzzes. I pick it up. "Who is it?" she asks.

"Text message."

"Read it to me." She sets up the film.

UNKNOWN: Sorry now? If not, you will be.

"Bloody hell. What is this?" I scroll back and see the previous message. I try to control my voice. "*Die bitch.* What the fuck?"

She shrugs. "I've reported them all to the police, but they haven't been able to trace them." Cress' nonchalant demeanor crumbles.

"Forget the film." I pull her shaking body into my arms.

Chapter 15

CRESS

Xposé is a few steps up from *Trash TV*. When the publicist told me, I laughed. She didn't join in. We tried for something more reputable, but Tina refused to appear anywhere else. A little research and bingo—the owner was part of her high school gang. *Shit.* I am so screwed.

I stare in the mirror, checking out the made-up version of myself. No wonder worker at this station. Tina prances in, tossing her long, dyed hair. She's dressed for a nightclub, not afternoon TV: short, sexy, low-cut silver dress, stilt-like heels, and diamond, or maybe pseudo-diamond, jewelry. She must have insisted on heavy makeup. It sits on her face like a mask. The short, flirty skirt allows her to show off her long legs.

She smirks at my understated royal blue silk blouse and gray flannel slacks.

"Still hiding behind the good girl mask. That ship has sailed."

"You look like a hooker."

Her tongue flicks over her lower lip. "You'll get yours."

Typical talk show set. Two couches on slants. A desk for a host in between. Assistants mike us up as the two hosts come on. We shake hands with Denise and Greg, then Denise sits next to me with Tina on the facing couch. Greg swivels his chair from side to side behind the presenter's desk. The director, who looks harried, comes on the set with last-minute instructions.

"There will be a voice-over intro, then the camera will start out with Greg. He'll introduce you then say a bit about the controversy."

I look at Tina. She gloats. "Just you wait." Her voice carries, and Denise shakes her head as the director starts counting down.

Voices, familiar voices—my voice and my father's voice —reverberate through the studio. To quote Dorothy Parker, *What fresh hell can this be?* A cold wave washes over me. This is a phone call from August, when the book hit the bestseller lists. The last time he asked for money, he must have recorded it. I listen with revulsion.

"Cress. Baby girl."

"Why are you calling?"

"You're on the bestseller list. Making boatloads of money. You owe me."

"I don't owe you anything. I don't see you unless I have a new book out. I'm not your cash cow."

"But, Cress, honey—"

"I'm not your honey. I'm barely your daughter. If you dropped dead tomorrow, I wouldn't cry. In fact, I'd probably throw a party. You're a sponger, a leech. Find some hole to crawl in."

I meant every word I said, but I never thought they'd be rolling back at me on TV.

Greg breaks in. "And now, our special guest, all the way from Jacksonville, Florida, Aaron Taylor."

Oh God, I didn't expect this. Why is he here? Then, as my gaze is inexorably drawn to Tina, I see her lip curl in a sneer.

My father walks onto the set. My jaw throbs, heart races, wetness spreads under my arms. I glance around the studio, looking for an escape. I can't just run away. Lungs constrict, and I can't take a deep breath.

"Thanks for inviting me." The way he says those few words tell you he is a snake-oil salesman.

Life is so unfair. Instead of an emaciated weasel, somehow his hard-living ways have only enhanced a feral silver-fox allure. His build is thin and wiry, not an ounce of body fat. How can a diet of bourbon and cigarettes make him a poor man's Anthony Bourdain?

As he runs his fingers down the lapels of his navy blue, chalk stripe jacket, I wonder where he got the cash to buy Hugo Boss. His gray hair is long, pulled back in a man bun, his face stubbled with silver.

At least he got rid of the Pancho Villa mustache. But the shaking hands belie his need for a cigarette or a drink. His voice sounds peevish, although I guess he is trying for plaintive.

"So, Cress. This purports to be an actual telephone conversation between you and your father." Denise is all team Aaron.

I clear my throat, trying to dislodge the softball there. "Uh, sorry, I, I…" This is a disaster. I don't even know what I am supposed to respond to. All I can see is Aaron Taylor, grinning at me.

"You bet it is. I called her last August when she was a *New York Times* best seller again. Wanted to congratulate her on her success. Called me names. Told me to drop dead. Her own father."

His fake wounded expression roils my stomach.

Denise looks at me and presses on. "Is it fair to say you and your father don't have a good relationship?"

I choke. Acid bubbles up into my throat. "What does my relationship with my father have to do with accusations of plagiarism?" I finally manage to squeeze out some words.

"Is it true that you refused your father's financial appeals?" Greg's gimlet-eyed stare is unnerving.

"He's a sponger." *Crap.* I'm whiny.

I sit up straighter, try to repair the damage. Before I can spit out another word, Tina breaks in.

"You're an ungrateful, untrustworthy, lying bitch. High-lights your character. You reject your father when he needs you." She manages to mix delight and disgust. "Why wouldn't you also be dishonest in your writing?"

Denise breaks in smoothly, "Mr. Taylor, you told us that after all you've done for your daughter, paying for all of her college education, including a doctoral degree from Oxford, she refuses to help you when you've had a financial setback."

My mouth drops open. My father starts talking.

"Denise." His voice drips with fake sorrow. "My daughter makes a lot of money. I supported her when she was young, and now she shows me nothing but contempt after all I've done for her."

Unfair. Why should he get to recreate the narrative? Portraying himself as the good guy and painting me as the ungrateful villain? My face reddens and I break, yelling over him.

"You bastard. You never did anything for me. Dumped us when Mom died, came around when you needed money. Financial setback." I snort. "You're a whoring, gambling alcoholic, never been able to keep a job. And I had scholarships for school. You never paid a penny."

He looks wounded. "You see, Greg, Denise, when Cress' mother died, I was heartbroken. Thought the kids would be better off with their grandparents till I could get myself back together. Sent money for them every month. Bet they didn't say anything about that. And they kept me away."

"That's crap. I'm sure he never sent money, in fact I know he contacted them over the years, asking for money. My grandparents did refuse to let him see us—not that he cared. After my grandparents died, I found the agreement he signed not to make contact. In return, they gave him a hefty payout."

My voice catches but I go on. "Tom couldn't wait to get out from under my grandparents' thumb. He found ways to contact Dad on and off throughout the years. Once Tom turned twenty-one, he left and turned over his inheritance to this great money manager. Who spent it all in a couple of years." I point at my father.

Greg cuts in. "We'll be back with more from our guests after these commercial messages."

The lights go down and we shift uncomfortably in our seats for two minutes. After the break, Tina repeats her accusations, my father continues to flaunt his hangdog expression, and we are done.

The torture is over, and I am wrung out. This was a farce. Nothing I said made any difference. No evidence was produced or demanded. I wasn't able to control my temper.

I am totally broken, my throat raw, as if I swallowed

sandpaper. My eyes are hot, red, and swollen. I cried on camera. How much guiltier can I look? How long will it be before my publisher drops me?

Outside, waiting for an Uber, my father sidles up to me. "I told you you'd be sorry for the way you treat me. I'll bet you are now."

"How did you get here?"

"Why, Miss Tina was kind enough to arrange it." He leers at the woman beside him. Her crocodile smile chills me. My father goes on, "She sent me a nonstop ticket from Jacksonville to O'Hare, got me a room at a fancy downtown hotel, took me shopping for this fine suit."

He sounds exultant as he caresses the lapels. "What a great show. I might sue you. With all the sympathy I drummed up, could be an easy win. You owe me."

"Owe you?"

"I figure you owe me a few hundred thou, at least."

"I owe you nothing. Not another penny. I paid for Tom's rehab, twice, after you squandered his inheritance. Sue me if you want, but you won't see a dime."

Tina thrusts her face into mine. "You never pay attention. Those text messages were only the beginning. Now the ball is rolling. Just wait. You won't have a career or a life worth living by the time I'm done. I'll ruin you, destroy you." Her expression looks almost crazed.

"Why this vendetta? What have I ever done to you? You were the popular one, the pretty one. Won all the beauty contests. Had all the cool friends. You were the leader of the pack. Why should you care about me? What difference does my life make to you?"

"The spotlight is on you, all the attention. No beauty pageants at our age. My dad went broke, so I never got the chance to go to college. I'm tired of low-wage jobs. I want to be a famous author."

She grabs my shoulders and shakes me. "I wrote a book, visited your publisher. Your editor laughed in my face, told me it was trash. I know you have poisoned the well. You are keeping me from being published. You were jealous of me in school, and you're jealous now."

I gape at her.

"You hide my light," Tina screams. "You hide my light."

"Fuck you." I turn toward the curb. The Uber driver has the door open, so I slide in.

Micki, martinis, and munchies at Bar Louie. Can't wait.

Chapter 16

MAX

I see the fiasco of an interview on my computer while I work on reports. Aaron Taylor is a wanker. How can anyone treat their daughter that way? All I want to do is rush to Cress, hold her in my arms, tell her everything is all right, make her believe she will overcome this.

My desire for her is almost overwhelming, distracting me from work. Both Clay and JL have complained that my obsession is interfering with my job. I need to resolve the conflicting emotions and pull up my socks.

I ring Cress' bell, tearing up the stairs as soon as the latch releases. Her door is open, but the cats are consoling a forlorn figure curled into the armchair wearing cute red cat pajamas. Her curls are in an unruly pile on top of her head.

"Got away as soon as I could." I shrug off my coat and kick off my wet shoes on her doormat. "It's snowing."

"I went to bed, but I can't sleep. The TV interview keeps running through my head."

She looks so sad that I want to hug the hell out of her then make out on the couch until she forgets all about her father and Tina, forgets about everything but me.

"I'm so sorry about how the interview went this afternoon." I pick her up and slip into the chair. "Do you think she's behind the threats?"

"She admitted she sent the texts today. But there's no other proof. The police haven't found anything to connect her, and she'd just deny it."

"Doesn't mean anything. She could be using a public terminal or knows how to mask the ISP."

"ISP?"

"That's the address of the computer that's being used."

"Oh." Her voice sounds flat, defeated.

"Why hasn't that woman been reported?"

"Reported?"

"Yeah. In England, we have Scotland Yard's Fixated Threat Assessment Centre. They'd have her watched or locked up by now. Don't you have an equivalent at the federal level, or even just in Chicago?"

"I don't think so." She scratches an ear. "Anyway, it's TV news. Not quite the same."

"You've talked to the police about stalking. You have the text messages and the note. All you have to do is listen to her and you can tell she's crazy. Also, I had no idea your dad was such a twat. I wanted to call him out I was so angry."

"He's not deserving of a duel."

"No, perhaps a punch in the nose, or maybe a kick to the balls."

"I can't believe you said that." Cress giggles. I'm happy to see her face brighten a bit.

In the background, a beautiful tenor voice sings in Italian. Goose bumps rise on my arms. "What's this? Music to sleep by?"

"*E lucevan le stelle.*"

"The stars are shining brightly," I translate.

"Puccini. It's from Tosca. This is Joseph Calleja, the Maltese tenor, singing Cavaradossi's aria before he gets killed in Act III."

"Isn't that what happens in opera? Everybody dies?"

Cress scowls but says nothing.

I rush to speak again before she can interrupt. "Guy did tell me one music joke that might be apropos. How can you tell if a singer is at your door?" When she doesn't respond, I continue, "They can't find the key and don't know when to come in."

She narrows her eyes. "There are various types of operas, and people don't die in all of them. Just like people don't die in every Shakespeare play."

"Okay, so explain that to me."

"Tosca?"

"No, opera. I have never known much about it, and I've only seen one. That was with Guy."

"No Covent Garden then? Or Glyndebourne?"

"The one we went to was some private production he did with friends. Can't say I enjoyed it. Some really dissonant stuff one of his mates wrote. Covent Garden for shopping and dining. Never been to Glyndebourne."

"The Royal Opera House is beautiful, and Glyndebourne is stunning. It's near Hastings on the south coast. When I went, I also visited Charleston. I'm a sucker for the Bloomsbury group."

I give her a quizzical look.

She shakes her head sorrowfully. "Virginia Woolf?

Vanessa Bell? John Maynard Keynes?"

"I've heard of Keynes." I rub a hand through my hair. "You're such a showoff."

"I'm sorry. I can't help myself."

I smirk. "It's cute. Now explain opera."

"You're sure?"

"If you go on too long, I'll shut you up with a kiss."

Her eyes are wide. "Ooooh, win-win."

"Yes. Rewards all 'round. Now bore the hell out of me."

"Robert Benchley said, 'Opera is where a guy gets stabbed in the back, and instead of dying, he sings.'"

"Cute. Who's this Benchley?"

"An American humorist. And John Philip Sousa…"

"The band guy who wrote the 'Liberty Bell March'?"

"How do you know that?"

I grin. "Monty Python. What else?"

"Ah. Anyway, Sousa said, 'Grand opera is the most powerful of stage appeals and that almost entirely through the beauty of music.'"

"You're saying I've missed out on something culturally important because I've never seen an opera?" I squeeze her.

"I'll order some Lyric Opera tickets so you can see what you've been missing." Cress picks up her iPad from the side table. Typing quickly, she brings up the website. "We could go see *La Traviata*."

"Tell me the story."

"You haven't heard of it? Have you heard of the composer Giuseppe Verdi?"

"Joe Green?" I tease. "Even I have heard of him."

"The story is about this French courtesan, Violetta, who falls in love with Alfredo. They move in together, and his father comes to break up the romance. She's suffering from TB."

I interrupt. "Isn't that the Dumas *fils* novel, *La Dame aux Camélias*?"

"You know the novel?"

"You look surprised. I do read."

"Really?"

"I studied languages. I've read lots of classic literature, mostly in the original languages. You know, *War and Peace*, *Madame Bovary*, *The Divine Comedy*."

Giving me a surprised look, she turns back to her iPad and buys the tickets online for a Monday evening performance. "We can have dinner at the Florian Bistro or the Pedersen Room in the Opera House. Joseph Calleja is singing Germont. How fortuitous is that."

∾

CRESS

JUST AS I finish the ticket order, a brick sails through one of my dining windows and lands on the table. The wood cracks. A moment of paralysis. I peek out through the hole in the starred pane. Paparazzi are milling. Did one of them throw it to attract my attention? Or was it someone else?

My first instinct is to run down the stairs and confront them, but Max grips my arm, fingers pressed tight. I shiver at the scowl on his face.

"I need to call the office. Some temporary security will probably encourage them to leave, at least for a little while."

"Shouldn't we call the police?"

"Yes. We'll do that too, but they can't hang around to keep you safe. Unless some of those jerks saw something, they won't unearth the brick thrower either. They can't even disperse those vultures. As long as the vermin stay on the sidewalk, they aren't trespassing." He pulls out his phone.

As I continue to stare out, the flash of a camera blinds me momentarily. Then the dazzle of broken glass that I've been standing on catches my eye. "I need to clean this up." I start to move toward the hallway for the broom and dustpan.

Max touches my arm. "Leave it until the police come. They're on the way."

I had ignored the lurid fake stories in the supermarket tabloids. Paul told me little vignettes still turned up on the news channels, but I stopped watching the news. Someone dug up old high school and college yearbooks and published sad pictures of my younger days.

Some reporter even dug up Kev, who didn't say much but left the impression that I was mentally unstable. Micki floated the idea of Paul making a statement as one of my oldest friends. He was willing, but I convinced them it wouldn't help. Obviously, the press was only interested in the bad, not the good.

But today's TV fiasco raised the stakes again. I focus on my window, where cracks like webs radiate from the hole. It's all too real.

Once a few security guys show up at the entrance to the building, Max comes back in with a couple of police officers and a man he introduces as JL Martin. JL shakes my hand and explains that he is the director of WatchDog, the business and personal security arm of GSU.

"Nice to meet you, Dr. Taylor." I discern a slight accent. He glances at the damage then leans against the corner of the credenza.

Max drops a kiss and goes to stand next to his colleague.

The cops take some pictures and ask what happened. After an hour of questions, they leave.

I stand at the window and watch the cars drive off. The squeal of their tires tears at my ears and the flash of strobes ricochets in my head. The street turns from blue to black.

My buzzer rings. JL casually walks over and pushes the door release. He's about 6'2" and solid muscle, wearing a white t-shirt and Levi's with well-worn cowboy boots under an unzipped Canada Goose Expedition parka. I'm surprised he isn't boiling.

His hands are shoved into the pockets of his jeans. Closely cropped brown hair and tattoos on both forearms make him look every bit the thug he isn't.

"What the hell?" I expostulate.

"Just the guys." He gives me a charming smile.

They are big, burly guys. Three of them are in rotation. JL introduces me to them, Dirk, Case, and Liam, so I'll know who they are.

"Just ignore them. They're your shadows. Assume they are around but do what you usually do. They'll be close by."

Then, with small waves, the four of them walk out.

A few minutes later, my buzzer rings again. Max hits the talk button. "Trent?" Getting an affirmative, he releases the building door. A minute later, two men in overalls walk in carrying plywood sheets. In half an hour, my window is covered with boards and the glass is swept up. Trent says they'll be back in the morning, and he and his guys remove the coverings from their shoes and take off.

Max slips into his overcoat. "We have a big push on for the next few days. My schedule will be crazy. Make sure you keep your phone off when you aren't calling out and avoid social media for a while. Don't ring in anyone you don't know. Stay in as much as you can."

The next few days are like a living in a surrealist painting. Trent replaces my window. JL stops by with a burner phone programmed with a number to reach Max. He cautions me not to use it for anything else.

The farthest I get from home is a garbage run to the alley. The shades are lowered. I can't write or concentrate enough to read. Instead, I binge-watch Britcoms and stuff myself with potato chips.

Micki sneaks in and out through the alley, keeping me supplied with junk food and carry-out. The paparazzi have thinned, but there are always a couple hanging around. Liam, Case, and Dirk are invisible.

My new normal is no normal at all.

Chapter 17

MAX

My day starts like shit. After all the drama at Cress' last night, I wanted her to come home with me or let me stay there. She let me stay, but after an hour, I gave up on the couch. The floor wasn't much better. I woke up with a headache, scratchy throat, and swollen eyes.

After an hour at work, the headache is a ghost, my throat is less sore, and my eyes aren't so scratchy. I manage to sit through two meetings, one with upper-level management and one a planning session with Jarvis and Eric.

Then it dawns on me that I had something else on my agenda for today. This might be a good time to make a call to Florida and implement another stage of Operation Get Cress.

Aaron Taylor picks up the phone. "Yeah?"

"Adam Taylor? Am I speaking to Adam Taylor?" I am pleased with the mechanical sound of my voice, complete with flat midwestern vowels. I've suppressed all traces of a British accent.

JL saunters in. I wave him to a chair.

"Aaron." A smoker's rasp.

I say nothing.

"Who is this?" His voice cracks.

I wait.

"I'm not buying anything if you're trying to sell."

He sounds a little rattled. Good.

I hang up.

"What was that?" JL's lips quirk.

"Just called Cress' father. The dodgy bastard needs a short, sharp shock."

I sit back and picture him shaking a little. A peek at the call log, seeing the number withheld. A picture forms. He runs his hands over his stubbly chin, pours a little bourbon into his coffee, lights an unfiltered Camel. Or maybe he's a Marlboro man, something he thinks gives him that macho aura.

The outline fills in, his day a combination of soaps and game shows. Looks over his shoulder for whoever is after him, because of course people are after him. I chuckle inwardly at this imaginary scenario.

"What's the plan, Max?"

"Shake him up, get him on edge. Then tell him Cress is going to sue him. Offer him a wad of cash to leave her alone."

"Does she know?"

"Once I have the signed agreement, I'll give it to her as a Christmas present."

"No, no, no. *Tu est timbré. Idiot.*" He loosens his tie and runs a finger around his shirt collar.

"Not crazy," I mutter. "I'm her white knight." The more he scolds, the more I dig in my heels.

"She won't thank you."

"I'm showing her how much I love her."

"Fine. Have it your way. I'll have fun watching you poke him, but I tell you, this will not end the way you expect."

All I hear is wah, wah wah wah, wah, wah.

Four more times I call him. Once he gets the warning out, JL is the ideal spectator. Eggs me on from one call to the next. I bet by now Aaron's covered in sweat.

I make a sixth call.

Cough. Hack. "Stop fucking calling me. You have the wrong number. Call someone else. Leave me the fuck alone."

He gasps. Heavy breathing.

"Aaron Taylor?" This time I use the right name.

He yells into the phone. "Look, I don't know who you are. Just tell me what you want. I'm not interested in playing games."

I use a different voice now, channeling my inner Scot. "Mr. Taylor." I emphasize the mister, rolling my Rs in a thick Scots brogue. "My name is Colin MacGuire. I represent your daughter, the author Cressida Taylor."

"Represent." Aaron repeats the word. "What the hell does that mean? You her agent? Lawyer?"

"It means your daughter is planning to initiate proceedings against you."

Aaron laughs, which transmutes to another cough. "Proceedings. You mean she's suing me. For what? She has money and I don't. No reason for her to sue me."

"She plans to bring a civil suit for harassment, libel, slander, and extortion. She will be asking for substantial damages."

Aaron is silent. I give him space to think over the implications. I'm sure he isn't worried about the money aspect. I've checked him out pretty thoroughly, and he doesn't own anything except his car. Maybe he wonders if this could mean jail.

I let the silence spool out for a bit. "Shall I go on?"

Aaron says nothing.

"I believe, Mr. Taylor, that your son, Thomas, is willing to testify on her behalf."

Aaron gives a short bark of laughter. "My druggie son, who lives with me, is going to testify against me? That's a joke. He knows which side his bread is buttered on. And if Cress plans to buy him, that's illegal." He sounds defiant, like he's scored a point.

"Indeed." I clear my throat. "Dr. Taylor would be amenable to a halt in these proceedings—"

"Oh, would she now?"

"Please let me finish. Dr. Taylor will stop these proceedings if you sign a document agreeing to permanently sever all contact and to not say or write anything public about her."

"She's my daughter. I have offers. A magazine interview, a book contract. I have a right—"

"You have no rights. Your daughter is an independent adult. She wishes to sever all ties. You can either come to an agreement now or see this through in the courts."

I take a breath and let the threat hang for a bit."

"Your daughter is more than willing to continue, no matter how messy and painful the trial. Personally, I would advise you to accept the offer I am authorized to make rather than go through the humiliation a public trial would bring."

"Offer?" His voice rises sharp with something that might be hope. "I get something for this?"

"Yes, I am authorized to offer you $100,000 if you sign the agreement."

Some noise comes through the phone, but I can't be sure if he's coughing or cackling.

"I do warn you, there are conditions." I pause. I let the silence accumulate.

"Conditions? What conditions?"

My voice is firm. "First, there will be no bargaining. This is a hard-and-fast offer, and my client will not raise the amount under any circumstances."

A choking noise comes down the line. "The book deal will bring more," he protests.

I snort. "Second, the penalties outlined for breaking the agreement are quite severe. If you renege, your daughter will pursue remediation in court and ask for repayment for any monies tendered over the years plus damages in excess of a million dollars."

"A million dollars." He laughs so hard he starts to wheeze. "Never going to happen." His voice is shrill. "The little bitch owes me—ME. I should have inherited when her mama died. All that money should have been mine. She owes me." He ends in a kind of sob.

"I have nothing to say about the disposition of your late wife's money. Your daughter knows you have no money. But if a judgment goes against you, it could lead to other consequences."

Bang. Bang. Sounds like he's beating his fists against a counter or some other flat surface. After a minute or so, the noise stops. "Go on."

"Third, there is to be no continuation of the collusion with Miss Tina Monroe." I conjure menace into my voice. "You have an hour to make a decision. At that point the offer will be reduced to $75,000. An hour after that, $50,000. Thirty minutes after, the offer will be withdrawn, and legal proceedings will be initiated."

There is a short silence. Dogs bark in the background. A slam. "Damn dogs. I keep warning the neighbors. Maybe I'll just pull out my shotgun—*bang*." He cackles. "I don't need an hour. I accept."

Short-term thinking, as I expected. Take the money, worry about the consequences later. I don't fool myself into thinking this is the last time Cress will hear from him, but I can afford to pay him. One less thing to agitate her.

"Excellent. I am pleased that we can conclude this agreement amicably. Give me an email address and we can settle everything quickly. You can print it out and fax the signed document back. Make sure you include your banking information so the funds can be transferred."

"Fine." He reels off a Hotmail address.

"You will need to have the documents notarized, but the library might offer that service. And you will need a witness. Once you have done all that, fax back the completed form. I will call you again in an hour to finalize the payment."

I hang up.

"Max, I hope this works, but I think you've made a mistake." JL shakes his head and walks out.

I know Cress will be pissed off when she finds out I bought off her father, at least temporarily, but I don't care. I know she'll forgive me.

Chapter 18

CRESS

Max is so busy at work that I've hardly seen him for the last few days. Paul and Ellie suggest we all go to Tiki Go Wild, a recently opened bar in River West. Micki jumps at the chance. Sam is out of town at another art show, and she's desperate to go out.

The paparazzi hung around for a while after the brick incident, but they have finally decamped. I still have a security detail so this should be safe enough.

Liam and Dirk drive me to the bar. Dirk is my designated date. Liam is the outside troubleshooter. We come in through an almost hidden alley entrance manned by a doorman. So cool. The stairs down to the bar are dark and atmospheric, and the music is mostly oldies.

The drinks are good—big, lavishly decorated with tiki swizzle sticks and hibiscus flowers and served in exotic barware. The decor is over the top with skulls and tikis, colored lights, and palms. We're crowded in a booth, looking slightly blue from the lights, the table crowded with pork belly buns, coconut shrimp, and crab Rangoon.

Fried food crunches in my mouth, the fat spreading on my tongue. Good prep for the alcohol to come. I pop a couple of shrimps, chasing crumbs of coating around the plate before I take my first sip of the most aptly named drink on the menu —a Painkiller. The name is perfect for my mood.

The combination of two rums, coconut liqueur, fruit juices, and cream served in a green, pineapple-shaped mug will deaden my pain. Dirk is drinking rum and Coke without the rum. I start to relax. Surely no one in the crowded bar will recognize me from the *Trash TV* feature or the tabloid coverage that exploded at the same time.

I'm usually a one-drink woman, but I'm so depressed that Paul talks me into a second. For this round, I choose the Tiki Go Wild. The original drink was invented during the Second World War by the famous Don the Beachcomber.

More rum, velvet falernum—a spicy rum-based liqueur— fruit juices, honey syrup, and Angostura bitters garnished with maraschino cherries makes a drink that smells like fruit cocktail, the taste of the alcohol masked in sweetness.

Drinks like that sneak up on you. This one knocks me on my ass when I get up to use the bathroom. Dirk goes with me. Balance eludes me, and I manage to trip and fall into a group of partying frat guys.

My knee scrapes against the tiles. *So humiliating to be groped by a bunch of guys barely old enough to drink when you're my age*, I think as Dirk pulls me away.

The raunchy comments let me know I am a joke to them. Was my generation like that? Probably.

Paul helps Dirk rescue me. Then the bouncers intervene and escort the troublemakers out of the bar as they loudly protest it isn't their fault. Micki grabs my arm and drags me into the ladies' room, a good thing since by now I can barely decipher the signs.

I emerge from the stall, stumble but catch myself, palm against the wall. A headache tears through me with no warning.

"Micki, I need to go. I feel awful." I hold her as we walk out. "Steer me to Dirk so he can drive me home."

But the nightmare doesn't end there. As I stumble out, grimacing from my headache, two couples block our way.

After the traditional polite jockeying, one of the women shrieks, having figured out who I am. "You're that woman, that writer, who was accused of stealing!"

I wince at a click. One of the men snaps my picture. I imagine my image all over the internet—slightly drunk, open-mouthed.

The man curses as Dirk grabs the phone and deletes the photo. He shuts up when he gets a good look at the mountain that is Dirk, who tosses the phone back. "No more photos. The next time I'll stomp the phone."

I run out into the alley. Dirk strides after me, and Micki, Ellie, and Paul chase. At the end of the alley, we run into Liam. "What happened? Why didn't you call me?"

Dirk holds up a hand. "Just a few people being jerks. No biggie. But Dr. Taylor wants to go now."

Out of the shadows, figures gather. Flashes blind me. Yells of "There she is!" Paparazzi everywhere.

Liam stands behind me, one broad palm on my back. Dirk moves in front of me. I'm a sandwich filling. The crowd presses close. Dirk moves forward like a tank.

"Out of the way you mofos." Sirens drown his warning. The crowd scatters to the wind.

Liam moves his hand from my back to my elbow. "Car's

right here." They walk on either side of me, help me into the back seat. I open the window and lean out, call to my gang, "I'm okay. See you tomorrow."

The plush SUV seat is like a hug. I breathe a sigh of relief. What I need is Max.

～

Max

ELEVEN PM and I'm still at my bloody desk. Reams of paper spew from the laser printer. Jarvis and MaryAnne, our current intern, collate the twenty copies of our completed proposal.

Three hundred pages of plans, diagrams, explanations, draft contracts. This could be the biggest contract we've negotiated since Clay started the company.

I tap my pen against the desk. Too late to see Cress. Again. Three days without her and I'm ready to crawl out of my skin. I snake a handkerchief out of my pocket. Hold it to my nose. The smell of Cress' perfume fills my nostrils. The bite of citrus with the heat of ginger permeates the cloth. I rub it against my cheek. Not a substitute for her cheek, but better than nothing.

My bed calls, but it will feel cold and empty when I fall into it because she won't be there. I need to touch her, hold her, kiss her senseless...coax her into my bed.

My phone buzzes. *Crap.* If this is another change, I'll...

Jarvis looks over. "We're just about done. Two more pages."

I pick up the phone. "Yeah?"

Shouts and the sound of feet pounding in the hallway. I look at my mobile.

Photos pop up. Cress in an alley, surrounded by photographers. Liam and Dirk scowl. *What the fuck is going on?*

JL skids through the doorway. His hair sticks up, untied tie slung around his neck, parka half on half off. "*Desolé. Pardonnez-moi.*"

He's sorry? Why?

MaryAnne is frozen, pressed against the laser printer, palms against her chest, mouth in an O, eyes wide.

"Cress is okay." JL's voice is hoarse.

I grab his shoulders. "She bloody well better be."

I glance at Jarvis. He flaps his hands. "We got this. Go."

Half an hour later we've careened up the Outer Drive, headed for Cress' place. Mark, one of our on-call drivers, pulls the SUV up to the corner. JL and I jump out. Liam is standing in front of the door.

"Dirk's up there with her. We didn't want to leave her alone. She's pretty shaken up."

When the door clicks, I bolt up the stairs. JL waits with Dirk, getting a full report.

Huddled on the sofa, Cress hasn't taken off her coat. Her eyes are hazy. The cats tangle in a heap on her lap.

"Cress." I stand behind her, stroke her hair.

"Oh, Max. I just wanted a couple of hours out with friends." Her intonation is slurred.

"How much did you have to drink?"

"Two cocktails. And I didn't even finish the second."

"People recognized her, started posting pictures to social media. By the time we got her out, a crowd had gathered."

"Come home with me."

She runs her fingers over the cat tangle. "I can't."

"It will only be a few hours, but we'll take them if you want."

"Need to lie down." She starts to slump over.

"Dirk, the carriers are in the closet at the entrance to the back bedroom."

"Got it." He sets a land speed record in carrier retrieval, scoops up Dorothy, and pops her into a case. Thorfinn struggles but fails to escape Dirk's grasp.

I go into Cress' bedroom, pull a duffle off the floor of her closet, stuff in pajamas, underwear, and a change of clothes. She's sound asleep, limbs sprawled out, head draped over the side of the sofa. Little mewling sounds tear at my heart. So fucking vulnerable.

Dirk slings the duffle across his chest then picks up the cats.

I cradle Cress in my arms, rub my cheek against her silky curls. Her scent envelopes me. "Safe. You're safe with me."

When we get to my house, I settle my sleepy girl in bed and leave her with the cats and a gentle kiss.

Dirk has already left, but JL is stretched out on the sofa when I go back to the living room. I open a bottle of *Brunello de Montacino* and grab two balloon wine glasses.. "How about a drink, mate?"

Chapter 19

CRESS

This morning was a mixture of disorientation and bliss. Dorothy draped herself over my chest in our accustomed wake-up ritual. The crisp blue sheets were unfamiliar. Fingers reached out, stroked Dorothy's soft fur. Warm breath tickled my ear.

"Morning, *la mia stellina*. Did you sleep well?"

I rub my eyes. Turn my head. "I don't remember coming here, so I guess so."

"Do you remember leaving the bar? The paparazzi?"

As I shift to my side, Dorothy digs her back claws into my stomach then rolls off the bed. "Yow, meow."

"There was a big crowd in the alley when we came out. Flashes. Yells. Sirens."

"Dirk and Liam got you home. Then we packed up the cats and brought you here. I didn't want you to be alone."

I snuggle against his chest, rub my nose against his throat.

His kisses set me on fire as he presses lips into mine, over and over, then pushes his tongue past my teeth, stroking and sucking. He tastes of sour cherry, aged balsamic vinegar, tobacco, espresso, and leather.

"You were drinking *Brunello*."

"Yeah. After you fell asleep, JL and I had a bottle." His eyes look a little bleary, but he doesn't seem hung over.

A voice blares through room. "The time is six oh five AM. You have a meeting at Global Security Unlimited in approximately two hours. There are no major delays on the CTA Red Line."

I can't suppress a moan of protest. "Max…"

"Right now in Chicago the weather is minus six degrees Celsius under cloudy skies. Today expect snow showers and a high of minus one degree. Have a good morning, Max."

"What the…"

"Special alarm." He rolls over and practically falls off the bed.

"What's the hurry?" My voice still sounds like sleep.

"Bugger. I need to get up. Stay in bed as long as you want. Your duffle is on the chair." He points to a corner of the room. "Just phone when you want Case to pick you up. He's your guy today."

A bit later, he puts a steaming cup of coffee on the night-stand and drops a kiss on my head. "Bye, *la mia stellina*." And he's gone.

Thank you, Max. I love you. Can't say it yet, but I feel it everywhere.

Then I pull out at the tickets Micki bought months ago for the Blackhawks game against Dallas tonight. Just three of us —Micki, Paul, and me. Ellie hates hockey, and her book club meets on Tuesday nights. Even though Max won't be there, I can't wait.

THE GAME IS at eight PM and Dirk shows up in another black SUV. After last night's fiasco, Max called me during a break in his meeting and argued that I shouldn't go at all. I stood my ground. Not missing this game. He arranged a ticket for Liam to sit near us and for Dirk to hang in the entrance area on the Madison Street side.

I'm sure the combination of hot hockey players and on-ice action will focus attention away from me. My Stan Mikita jersey and a hat change my look. No curls are visible.

My Hawks sweater makes my body shapeless. Micki painted my face with some black, red, and white stripes on each cheek, with 50 on my left cheek and 10 on the right, above each red stripe.

I relax, sip a bottle of water, drool over Patrick Sharp. Who doesn't? Fangirl Corey Crawford. Yay Crow. I have a weakness for goalies. We're down near the glass, a surprise since I usually sit near the top of the third tier. We watch warm-ups and join in the craziness during the singing of the national anthem.

I can't see the action unfolding as well, but the players are almost close enough to touch. Patrick Kane flips a puck over the glass, and it lands in my lap. *Oh my God...*

"He's my favorite." Micki's grabby hands reach for the puck.

"Too bad. It's mine." My fingers cover the coveted piece of rubber.

Once the game starts, I grit my teeth listening to the know-it-alls behind me comment on the action. Just because these guys are season ticket holders, as they keep reminding the rest of us, doesn't mean they have to be obnoxiously loud and usually wrong.

Relieved that Sam is still MIA, I tune them out along with Paul, who is constantly yelling for the players to shoot, even when they have no chance to make a play.

Five minutes from the end of the period, a fight breaks out between the Hawks' Andrew Shaw and the Stars' Antoine Roussel. Even with his sweater pulled over his head, the Mutt lands a flurry of blows on Roussel.

The officials eventually separate them, one of the linesmen wrestling Shaw to the ice. As he leaves, the Mutt salutes the crowd. We roar our approval.

I turned on my phone when I called Micki this morning, but my heart still races when my texting app sounds.

MAX: Liam tells me he has eyes on you.

I start to answer, but the Hawks are really pushing in the offensive zone. He will have to wait.

In the first intermission, I buy nachos to share with Micki. My phone dings with another text. Has to be Max. I forgot to answer in the excitement of the first period. I crunch on nachos while I swipe the screen.

MAX: What do you call a grumpy hockey player?

ME: NO NO NO

MAX: No more Mr. Ice Guy!

ME: …

MAX: That was funny.

ME: Not.

MAX: Where is the best place to shop for a hockey shirt?

ME: STOP…

MAX: New Jersey.

ME: Please stop.

MAX: Come to my place after the game.

ME: I took the cats home.

MAX: I'll fetch them.

ME: You don't have a key.

MAX: Not a problem.

Wait—what? He can get into my place? A prickle of unease runs down my spine.

MAX: Cress…

ME: You can stay at my place.

MAX: Your floor is uncomfortable.

ME: We can share my tiny bed.

MAX: *text bubbles*

MAX: *text bubbles*

MAX: *text bubbles*

MAX: I'll be waiting.

I tap Micki on the shoulder and hold out the phone so she can read the conversation.

"A sleepover huh?"

"Am I making a mistake?"

"Go for it." Micki's yell makes everyone in the seats around us turn.

Then they all yell, "Go for it!" Of course, they're egging on the Hawks, not me.

The Hawks lose 4-3. Paul offers to drive Micki home, and Liam walks me out toward the SUV. Butterflies swarm in my stomach and caterpillars crawl up and down my spine. My heart races.

MAX GETS OUT of his car and crosses the street.

"You didn't go in?"

"Don't have a key, remember."

"But you said…"

We make a pillow nest on the floor. My furniture really isn't suitable for two. A new couch might be in order, if I can figure out how to make it fit in the room.

Max nuzzles my neck. "The floor seems more comfortable when I share it with you."

"Ummm, the bed would be better."

He doesn't have to go in early, so we sleep late then bundle up and walk down to the lake. Huddled in our parkas, we stand on the pedestrian path above the deserted, snow-crusted sand, arms around each other, watching the high winter waves batter the shoreline. We are so close now. I want him to show he trusts me as much as I trust him.

"Tell me about the motorcycle accident."

Max clenches his teeth. A sharp pain strikes my chest as he releases me and moves down the path. His arms wave in a conversation I can't hear.

When he stops, I run into his back. He is immovable, standing with his back to me. He raises his voice over the crash of the surf. "You want to talk about this now?"

Even though it wrenches my gut, I yell into his back. "Yeah. I want to know."

His muscles bunch under my cheek. I step back so I don't fall down if he moves forward.

Max walks out a little farther before turning to face me, body stiff, legs apart, arms folded. I wish I could see his eyes, but he's just far enough away that they look like black pinpoints, barely visible through his lenses. We stare at each other. He collapses to his knees and starts rocking back and forth on the ice-coated sidewalk.

I walk toward him. He holds his arms out, palms toward me, warns me away.

"I wasn't doing well after Guy's death." His voice is slow and rough. "I was in therapy. Nightmares almost every time I tried to sleep. Death always on my mind. Grief mixed with rage. I resisted help at the time. I didn't want to pick at my feelings. I wanted to bury them, bury the pain, bury me."

He pushes up, staggers. His khaki slacks are wet, smeared with mud. He must have scraped the hell out of his knees. I can see red streaks leaking through the fabric. I cram a fist against my mouth as Max pivots to contemplate a gull turning cartwheels above the gray-green foam. When he turns back, he takes off his glasses and tucks them into a pocket as he walks a few steps back toward me.

"I was on leave from the job, hid from everyone—family, friends, colleagues. I rented a cottage near Ely, in the fen country." He moves closer, voice low.

I strain to hear over the crash of the waves and the screams of the gulls mixed with the clamor of traffic in the distance. I sniff the air, but it just smells cold.

"Three times a week, I went into Cambridge to see a therapist arranged for by MI6, someone also covered by the Official Secrets Act. I spent my time seeing the therapist, ringing bells, and riding my motorbike."

"You're a bell ringer." I grab his hand if it was a bell rope and start swinging it. "I always wanted to try that. *The Nine Tailors* is one of my favorite books."

He pulls away. "Never read it," he growls, staring at his arm, which is swinging of its own volition, oscillating like a pendulum. He clamps his other hand over his forearm, forcing it to stop.

"I did a spot of ringing in my undergrad days, and the therapist suggested I give it a go. Ringing those bells was therapy, and strenuous exercise too. Helped me sleep. I joined the ringers at Ely St. Mary's. That was about all the social contact I had outside the therapy sessions. Change ringing is very mathematical and you really have to concentrate, especially with call ringing. It gave me something to engage my mind and block out the memories."

I grab his hand and entwine our fingers. His hands are

rough, with a hint of the callouses he must have developed pulling the ropes.

"What about your family?"

"They were told not to contact me while I was in treatment."

"What the fuck." I can't keep the anger out of my voice. "That's inhumane."

"I think the MI6 were worried I would completely break down and spill all my secrets."

I'm shaking with anger. Max starts to move toward me, then changes course and moves a few paces away.

"Shall I continue?" He sounds as if he hopes I've heard all I can stand.

I shift from one foot to the other, dislodging small rocks from the path. I swallow my ire and give him a reassuring look even though I'm very far from smiling. "Might as well."

His expression is granite. "I was feeling pretty hopeless. One particularly bad day, when I was out riding, I started thinking about T. E. Lawrence."

"Oh no." I think back to the death of the famous archeologist, diplomat, and one of the leaders of the Arab revolt against the Ottoman Empire during the First World War. In 1935, he lost control of his motorcycle and was thrown over the handlebars, dying of brain trauma a few days later.

"The weather was bad—rainy, foggy, slippery road. And here I am, riding my Ducati 750GT, depressed, going too fast, thinking about a bloke who might have committed suicide on a motorbike."

I move closer and grip his hand.

"I don't remember much. I was told the bike skidded and slammed into a drystone wall. I was wearing a crash helmet. That probably saved my life. As rain poured down, trapped under the bike, all I could think was, *Shit, can't even kill myself properly.* Then a farmer drove by, found me. Called 999. Police cars, an ambulance, and off to the local hospital. The Ducati hauled off for scrap."

He's silent for a few beats. "When I recovered enough, I went to a residential facility for therapy of all kinds, even handbells once they knew about the ringing. Once I was out of captivity and MI6 was informed that I could go back to work, I requested approval to go to Oxford to study cybersecurity. My bosses didn't want me anywhere near fieldwork, so everyone was happy with that solution. I could still be useful. No way I was ever going to be allowed in the field again."

"You're okay now." I stroke his cheek.

"Better."

Chapter 20

CRESS

My phone rings, an unreasoning flutter in my throat. I check caller ID: Paul. Voicemail. My agent—voicemail again. My editor—same. The hopeful flutters have given way to resignation.

I haven't heard from Max. The walk on the beach convinced me we were on the same page. His silence sends a different signal. I let my ice walls melt, but his fortress is made of stronger stuff.

Another call. Number withheld. That's the fifth time in the last few hours. My mind shifts to Tina. She's been quiet since the TV confrontation. Not what I expected. After the clusterfuck outside the tiki bar, I figured she would really push the envelope. A deluge of social media posts, short interviews on internet news outlets. Instead, silence. Just like Max.

I look over my shoulder all the time. The security detail

doesn't make me feel secure. I need Tina gone and Max here. Right now I hate my life. Hate it, hate it, hate it.

And it's my birthday. Forty-six today. Mine falls at the worst time, in between Thanksgiving and Christmas. Who needs another celebration? *Non, merci. Hayır teşekkürler. Nein danke.*

A party when I was six. Mom baked a Barbie-decorated cake and invited several girls from my first-grade class. My seventh birthday was forgotten. Mom started chemo, could hardly keep any food down, and was weak. My dad was never around. My grandparents' contact was sporadic. Did I care? I can't remember.

Soon after my eighth birthday, Mom died. Birthdays and Christmases vanished forever in the cremation flames. Except, this year, I kind of hoped...not that Max would even know that today is my birthday. No, not going there.

Darkness steals in and I move toward the windows. Time to pull down the blinds and think about dinner. I haven't had anything all day. Pizza? Do I have one in the freezer? Maybe just get Giordano's delivered. I slump to the couch, too dispirited to turn on the lights.

Commotion filters in from the street. Music? Probably just a blaring car radio. The volume increases. The hubbub is right outside my window. I manage to pull myself upright. After the brick, I'm wary, so I creep across the floor on my hands and knees then peer under the partially open blinds.

On the sidewalk I see a band, flames, signs. Is this a witch hunt, a book burning, a lynching? Has the time-space continuum been breached?

Fuck, this must be Tina's latest stunt—a protest over my book. A volcano erupts in my chest. I can't stand any more harassment. I write fiction, for God's sake. Fiction. These plagiarism accusations are bullshit. It's all innuendo, baseless allegations with no proof, or even an attempt at proof.

I hear a chant. My name? Or is it "Burn her. Burn the book." Too indistinct to tell. Maybe I should go out and confront my nemesis. Violence isn't my style, but at this moment, hitting someone sounds good. My vision clouds. The burning in my chest is intolerable.

I throw caution to the wind. Push up the window and stick my head out. "Fuck off, Tina."

"Cress? Are you all right? You sound ill."

Sounds like Max. Hard to tell over the pandemonium. Trumpets? Singing?

Everything goes quiet. Has the noise stopped or am I deaf? I roll my head, pushing against my ear canals, trying to clear them.

Knock, knock. I open the door.

Thousands and thousands of balloons float up toward the ceiling. Or twenty.

"I'm so sorry." Max pulls me into a hug. "Micki told me your birthday is all sad memories, so I thought I'd change the dynamic. Clean the slate, start some *beaux souvenirs*. Have a band play 'Happy Birthday' and bring you a bouquet of balloons—I even hired a fire eater. Thought that would be cool."

"A fire eater? I saw one in the Marais, in Paris, years ago. It was magic. You did all that for me and I missed it."

"It's all right. We'll go to Paris and find one."

We walk over to the window. The band is packing up. The onlookers meander down the street. The fire eater pulls his shirt over his tattooed arms, his flames doused.

"Once everything was in full swing, I planned to take you downstairs to celebrate."

I gaze at the balloons floating near the ceiling, silver

Mylar ones saying *I Love You*, multicolored ones shaped into flowers. Dorothy is on top of the mantelpiece, trying to catch one.

A piece of white cardboard lies on the floor, half covered by Thorfinn's butt. I nudge him aside and bend down to pick it up.

A drawing of a cake that looks like it was done by a five year old says *Happy Birthday Cress* in green marker, with flowers drawn around the edges.

Max is still talking.

"Sorry. Distracted. What did you say?" My throat hurts as I try to swallow.

"Zoolights. Then dinner at Bavette's with Micki, Sam, Paul, and Ellie, and JL and whoever he's seeing just now. I'll call Micki and cancel."

"Forget that. You gave me what should have been the best birthday of my life, and I missed it. Let's enjoy what's left of your surprise."

He leans against the curio cabinet. My gaze roams over the lean muscles in his biceps, down the tight stomach, lingers on the overdeveloped quads and sculpted calves.

I want to run my fingers everywhere. I glance up to his face. His eyes, the soft gray of mourning doves, transfix me.

"I had a videographer, so you can see the spectacle over and over on your DVD."

"Not the same, but better than nothing. I regret the fire eater. That would have been amazing."

Max checks his watch. "So, Zoolights? We can duck out back and down the alley. I'm parked in the next street."

"How much time do I have to change?"

"Fifteen minutes?"

"More than enough. I love Zoolights."

"By the way…" He brandishes a large, cream envelope. "I have another surprise for you."

It reminds me of the nomination I received a few weeks ago. Seems like forever. "What is it?"

"Open it."

Inside is a large, cream-colored card with the crest of the British Consulate at the top. I look up at him. "Is this a joke?"

"No." Max frowns at me. "My brother Ian is in the diplomatic service. He wants me to attend this event the consulate is holding. The cause is near to his heart. I told him I would, but you had to receive an official invitation of your own."

He pulls the envelope and card out of my hands, puts it on the small table next to the couch. "Please come. It's a private fundraising event for a research lab, but the couple involved are also very interested in literacy projects. I'm sure they would be thrilled to meet you."

I'm not so sure about that. "This sounds very posh."

"Oh, it will be, so you will have to go buy a fabulous new frock."

I swallow my misgivings. "Sounds like the best night ever."

MAX

BACK AT MY HOUSE, I stretch out on the couch, pulling Cress in next to me. We've been sipping hot toddies, being cozy. I'd never been to Zoolights. We had a ball roaming the grounds of the Lincoln Park Zoo, looking at animals made out of wire and twinkly lights. Delighted screams of children filled the air. So festive.

"That was the best birthday ever. Thank you."

"I'm glad you liked the last part. I was a fool to think a surprise was a good idea." I give a little laugh. "Dinner was brilliant, however."

"I had a great time getting to know JL. But what's the deal with his girlfriend?"

"With that sexy French-Canadian vibe, picking up women is easy. He's not into long-term, though, so he picks women he doesn't like very much. That way he can drop them after a date or two."

Cress wraps a curl around her finger and gives me a come-hither look. I prepare for a kiss.

"Tell me about the guy who was with you at Oxford. I thought you were a supercilious jerk, but he was a sneery asshole."

My lips twist. Not what I expected. "You don't pull your punches, do you? The sneery arsehole was my cousin, Guy."

"You mean the one you were talking about at the beach? They were the same person? I didn't realize…" Her eyes squeeze shut, and a tear drips out of the corner of one. I brush it away with my thumb.

"Funny you should bring him up. I wanted to talk about him."

She tilts her head to the side.

"We were pretty close."

"Were close? You're not close now? His attitude drove you away?"

"No." My vision blurs. "He died."

She gasps in surprise. "I'm so sorry. Was it an accident?"

"No." I roll my shoulders and move over to the chair, taking a few ragged breaths. "We grew up together. His father was a diplomat, posted all over, and Guy mostly lived with us so he could have a more stable life. He spent holidays wherever his parents were, but the rest of the time he was just another brother to me. All our schooling was together. We shared digs at Oxford. He was an organ scholar."

"I remember you mentioned him in connection with music, but I wondered because I thought you said no one in your family had any interest in music."

"That's not exactly true. My mother trained as a pianist and her uncle was too. But Guy was exceptional as a performer and as a composer. He was always an exception to everything. And then he died."

"Oh God, I'm sorry. I didn't mean…"

"Yes, you did. And he was. He could be an insensitive, prejudiced, misogynistic arse."

"But he was your cousin."

"Yeah, and in spite of all his flaws, I loved him." I pull a worn, folded piece of paper out of my pocket and slide it over to her. "He could be pretty thoughtful and even, dare I say it, philosophical. His writing was eloquent. The letters I got when I was traveling were a lifeline since I could seldom phone anyone or even go home. He sent me this while he was undergoing cancer treatment."

DEAR MAX,

Music and cancer have become intertwined for me in recent times, and especially since the beginning of this year. As you know, I mostly gave up music after Oxford and went into the family business. I still composed and played a little, but music became a grace note in my various postings.

I was diagnosed with an aggressive form of prostate cancer a couple of years ago. But like my sporadic compos-

ing, I saw this as an isolated fact in my life. *Surgery and radiation weren't fun, but they were over quickly, and I returned to a normal life. I used music as a kind of therapy, and composing becoming my drug of choice, until it was obvious the early treatments were not successful.*

It was only recently that my cancer treatment itself has come to take over so much of my life. Now that I'm on chemotherapy, my treatment has become the undesired center of my schedule. Each infusion is followed by about two days of emotional misery, followed by two to three days of utter exhaustion. Gradually, the exhaustion gives way to a generalized fatigue. This fatigue is not so debilitating as the first few days after treatment, but it robs me of any stamina for extended effort, physical or mental. As a result, I cannot compose now; that takes too much sustained effort. So, cancer has displaced music as well as my full-time job, and I hate that. I really want to compose, but I can't summon the energy.

I recently made a list of things that make me feel better. This ranges from ice cream to Monty Python to, of course, listening to music. And when I feel really bad, I like very aggressive music. Bartók's Miraculous Mandarin is ideal for those occasions. When I'm not so down, I listen to a variety of things, too wide a list to detail here.

But listening to music isn't the same as composing. If I have temporarily given up composition, I began with a rationalization. I told myself it's always good for a composer to take a break, to write less and listen more. There is no better way to learn music than to listen, and to listen broadly. But after almost two months of chemotherapy, I'm beginning to doubt my rationalization. Listening to music for me is an active process. When I listen to music I don't know or rehear music I do know, I'm actively engaged in the music. Now I can't summon the energy even for that.

Music is a constant in my life, in recordings, in performances, on the radio, and in my mind. And yet, now I'm not listening very deeply. I don't have the stamina to listen in any depth. I can only hope the good listening does for a composer will somehow reach me by some sort of osmosis. But that will inevitably be in some diluted state, since more passive listening is all I can do, at least until my treatment is over.

You once said I was the kind of person for whom music is a sort of life force. Of course, it's facile to contrast that with cancer as a death force, but the intersection of music and cancer in recent years seems deeper than that. They represent the years-old conflict of pursuing and ignoring music that I lived with when I was involved in a career outside of music. It's a connection I would never have expected, but that's the nature of cancer. And the unexpected is in the nature of music too.

Surely cancer will change me in ways I can't anticipate; it's already changed me, and surely that will affect my music in ways that are even more difficult to anticipate. One friend has already asked me how cancer has changed my music, and I haven't been able to answer him yet. Although I was diagnosed two and a half years ago, it's only this year that cancer has taken over my life so fully, and only two months that I've been on chemotherapy, so it's difficult to predict how it will change me in the end. It's clear that music and cancer are strangely, absurdly, and intimately intertwined in my life and will remain so permanently.

I hope you will be able to slip out of your shadow life and spend some time with me in the Highlands soon. If I have the energy, I'll play some of my compositions for you.

Guy

CRESS PUTS the letter back on the table. Her head hangs down; her shoulders shake. I move over to the couch.

"Oh my God. I can't believe I said such insensitive things about him." She wrings her hands. "This is why you don't listen to music."

"I never thought of it that way, but maybe so. I only listened when Guy was playing something. Then again, he almost always had music on, and I never have music on. It was almost painful when you turned on the radio the other day."

"How old was he?"

The ensuing silence presses down like a weighted blanket, all-encompassing, but stifling rather than comforting.

"Thirty." My throat closes up like I'm choking on bile. "It's a travesty to die of prostate cancer at thirty—an old man's disease."

She takes my hands in hers and rubs her knuckles up and down against my fingers.

"You spent time with him at the end." It's more a statement than a question.

My eyes squeeze shut. I shake. Christ, I haven't felt like this in years. All the memories pour in, fresh as when we experienced them. My heart aches.

"Max." Her voice is sharp. Swallowing, she tries for a gentler tone. "Max."

"No. I couldn't bloody go home. I was overseas." I pause, look anywhere but at her.

"Even so…"

"The job was delicate. I asked to go home for a bit, but

my masters said they needed me there. Too much at stake. A dying cousin, weighed in the scales of foreign relations, was like measuring a feather against a rock. By the time I was home, by the time I could reach Scotland, he was dead. I've never forgiven myself for not leaving. My family should have been more important than my job."

"Oh, Max. Now I understand what you were telling me about your accident." Her cry cuts me to the heart. I hear her grief for a man she never knew, and for me as well. My hands are clasped so tightly the tips of my fingers are white.

"Oh my God...I can't believe anyone would be that heartless. You worked for assholes."

"Intelligence agencies are all the same. It's part of what you sign up for."

Chapter 21

Max

Friday. Finally. I leave the office, exhausted and starving. No way I can cook. Leftovers are unappealing. I pick up samosas, lamb biryani, butter chicken, *saag paneer*, and *gulab jamon* on my way home, dump it on the kitchen counter. "Scots Wha Hae" brays out of my laptop. I grab my heaped plate of samosas and chutney and a bottle of cider.

Without even checking, I hit accept, and my older sister shows up on the screen with her wide sharky grin. Slightly smeared red lipstick mars her teeth, gives them a blood-stained look.

"Hey, Smiley. Where have you been hiding?"

I wince at the stupid nickname. When I joined MI6, my family christened me Smiley, after the John Le Carré character. "Miss you too." I shift on the sofa, continuing to look into the screen propped on the coffee table. "It's late. Long night at the palace?"

"We had an event." She changes the subject. "Hope you're planning to come home for Christmas this year." Meggy's loud voice is an assault.

I give her a thumbs-down. Dip my samosa into the bright green coriander sauce and take a bite.

"You're eating."

"Dinner time. Takeaway curry. The smell is amazing by the way. Wish we had smellavision so you could be even more envious."

Meggy sniffs. "Sorry. No wonderful cumin and hot chilis coming my way."

"Too bad but you probably don't want that late at night. Anyway, I can't come over this year. With this big software upgrade rolling out, I honestly don't have the time."

"Seriously, Max. It's been at least two years since you were here last. Mum and Dad won't say anything, but they're getting older, and they miss you. Your precious job can let you go for a few days."

"Guilting me is not the way to my heart," I growl.

A tickle of unease makes my neck itch. It's true that Mum and Dad aren't getting any younger and Dad's health isn't great. I take another bite of samosa.

"Are they okay? Has something happened?"

"Would you come home if I said yes?"

"Would you lie to me?"

"Maybe." She giggles. It's a sound unbecoming to one who works in the queen's household.

I press my hand to my chest and roll my eyes. "Are you trying to give me a heart attack?"

"Heart." She's glaring now. "I don't think you have one. Sometimes I think you've forgotten us altogether. All those years in that secret life…you need to come home, reconnect, stop being an arse."

"Thanks for being so frank."

"You're welcome."

Ah, the joys of Skype. Communication is so visceral.

"Do you know you are making monkey faces?" I jeer. "I'm not ten years old and at public school anymore. Save them for your nephews. A much more appreciative audience, I'm sure."

She cackles, a sound even more disturbing than the faces.

"I Skype every week." I throw out my hands, palms up. I know I'm not the model son.

She sniffs then sticks out her tongue in derision.

"How old are you, six?" I grouse.

"If I'm six, you're only a wee bairn of one. Still in nappies." The laughter melts away. "Skype is a stopgap. *Mamushka* and Dad want you home for the Sunday roast, to go to the rugby match, have a pint at the pub, play with your nieces and nephews. Save Mum by going racing with Dad. Share some hugs. Show some family feeling."

"Things are complicated."

"When aren't they complicated? That's an excuse, a screen. Come out from behind the curtain, O Great Oz."

"I'm tied up with things."

"Work things." Her voice is flat.

"Yes…but there's something else." *Shit.* Why did I say that? Give my sister an opening and she'll stick in the knife.

"Personal? Have you decided to come out of the closet?"

I can't believe she's said that. "What are you talking about?"

"You've never had a girlfriend, so excuse me if I assumed—"

Cider. The hint of bubbles and slight astringent burn from the fermented apples cool my throat. "Don't assume."

"You have a girlfriend." Now she sounds gleeful.

"What, I—fuck, Meggy. Just stop prying."

"Bring her with you. That will solve everything."

"I'll see what I can do in the new year about making a short trip. Let you know when I make some concrete plans."

She snorts in disbelief. "Keep telling yourself that, Max. Meanwhile the parents keep getting older. And if you do happen to have a lady love, they'd love to meet her, I'm sure."

"Look, don't tell them. I'll call and let them know."

"Yeah, sure," she says. But I don't really believe her.

I end the call with relief, but also lingering guilt and depression as I shut down my computer. I go into the kitchen and look at the heap of containers, wondering why I bought so much. I've lost my appetite.

I MULL OVER Meggy's call, trying to figure out what to do about Christmas. Saturday I'm back in the office. Admin never ends and so few people are around I can really dig in, but thoughts of Cress and my family make concentration difficult. Cress and Micki have a girls' night planned, so I rope JL into dinner and a film.

After my Sunday morning run, I decide to make a Skype video call to my family before Cress arrives for dinner. The six-hour time difference works perfectly. It's the middle of the day here, and well into the evening there. I launch into my first joke.

"Knock, knock."

"Who's there?" That's dad.

"Arthur."

"Arthur who?" Ian chimes in.

"Arthur any mince pies left?" Dad cackles, beating me to the punchline.

Mum's face twists in mock pain. A call with my family means a lot of bad jokes.

The family groans crescendo. Ian pumps a fist. "I told you no one misses your jokes."

Dad breaks in. "What do you get when you cross a Christmas tree with an apple?"

Silence.

"No? No guesses?" He laughs.

Silence.

"A pineapple!"

"The apple doesn't fall far from the tree." Meggy's joke is a little flat, but we roar our approval anyway.

I clear my throat, rushing to forestall what's coming next. "I can't come home for Christmas."

"Oh." Mum can put so much meaning into a two-letter ejaculation.

"I have obligations."

"That's no exaggeration." Meggy grins.

"What might these obligations be?" Dad chews on his pipe.

"A girl, living with him." My meddling sister sounds gleeful.

"Oh?" Mum again. She has so many meanings with that word.

I swallow, try to relieve my dry throat. "She's not living with me." Silence rolls in like a pea souper. "Remember my bicycle girl?"

Initial looks of mystification slowly morph into understanding.

"From twenty years ago?" Diana's squeals are ear-splitting. The slack-jawed faces are priceless.

I smirk. "Exactly. Anyway, she lives in Chicago. I saw her on television and found a way to get in touch. We met properly not quite a month ago."

The cacophony is deafening.

I shout over the crowd. "She's a writer. Very smart. Very serious."

"Yeah. Older than my dear brother."

"Just shut up, Meggy."

Everyone starts talking at once.

Mum finally breaks through. "It's been too long."

"Twenty years is nothing."

"Not that. It's too long since you've been here. We need to see you. In person, not this virtual *chepukha*. Figure out some way to come home." The longing in her voice cuts me to ribbons.

"Doesn't this girl have family and friends to spend Christmas with? Surely, she can manage without you for a few days. Or bring your *lyubimaya devushka*, your girlfriend, along. Your dad and I are not getting any younger, Max."

Wincing as if she slapped me, I try cajoling her. "Please don't try to guilt me about this, *Mamushka*. I'd love to be home with the family."

"Not enough, apparently, to actually come home." A shiver runs through me like a wind blowing in from the Sahara. Dad's good at guilting me too.

Now, how to put the rest? I rub the back of my neck then draw a deep breath. Then I confess, "I don't know if she can be without me, but I can't be without her."

The raucous hooting from my siblings is superseded by Mum's snort of displeasure. I fall silent, thinking furiously about some way to placate her.

The silence that follows is deadly. We all watch each other shift uncomfortably on our seating of choice. Mum is obviously furious. I can see it in her face as she glares into the computer screen.

Then I try the last-ditch gambit I concocted last night as I sat around, wallowing in too much Indian food. "Darling *Mamushka,* you and Dad could come to Chicago for a few days right around Christmas."

"Yes, let's do that," Meggy bellows into the phone.

"I didn't invite you." Bloody hell. Now the whole family will turn up.

"You know your dad doesn't fly now." Mum's voice is strained.

Dad huffs. "I'd be willing to go to the States for a chance to see Max. A few days in Chicago might not be too bad. It's the flights I can't stand, but I'm willing to put up with the discomfort if we have no other way to see you and meet your girl. Maybe the doc can give me something."

Besides the physical challenges posed by flying, Dad can hardly bear to see a runway. Stepping on a gangway is sheer torture. Two near-death crashes can do that to you. He walked away unscathed but shaken from the first one, joking about being a modern Antoine de Saint-Exupéry, but the injuries he endured in the second were devastating.

"I can book you on the Queen Mary II out of Southampton. You can do a round trip and train from New York to Chicago. No flights, plenty of chances to walk around and relax. Kind of like the early days of steam. I know you'd be cutting it close to arrive here by Christmas, but it's possible. How soon can you be ready?"

Mum looks thoughtful. "What do you think, Brian? It would make up for the round-the-world cruise you keep denying me."

Dad pulls his ear, pretends to be reluctant. Mum elbows him in the solar plexus. Finally, he grunts, "I'm game."

We cheer loudly. Video calls are the next best thing to being there.

"We can meet this new, important person in your life. Get us the earliest date you can, Max. Tuesday, if that works. I'm pretty sure there is a sailing Tuesday."

What? Were they expecting me to tell them I wasn't coming home for Christmas? Of course they were. Meggy would have told them. Has he manipulated all this? Doesn't matter, I decide, happy they are coming. I pull my attention back.

"We can easily make it to Southampton in time. Doesn't take long for anyone in this family to be ready to move. We'll arrange the train."

I pull up the Cunard website. God, I miss my big, noisy, messy family. "How many cabins, then? Will everyone come?"

"All of us, yes. Frank and Liz and the kiddies, Meggy, and Les and Diana and Sean. So, four cabins should do it if there is a big enough stateroom for Frank's family and a triple for Les and Diana."

"What about Ian?"

"I'll already be in Chicago by the time you arrive, *Mamushka*."

"What?" The shouts come from all sides.

"I will be the temporary consul in Chicago for the next three months. I was planning to surprise Max, but I guess you all know now."

"Fine." I type furiously. "I'm sure I can arrange something satisfactory for everyone else. I'm on the website with Cunard right now, chatting with an agent." The clicking of my keys is loud in the silence. "And surprise—it does look like there is a sailing Tuesday. I'll text you the arrangements as soon as they're made."

"The kids are dancing." Liz turns the camera so I can see. "This will be such fun for them."

"Maybe we can even go for a spin while you're here if the weather isn't too bad. I have a couple of cars you'll be interested in trying out, Dad." I try not to double up at the expressions on my parents' faces, Dad's one of anticipation and delight and Mum's of resignation. Dad might not be able to tolerate flying these days, but he is still up for short rides in fast machines.

He treats us to a last joke. "What do you call Santa's little helpers?"

"Subordinate clauses," Sean shouts out in the background while Diana scowls. The kid is definitely a Grant.

Dad laughs. "Make the arrangements, son."

"Train tickets are done." Meggy beams with satisfaction. "I'll pick you up at King's Cross tomorrow, and we'll all travel down to Southampton Tuesday morning."

"We can't wait to see you." Mum throws a kiss.

Chapter 22

CRESS

When I show up for an impromptu meal, I surprise Max by bringing the cats and an overnight bag that includes my dress for the opera. We cuddle for hours on the couch. The way he strokes my body, and his deep kisses, heat me up and make me regret my decision to sleep in the guest room.

After a restless night, I wake up early. I'm starved even though we had a huge meal last night. I mix up an oven-baked frittata. Heat rolls out as I open the oven door. Just as I pull out the pan, two arms slide around my waist and soft lips kiss the nape of my neck.

"Sleep well?" he asks.

I pull away to put the baking dish down. Quick as the brown fox, he traps me against the counter.

He's wearing flannel sleep pants and a short-sleeve gray tee that matches his gray eyes. Unshaven, hair standing in little peaks, his rumpled look makes my skin heat. I run my fingers down his face and neck and drop light kisses on his chest. "You look yummy."

He straddles one of the bar stools and nudges me between his legs. Cups my chin, tilts my head up. I'm lost in his liquid-silver gaze. The oven chimes.

"Let me put in the casserole and we can fix some breakfast beverages." He laughs when I say breakfast beverages.

When he nuzzles my neck, I squirm, and he releases me. I slide the baking dish into the oven, find a paper towel, and wipe my face. The open oven door adds exponentially to the heat flooding me.

Looking at the eggshells, remnants of chopped vegetables, and an empty packet of grated cheese on the counter, he makes a sweeping gesture. "You could have chosen a bowl of cereal or a container of yogurt. The fact that you went to the trouble to cook for both of us is so much beyond that. I can't tell you how happy it makes me."

I choke up, my whole body tingling. I squeeze his hand and put a capsule into his tiny coffeemaker. We sip our respective drinks and luxuriate in the silence until the frittata is ready. Then we dig in with moans over the deliciousness that is eggs, spinach, onions, mushrooms, and pancetta baked in a pan.

The bitter tang of coffee mingles with the cheese and onions to create a fragrance that could be bottled in a diffuser and called Morning Joy. Maybe I need to make a proposal to Bath and Body Works.

Max stuffs a piece of frittata in his mouth and washes it down with a gulp of tea. "By the way, my family is coming over for Christmas."

"Your family?" My fork clatters to the table.

"When I told them I couldn't come home, well, things got out of control."

"When?"

"They arrive from New York on the twenty-first." He scratches his stubble.

"New York? I thought they lived in Scotland."

"They do. At least, my parents do. Ian, Meggy, Frank, and Diana live in London. They're taking the Queen Mary II to New York and the train from there. Except Ian. He'll be in Chicago in a few days as acting British consul."

Wait—this is an avalanche. We've only known each other for a few weeks, and now his whole family is coming. "How many people are we talking about?"

He holds up a fist. "Mum, Dad, Ian, Meggy, Frank." Five fingers extend. He starts on the second hand. "Liz, Diana, Les, Sean, and the four little kids."

Thirteen. Oh my God. And four of them little kids. "How little?" My voice is faint.

"Three, five, eight, and ten. Those are Liz and Frank's kiddos. Diana and Les just have Sean, who's almost fourteen."

I press my thumbs against my eyes and rub my temples. I can't do this.

"Calm down. I know this is a lot to hit you with all at once, but we can control all this. You can always retreat to your condo when you need an escape from the Grant carnival.

My mum and sisters will want to shop, and you can plead deadlines. My brothers will be tasked with entertaining the kids. Ian will be working. The big Christmas Day set piece will be the only real test."

Okay, Cress. You can deal. You want this man, the relationship, everything. So suck it up. Family is supposed to be a good thing. I lean toward the hot man across the table. "Tell me about your cars."

Max does a double take. "Really?"

"Cars are important to you. How did you get interested?"

"Don't all boys love cars?"

"I don't know. I don't know many boys, but I guess the ones I know do. Paul, my dad, my brother all do. So, maybe?" The question mark hangs in the air, almost visible.

He snickers. "My dad is a car nut. Planes too, but he was a pilot, so that goes without saying. Ian, my older brother, drives a sports car, but he prefers train spotting. Frank, my younger brother, likes cars as well—and motor bikes. He's a dirt racer in his spare time."

"Isn't that dangerous?"

"Not if you know what you're doing. Anything can be dangerous, but you if never do anything risky, you're probably not living."

I'm not convinced. After all, he used a motorcycle as a deadly weapon, against himself.

MY OPERA-GOING dress is hanging in the guest room closet, the black sanded-silk garment I wear everywhere when jeans or sweats won't do. Will Max remember that I wore it at Everest? I slip it off the hanger, hold it against me, and pretend I am one of the Sufi dervishes. Twirl slowly in meditative silence until I'm dizzy. Fall spreadeagled on the bed. The dress slips from my hands and forms a black pool on the floor. After I'm showered and dressed, I go back to the living room. The cats are sprawled over the back of the humongous couch.

Max comes in looking like he's ready for the catwalk. I can't take my eyes off him. He's wearing a bespoke charcoal gray suit with a subtle stripe, a dark blue shirt with French cuffs and heavy gold cufflinks, and a silvery gray silk pocket square with a matching tie held by a fancy sapphire tie pin. Instead of his usual Rolex, his wrist sports a *Vacheron Constantin* watch.

"You look beautiful, Cress. I don't know why, but black really suits you. So French. So chic."

Heat rises in my face. Fingers crossed he won't twig that this is the Everest dress.

He rubs his chin. "This is the dress you wore at Everest, right?"

Damn. "Yes. It's the same one. My only dress-up dress."

"If you can only have one, that's the one to have. It's flirty, sexy, and fits you like a glove—a glove I'd like to peel off you." The light in his eyes is a little bit wicked and a lot mischievous. "Can we skip the opera? There are plenty of things we could do here."

I narrow my eyes and purse my lips. Then I point to his wrist. "Did you know Napoleon owned a watch like that?"

He slips a hand into his jacket, affecting a Napoleonic pose.

"Do you have your clothes custom tailored?"

"Yes. Even my shoes."

"And your socks?" I glance at the highly polished black brogues and striped gray and blue cashmere-blend socks that complete the ensemble. "I could make you socks like those."

He throws me a speculative glance. "Could you?"

"I could. Doesn't mean I will."

"Tease."

Socks go on the to-do list, cashmere sock yarn on the shopping list. I'll have to measure his feet—his very long feet. Or steal a sock.

"I have a bespoke bootmaker and everything."

I jerk my attention away from soft cashmere to shiny

leather. "I could see you moonlighting as some sort of fashion model."

Max shakes his head. "I'm a chameleon."

"Chameleon…so always changing. Not sure I like that."

He shrugs as if it is no big deal. "I decide who I want to be, then I dress for the part."

"And today you're a model, a clothes horse…" I trail off. My heart sinks. If he is all façades, how will I ever know if he's telling me the truth?

"For the opera I'm the suave, sophisticated, rich professional man, trying to impress the hell out of the unobtainable woman he wants."

"Is that a joke?" I remind myself how much I hate his jokes.

"No. This is what I do, play parts. A hard-to-break habit."

"I thought we agreed not to play games."

He shifts from one foot to the other. "Guess the habit is harder to break than I anticipated."

I draw up my lips in a thin line. "Sorry, I'd be more impressed by the honest, straightforward guy with no pretense."

"I can do that."

The silence stretches as we assess each other. Disappointment rolls over me like a tidal wave. "You're treating that as another role. I can't trust you, Max, not if you still see yourself as an actor, all façades, everything to everyone."

I carefully wipe a little moisture out of the corner of one eye. "I want you, not today's façade or tomorrow's mask. Just you, the man underneath the player. Trust is everything to me. I've told you."

He turns away and gathers up our coats.

A horn sounds, heralding a black SUV. Max takes my arm, and we walk out.

Just as he starts to help me in, I turn and kiss his cheek. "I'm sorry, Max. I overreacted."

He brings my hand to his mouth and kisses my fingers.

Max

AFTER CRESS GETS into the car, I stand on the pavement and scan the street. I may be crap at relationships, but I still have a few skills. My glance flits over a few pedestrians out for a stroll. A couple of dog walkers pass by, and a cute Lhasa Apso sniffs my shoes. I look for a woman in a big hat and a long coat with a fur collar.

Tina's continued radio silence unnerves me. My unease grows with each day that passes without a new action from her. The brick throwing was an escalation into violence. As pressure builds, I worry about a geyser-like eruption.

I draw in a deep breath. She's not stalking my house, not now anyway. No way she knows we're going to the opera. Need to check the exterior camera footage when we get back.

As we drive up Madison Street, I focus on the tall building looming up at Wacker Drive. I've passed by the Civic Opera House many times but never gave it much thought. Cress explains that the lavish Art Deco building ironically opened just after Black Friday in 1929 and cost over $23 million to build—over $350 million in today's money.

"The architects also designed the Wrigley Building and the Field Museum. In the '30s, they designed the Merchandise Mart. Can you see the chair shape? It's a giant throne."

By this time, we are at the drop-off, so I no longer have a perspective.

I put my hand under her elbow as I help her out. "I was more focused on the sculptures."

"They were created by Henry Hering. He was from New York, but he had a bunch of commissions in Chicago, like the figures of Day and Night at Union Station and Defense and Regeneration on two of the bridge houses on the DuSable bridge."

"I might have seen the bridge ones since I'm on Michigan Avenue a lot, but I'm sure I didn't pay attention. And I've never been inside Union Station."

"You will be when your parents get here."

I throw a quick glance in her direction. She's smiling. Thank God for that.

Under the portico, music pours out to entice passersby to consider an evening at the opera. We join the end of the queue to enter. Cress pulls out the tickets and rubs her fingers over the cards. I rock back and forth, heel toe, heel toe. I'm starting to listen to music with Cress, but I'm still not totally at ease with it. Memories flood in too often.

"It's the second largest opera auditorium in North America after the Met in New York. Wait until you see the interior. It was designed to look like the Paris Opera House."

She draws a breath. "The grand staircase and beautiful Art Deco features accentuate the palatial feel. It's an opulent space for an opulent art form."

I can tell how much Cress loves this place. Her eyes sparkle as she holds out the tickets to be scanned.

"Anything else I need to know?" I'm happy to facilitate her tour guide tendencies.

"The opera house was the inspiration for the one in *Citizen Kane*. The man who had the opera house built,

Samuel Insull, provided one of the plot elements. While he didn't build the opera house for his wife, an unsuccessful ingenue, he did try to relaunch her career in 1925 and 1926 at the Studebaker Theater."

"Interesting." Protracted exposure to the music makes my skin crawl, so I focus on the Art Deco ornamentation of the lobby.

"Insull was one of the villains of the stock market crash in 1929."

"You're joking." I tear my eyes away from the awesome decoration. Her face is serious.

"Nope. No joke. But we're here for glorious architecture and divine music, not an economics lesson."

She leads me to the opulent Sarah and Peer Pedersen room, where we have a very nice prix fixe meal designed to move diners in and out in time for the performance.

Once we're in the auditorium, I check out the staggering amount of gold leaf in the decor and the painted fire curtain that depicts the parade from *Aida*, the first opera performed in the building.

Our seats are at the back of the main floor, which Cress tells me is called the balance for some reason. She's been clever with the seats and arranged for us to sit in the last row so my height won't be an issue for other audience members.

My seat is on the aisle with no one directly in front of me except a wheelchair space, empty for this performance, which gives me plenty of space to stretch my legs.

I fidget during the first two acts. My neck itches. By the end of act two, damp patches make my shirt cling to my chest and back. This much music is overwhelming. I want to leave, but Cress is entranced by the performances, and I can't bring myself to tell her.

We walk out to the lobby. I squeeze her hand. "Can I walk outside for a bit of air?"

She rummages in her bag and pulls out a ticket. "Just in case."

The cold air slaps me in the face. I take in deep lungfuls, walking up and down in front of the building for a few minutes. Then I straighten my spine, roll my shoulders, and walk back in to face the last act.

I stop at the gift kiosk and buy Cress one of the silk scarves with a reproduction of the curtain, then I stop by one of the vending counters and buy two glasses of champagne.

I drape the scarf around her shoulders and kiss her neck. We sip our drinks and watch the parade of opera aficionados. Many of the women are decked out in designer gowns, furs, and opulent jewelry.

"You look pale. Should we leave?"

"I'm fine." I give her a weak smile.

When the last act is announced, I trail in after her. In the now-darkened auditorium, I shift and bounce my knee. Cress rests her hand on my bicep. Her touch calms me for the moment.

As the action moves inexorably to what must be Violetta's inevitable death, I fidget more and more. She begins singing "*Addio, del passato bei sogni ridenti,*" which translates as *Farewell, lovely, happy dreams of the past.* I choke and run out of the hall.

Case perches on a chair next to the exit door to our aisle. When I push out, he grabs my arm and drags me over to the chair. I last about two minutes before I rush down to the toilets. Five minutes later I struggle up from the floor and wipe my mouth before I stagger back into the lobby and collapse back into the chair.

The music crashes out into lobby as it reaches a climax.

Shudders roll through me. Cress is so involved in the drama that I'm sure she hasn't even noticed I've left. Maybe if I sit here quietly, I can process what happened.

The fiction of the death in the opera hit me like a shot from a catapult. The intensity of the music and the death from illness are parallels. Guy is not far from my mind, but this reaction is too extreme.

Then understanding floods through me. The opera is all about loss. My reaction is all about loss, people being torn from me. Outside my immediate family, the only close relationships have been my cousin, my public-school roommate, and the woman I thought I was falling in love with in Turkey. All dead.

I shudder at the vision of the explosion that killed Zehra. Preston hanging from the rafters of our room, the chair kicked over. Guy's deathbed in Scotland while I was thousands of kilometers away. But it's not just loss—it's fear too.

The next attack on Cress could be a sniper with a rifle on a roof or a Molotov cocktail. My head drops into my hands. No matter how much we try to protect her, no one can completely ensure Cress' safety, and I can't bear the thought of losing her.

Chapter 23

CRESS

The silence in the car is stifling. I hold his hand, trying to silently tell him everything is okay. I can see why Violetta's death scene was so traumatic. I should have anticipated his reaction and suggested a different opera, maybe a comic one instead.

After the endless fidgets, I wasn't surprised when he walked out of the auditorium. When he didn't come back, I wanted to race out and make sure he was all right, but then I thought maybe he needed a little time alone.

Being in the back meant I could slip out easily during the curtain calls. Case called over to me as I exited. Max's face was the color of skim milk, white with that slightly blue undertone. A sudden pain ripped through my chest. Max didn't look up as I stroked his hair.

We waited under the portico while Case retrieved the SUV. The cold air helped, but Max's eyes were sunken, and he still had no color in his face. When I slipped my arm around him, he was trembling.

When we went to bed, I held him all night.

After Max leaves for work, I feed the cats and try to figure out my day. I should go home, but somehow that is unappealing. I make coffee and text Paul and Micki. I need company, advice, and solace. They both answer within thirty seconds. Micki begs off, client meetings all day.

Paul offers lunch and a sympathetic ear if I come to Cafecito in South Loop. I gulp down the still-hot coffee and swear under my breath as I burn the roof of my mouth. I check the schedule and contact Liam to drive me. I plan to go home after I meet Paul.

I walk carefully down the steps and out to the SUV with a carrier in each hand and my duffle over my shoulder. Liam assures me that he is fine in the car with the cats. I promise to bring him a sandwich and his choice of drink.

I'm early so I have time to order a Cubano and coffee and bring it out to him. He's sitting in the back with the cat carriers.

"Hey guys. You okay in there? Wish I could let you out. Bored, nowhere to go, nothing to do." His voice is melodic as he croons to the cats. They meow in answer to each new phrase. I hand him the food and he gives me a small salute.

When I get back, Paul is at the door. We place our orders at the counter and slide into a booth.

"Cress. What's up?"

I open my mouth, but I'm at a loss for words.

He looks me up and down, his face twisted in a grimace. "You look like you're losing weight. The dark circles look like bruises. Did Max upset you? Or Tina? Or your dad?"

"No. Max had a meltdown at the opera last night. God, Paul, I'm an idiot, taking him to see *La Traviata*. He was devastated. Somehow, I couldn't see that would happen." I pull my napkin back and forth through my fingers.

"I keep pushing for him to completely open up about his life, spill his secrets. I tell myself I can't trust him when he never does anything untrustworthy except not tell me everything about his past. Then he tells me something major, and I ignore it then drag him to the very thing to bring back all those memories."

My voice catches in a sob. Paul hands me his silk handkerchief, but I am reluctant to mess it up with tears and snot.

"Just use it, Cress." His voice is as tight as a violin string. "I'll send it to the cleaners."

I fall silent as the server brings our lunches. I cut my grilled cheese sandwich into tiny squares and start peeling the bread away from the cheese. I can't swallow a bite.

"I take it you haven't told him everything about yours either," Paul mumbles through an enthusiastically big bite of his Cubano.

"My problem isn't that I keep secrets. My ice wall is too thick." I stare at my plate, fiddle with the coagulated cheese.

"Ah, the famous ice wall. Has he already put in the crampons? Maybe Max can eventually be Shackleton on South Georgia and scale your wall. Fingers crossed. Many have died trying."

He puts my plate on top of his empty one and moves them to the side. "No matter what he does, you freeze him out?"

"I thaw and refreeze, over and over. It's an ice wall with barbed wire and metal spikes. I don't know how he can even be interested in me at this point."

"I guess he sees, or wants to see, something salvageable. Love will do that." He glares at me. "Jeez, Cress, you were like this at ten." He hits the table with his fist, knocking his fork to the floor. The people at the tables around us look over, startled.

"Sorry," he mutters, the tips of his ears glowing red. He rubs his bald spot and looks at me sadly, with the affection of years of friendship. "I've known you most of your life. We're the Inseparables, Athos. Micki and I both want the best for you, and we see Max as the best—maybe even D'Artagnan."

I snicker.

"Well, maybe he's not poor, but he's noble."

"Are you recasting me as Constance?"

Paul waves the comment away. "Of course not. That would make this a tragedy. As Porthos, I'm all about farce. Just know we'll be there, whatever happens."

"I'm so angry with myself for being such a bitch. I need to do better, but I'm not sure I can figure out how."

"Puhlease. Grow up. Let go of the past. Acknowledge it and move on. I can't believe you still think everyone is out to hurt you—except Micki and me, of course. I know that sounds glib and easier said than done, but you're not twenty-five anymore."

He takes another bite of his sandwich and washes it down with iced tea. "Kev is so far in the past that you can't even see him in a rear-view mirror. You've got to try. We'll help where we can."

He leans forward and grabs my hand.

"Talk to Max. Not in an angry, confrontational way. Come out of the snow cave. Stand closer to the fire. And even if things aren't forever, don't hide. Because what if they are?"

"Are what?"

"Are forever. What if Max loves you? If you don't take the chance, you'll never know. I'd hate to see you become the old, bitter, crazy cat lady. Call him up or send him a text. Let him know you want to melt."

PAUL WALKS ME OUT, waves, and walks back toward his office. I contemplate the SUV, then I drag myself to the curb, exhausted. I tap at the window and Liam hits the lock release.As I slouch in the back of the car, I anticipate a quiet respite with the cats, a cozy fire, a hot cup of tea, and a nap. I never nap. Well, I'm napping today.

The cats whine in their carriers. My eyes feel swollen. Hard for me to focus when I try to stare out the window at the lakefront. It's a blue-gray blur. A cold washcloth would be bliss.

We pull up in front of the building, and I stumble out between the parked cars.

"You okay?" Liam calls out.

"I'm fine, just a little tired."

"Okay. As soon as you're inside, I'll park."

I wave as I clear the curb then wrinkle my nose at an unfamiliar reek. No, not unfamiliar—unexpected. I smell smoke. Maybe someone is illegally burning trash in the alley.

I fumble with my key, struggling with the lock. We need to repair or replace the door. The faint odor of smoke is stronger as I enter the lobby, a smell like paper burning.

As I climb the stairs, a cold chill sweeps through me. My door is slightly open. Hyperventilating, I throw myself back down the stairs, stumbling on the next-to-last step.

Pain shoots through my ankle as I push myself up off the tiles. I run out of the building. My ankle gives out and I collapse on the sidewalk. I brush at the debris scraping my knees.

Deep, ragged breaths tear at my chest. Liam looms over me.

"You okay, Dr. Taylor? What happened?"

"I think someone broke into my condo."

"I can't hear you. Why are you whispering?"

I rub my eyes, try to refocus, then look back up at him. I try to speak louder. "I found my door ajar. I smelled smoke. I think someone broke in."

Liam has his phone out before I finish. He holds up a hand to stop me. "JL, looks like someone might have broken into Dr. Taylor's place."

He pauses, listening to the voice on the other end. "She went upstairs then came running out. Her door was open, and she smelled smoke." He turns back to me. "Did you go in?"

I shake my head no.

"No, neither of us." He listens some more. "Okay. I'll call 911. See you soon."

I've managed to struggle off my knees by this time, but I wobble and grab Liam's arm.

"Let's go to the Escalade. I'll call the police and keep you warm until they arrive. JL's on his way."

I tremble in the back seat. Thank God Max wouldn't let me cancel my security.

The street fills with fire engines, police cars, and an ambulance. A wall of sound pins me to the seat. I cover my ears and close my eyes.

Noise and light sift through anyway. Windows crash as streams of water hit the building.

Time is elastic. Fast, slow, fast again. I have to wall off my emotions, be the ice queen.

JL shows up, but my heart plummets. "Where's Max?" I ask.

He peers in the window. "*Calisse de tabernak.* You are white as new snow."

I wipe my hand over my face. "Max didn't come with you?"

"He had meetings out of the office this afternoon. I'll let him know later. Not something where you want to leave a voicemail."

MAX

A TEXT ARRIVES FROM IAN. Unbelievable. Sometimes fate gives you what you need, even if you don't know you need it.

IAN: Just landed at O'Hare. Dinner?

ME: Brilliant. Spiaggia 7:30. You make the reservation. On my way to a meeting.

Then I turn off my phone, shove it in my briefcase. GSU policy mandates no phones in meetings.

I walk into Spiaggia, slip off my overcoat, and tell the maître d' that I have a reservation for Grant. I need advice. I've been in a quandary about who to talk with. Usually, I'd talk with JL, but he's out somewhere, and Ian is one of the few people in the world I can confide in even though I haven't seen him in at least three years. Every time I've gone home, he's been stationed somewhere inaccessible.

"Your party is already seated." He motions over one of the staff. "Table 15."

"Max." Ian stands up from the table. "You look like crap."

I grab his hand and squeeze hard. "Contraceptives should be used on all conceivable occasions."

Ian groans. "Really? Spike Milligan?"

I grin. We both have a soft spot for *The Goon Show* and Milligan's madcap humor.

"Can't you come up with your own jokes?"

"No point bothering when the perfect joke is already available."

He pulls at his lower lip. "Maybe I shouldn't have told you I was coming."

"I know you love my jokes. But, moving on, the horde is on the QM2. I heard from Dad just before they left Southampton."

He looks me over. Not sure what he expects to see, but I guess he doesn't find it when he shakes his head. "I've finally been sent somewhere nice for a change. Having you on-site makes it that much better."

"Any drinks, gentlemen?" A slight French accent surprises me.

"Saved by the sommelier." I wipe my brow.

Ian consults the wine list. "Let's be celebratory. We'll have a bottle of the *Prosecco di Valdobbiadene brut Crede, bisol, Veneto* 2011 to start."

I can't help smirking. "My brother can't help showing off."

The sommelier regards me impassively then turns to Ian. "Very good, sir. Would you prefer champagne coupes or flutes?"

"What do you think, Max?"

"I don't care."

"Flutes."

I make a punching motion toward my brother's shoulder. "Might as well have a long, boozy evening. Maybe getting drunk will cheer me up."

Ian considers me, lips pursed. "And why is that?"

"I'm in over my head." I sigh and pull out my phone to show him a photo of Cress. I notice I have a few messages. I ignore them and go straight to my photos, bring up the one from Cress' birthday dinner. I run my fingers down the screen. It's a totally candid shot and she looks incandescent with happiness. I pass over the phone.

"Nice. Is this the girl Meggy mentioned? She's important, yes?"

Now that I've intimated that I'm in difficulty, I panic. I see my brother as a life raft, and now I wonder if drowning wouldn't be preferable. Telling Ian anything is a mistake. He is the high priest of gossip in our loose-lipped family. I can't cut and run, so I need to de-escalate fast.

"She's a good friend."

He rubs his hands in gleeful imitation of Uriah Heep. "You're a bad liar, Max."

I grace him with a look of deep displeasure. "I might need some advice."

"Just what older brothers are for, heh-heh-heh. Just no tech or politics."

I bring Ian up to date on developments twenty years on.

"Well, I'll be damned. But you said you need advice. You re-found the girl of your dreams. What's the problem?"

"Frankly, trying to figure out how to have a relationship scares the shit out of me. I wonder how much of myself I'd be willing to give . I've always felt there's no point in getting attached to anyone when so many couples crash and burn. I've poured my energy into work, rugby, running, and cars."

I pull out a glass-cleaning cloth and start polishing. My brother slaps my hand.

"Stop faffing around and tell me the point."

"Now that I'm out of the spy game, I don't need to live a secret life anymore, but breaking the habits of a lifetime is almost insurmountable."

My voice catches. "I don't want to be alone anymore, and I have no experience in being with someone. I want her, but

I'm terrified if I tell her everything, she'll leave." Ian starts to answer, but I go on. "She thinks I'm an untrustworthy arsehole."

He raises an eyebrow. I give him the gist of the chameleon conversation and my breakdown at the opera.

"I'm amazed she hasn't ended everything," I tell him.

"You are an arse, Max. Don't you know anything about women?"

"Evidently not."

Ian gets up, rounds the table, and pulls me to my feet. "Do you know what you want?"

I lean into his face, my voice low. "I want her."

He shakes me then sits down.

I subside and start brushing breadcrumbs around my plate.

"Are you sure she's worth it?" He looks genuinely curious.

"Worth it? She's literally haunted my dreams for twenty years."

"And yet you've never done a thing about it." His voice sounds like sandpaper scraping my ears. "If you could go without her for that long, I don't understand why you can't drop her now."

Tension builds in my neck and my eyes burn. A new headache is brewing. This conversation is not going the way I expected. Despite that, I drain my wine glass and pour the last of the excellent Prosecco into it.

I keep my voice steady. "She and Guy have been the two biggest regrets in my life. It's too late to do anything about Guy, and I am fucking afraid I'll lose her again. My whole life has been about secrecy, about hiding and lying. Every time I think I've made progress on convincing her I'm a good guy, I screw things up."

"My advice is to tell her that. If you have any chance with her, she'll understand."

Just for a distraction, I pull out my phone. My voicemail is flashing with JL's number. I listen to the message, my napkin crumpled in my fist.

"I have to go." My throat is tight.

"Let's go then." He calls over the waiter, explains we have an emergency, and pushes money into his hand for the wine. We don't actually run, but almost.

∼

CRESS

HOURS AT THE SCENE, but so much is going on between the firemen and the police that I still haven't been questioned. My neighbors come home from work, but no one is allowed inside. Tape blocks the door to preserve the scene for the investigative unit.

The police let Liam and JL take me to Micki's place where we talk about next steps. I have no idea about the extent of the damage.

The investigators show up a couple of hours later. I've been curled up on the loveseat, an ice pack on my ankle, drinking coffee. Micki's furniture is so her. Bright, weird shapes. A showcase for modern design, so different from my English country cottage style. A sob catches in my throat.

The officer drops a glance at my hand. I guess he wants to check for a ring. "Miss Taylor, when did you say you arrived home?"

"It's Dr. Taylor." JL throws the cop a pointed look.

My voice is raspy. "Probably around two. I met a friend for lunch. Then Liam drove me home."

"That's right. Dr. Taylor and her cats." Liam straddles a dining-room chair.

"I smelled smoke when I got inside, wondered if someone had been smoking in the hallway or was burning trash. When I got to the landing, I could see that my door was slightly ajar, so I knew something was wrong. I ran back outside, and Liam called 911."

"You didn't go in?"

"No. I tripped on the stairs on the way down, sprained my ankle. Fortunately, Liam found a parking space and saw me stagger out of the building."

The officer who is interviewing me looks over. "You Liam?"

"Yeah. I work for WatchDog Security. I'm Dr. Taylor's assigned bodyguard." He looks at his watch. "Actually, my shift ended half an hour ago. Dirk should be here already."

JL breaks in smoothly. "You'll get overtime. As soon as the police are finished, you can take off. Case and Dirk will cover tomorrow."

"But Dirk's on tonight," Liam protests.

"I'm taking over tonight."

The cop looks at me. "WatchDog, huh? Why do you need security?"

"I've had some threats, so a friend suggested hiring a security firm for protection."

Micki glares at me. "What the fuck? Max is more than a friend." She makes quotation marks with her fingers as she says friend.

"Not the time for this discussion." I fold my arms across my chest. My shields are activated and repel her glare.

"The fire department won't let us in until tomorrow, but

I've been told the damage is extensive." JL breaks into our staring contest.

I can't hold back a small cry of distress.

"Pretty sure we're looking at arson, although, as I said, the investigators can't get in yet."

I startle. Forgot the police were still in the room.

"Who has it out for you?" The cop's pencil is poised over his notebook.

"I think the person who has been threatening me is the likely candidate."

He frowns at my useless response. "Are these anonymous threats, or do you know who it is?"

I lick my lips. How much should I tell them? Might as well get it all out there. "The threats themselves have been anonymous, but a woman named Tina Monroe has been trashing my name and reputation in the media."

My eyes are closed as I slouch deeper into the chair. "She admitted privately to me that she sent the threats, but it would just be her word against mine. I'm sure she'd deny it if I accuse her. Someone threw a brick through my window. Someone vandalized my place. I don't have any proof, but I can't believe these are different people."

I let out a deep sigh. "I did report all this to the police."

"Motive?"

This sounds so stupid, but I tell him anyway. "She thinks I've destroyed her chance at a writing career."

"Oh?" He leaves the question hanging.

"I'm a successful writer. She's...not. Somehow she has put these two unrelated facts together and decided her failure is my fault." I put my head in my hands.

"Do you know where she is?"

"No," I mumble through my fingers. "I guess you could contact the offices of *Trash TV*. She's been on there several times with her accusations of plagiarism. I'm sure they have contact information, unless they pay in cash."

He stands up, closes his notebook, and puts on his coat. "Thank you, Dr. Taylor. Someone will be in touch."

"When will I be able to check out my condo? I need to have the insurance company look at it then find a service to clean up."

"Probably sometime tomorrow or the next day. How should we contact you?"

"My cell number is fine."

"Okay. We have that."

I bleakly contemplate my immediate future. The break-in is the icing on a cake of shit being forced down my throat.

"Dr. Taylor." The cop taps my arm to draw my attention.

"Sorry."

"Are you staying here?"

I start to stand up, but the pain in my ankle forces me back down. "No, I can't stay here. I'll need a hotel room."

"Okay. Just keep us apprised." He shoves his notebook into a pocket then motions to his partner. My breath whooshes out of my lungs as they leave.

Micki walks into the living room with a new mug, takes the one in my hands, then proffers the replacement. "I know tea won't stop the hurt, but it might be marginally soothing."

The warmth is welcome. "Thanks. I'm so cold. Can't stop crying. Everything hurts so much."

"Do you want to call Max?"

"I should." A breathy catch in my voice forces a pause. A little cough clears my throat. "Where's my phone?"

JL calls over. "I left him a message to call."

"You think Tina broke into your place?" From her expression, Micki looks like she's ready to take Tina apart.

"Who else?" I may not have many friends, but I have fewer enemies.

"If the building is still too hot for the investigators to get in…" Micki rubs the back of her neck.

"I still can't believe she thinks I can keep her from being published. She's always hated me."

"You're everything she's not."

"She was the beauty queen, the popular girl. I was the outcast."

"No one can be the beauty queen forever." She drops to the purple couch and tucks her legs under. "It's so twisted. Guess she thinks if you are gone, she'll have no competition."

"Competition?"

"Your books, your awards, your success."

"It doesn't work that way. My success doesn't mean her failure. They don't have anything to do with each other."

"Right. That's logic. Tina's mind doesn't work on logic. You win, she loses. She eliminates you, she wins. It's a zero-sum game."

I scoff. "She's a narcissist. She doesn't envy me."

"Narcissists are deeply insecure."

"When did you become a psychologist?" I snarl.

"Did you forget I was a psych major as an undergrad? It's certainly helped me as a lawyer."

"She's right." Our heads swivel to JL. "I am a psychologist—one of my many roles. While I can't give you an official diagnosis, she certainly exhibits many narcissistic traits. If she's thwarted, a narcissistic rage can result. Very destructive. I told Max this a few days ago."

"Sorry. I shouldn't have been so dismissive."

JL's phone trills. "*Oui?*" He looks over at me. "*Cress est chez Michelle. Viens ici maintenant. C'est très important. Vite.*" He slips the phone into his pocket.

I'M CRASHING. Micki walks in from the kitchen. "You okay?"

Her buzzer sounds, making us both jump.

"That must be Max." JL goes to the intercom and pushes the door release.

"Where is she?" Max sounds hoarse. I can hear his heavy breaths.

"The living room."

Hurried footsteps make my ears ring. Max drops to his knees beside me and touches my ankle. "What happened? Did you have an accident? How serious is it?"

"She tripped running out of her building but forget about her ankle. Her condo's been vandalized. We've spent hours with the police, and now Cress needs a place to stay." Micki brushes her hair back.

"I can stay at a hotel."

Max shakes his head. "You'll stay with me."

"I'll be fine at a hotel." The idea of moving to Max's house terrifies me. One commitment too far. When I've stayed over, I could always go home. Now I have no home.

Micki interrupts. "This won't be a few days, Cress. From what the police said, your place may have to be gutted and completely redone. Staying at Max's makes sense."

A deep bass voice breaks in. "You'll be much safer with him."

I look up and see a slightly shorter, sandy-haired version of Max. "Who are you?" Squeak, squeak. *Shit.* I sound like a mouse.

"This is my older brother, Ian." Max sounds contrite. He gestures to the man in the impeccable Harris tweed suit.

Ian comes over to me; amusement crinkles his crystal blue eyes. "I'm the good-looking one."

As Ian preens, Max makes a face, and Micki and I titter. JL mutters something unintelligible in French.

"He's been appointed acting British consul in Chicago. We were having dinner when JL called."

"I called and texted all afternoon."

Max holds up a hand in apology. "You know Clay wants all phones off at meetings."

"Do you want something to eat?" Micki sounds flustered. "We could order pizza, or I can scrounge up cheese and crackers."

"Thanks, but don't bother. Once Cress is settled at my place, we'll figure something out."

"Or we can take her to Spiaggia and finish our meal." Ian's expression is smug.

"You're a facetious arse."

I've lost the thread of the conversation. I study Max's brother. His hair has more gray, deep lines frame his mouth, and his eyes look red-rimmed with dark circles. Unlike Max, he doesn't wear glasses, but he might have contacts instead.

Max grips my hands.

"All right, Cress. No more arguments."

I remove the ice pack, jam swollen feet into my shoes, and struggle out of the chair. Micki brings over my coat and purse then retrieves a duffle that she hands to Ian.

"I know most of this will be oversized, but I packed up some clothes and a few toiletries."

"Thanks, Micki. You're the best friend in the world."

"Of course I am." She folds her arms and smiles.

Max helps me hobble toward the floor just as Sam walks in, a thunderous expression on his face.

"Where the fuck have you been? I expected you at the studio hours ago. You haven't answered my texts or the phone." He looks at our little group. "What are all these fuckers doing here?"

"They're just leaving." Micki walks over and pecks his cheek. "I'll explain later."

"If they're going, I don't care why they're here." He thumps down into a recliner I know Micki bought him. "Just bring me a beer."

My face scrunches. "Thanks for everything, Micki."

"I'll walk you out. Be right back, Sam."

We hear him yell, "Get me the damn beer first." The door slams behind us.

Two hours later, Ian has left and I'm sitting on the edge of Max's couch while he kneels in front of me and rewraps my ankle. All the ice packs and judicious amounts of ibuprofen have brought down the swelling, but I still can't put much weight on it.

Finished, he stands up and stretches. "Okay or too tight?"

"It's fine." I yawn. Dorothy is on my lap, and I pull her up so I can rub my nose against her head. She squirms off and jumps down. If she could talk, I'm sure she'd be asking what the hell I think I'm doing. "Just be glad I love you. If I hadn't brought you with me the other night, you'd be burnt to a crisp."

She gives me the kind of look only cats can carry off then flounces out of the room.

I yawn again and stretch my arms over my head. "Could you help me up?"

Max grabs my arm and pulls me up. I lean against him. Then he scoops me up and carries me to bed.

～

IN THE MORNING a call from the police department tells me I can go back to my condo in the afternoon. I need to document the damage for both the police and the insurance company.

I start a mental list of the most pressing to-dos. I can hire a service to clean the place, hire workmen to repair any damage, and start claims for replacements. Micki will come with me, partly to help and advise as my lawyer, and partly for moral support. Max insists on coming too.

I still smell smoke, so I take another long shower, washing my hair again. A vision of my lovely three-flat building, water being poured in through the windows, hits me like an Acme anvil.

I'm haunted by the faces of my neighbors, shock and sadness etched into their expressions as we contemplate our loss, holding up crossed fingers as we all make a wish that the building can be saved.

The area around us is covered with thick ice from the thousands of gallons of water that were pumped into the building. Standing in a clear patch on the street in front of the flame-scarred building, a hint of smoke still in the air, I am swimming in the sweats Micki lent me.

The sleeves are rolled up, as are the pant legs, and I consider that I need shorter friends in case I ever have to borrow clothes again. I pull up the hood on my parka, trying to keep my ears from developing frostbite.

Eventually, two policemen arrive. One is tall and heavy, the other short and thin. They aren't the ones from yesterday.

"Dr. Taylor? Officer Green and Sergeant Neill." They pull out ID. "Shall we go up?"

Another man walks up. "Fire Marshal Miller. I'm the arson investigator."

After the tape is removed, I pull out my keys, and we troop up the stairs.

"What happened with my neighbors?" I ask.

"Right now, the building is uninhabitable," the fire marshal tells me. "It needs to be evaluated for damage. No one will be living here for a while."

We skirt shards of glass from broken windows, mirrors, picture frames, and the seldom-used TV. Someone has taken a hammer to anything breakable, including the furniture. Fabrics are slashed, stuffing pulled out of cushions and pillows.

Heaps of multicolored fragments are the remains of my prized Murano glass collection. Ribbons of canvas hang from the frames of oil paintings done by artist friends.

Everything is charred. Plastic and some glass are melted to the hardwood floors. My life has been reduced to a pile of rubbish. I stand tall and view the devastation with dry eyes.

That is until I walk into my office. Now, standing in the wreckage of my library, I'm sobbing. I picked out the now-broken furniture with loving care. The ruined oriental rugs were cherished memories of trips abroad.

My books—torn, trampled, ripped apart, and burned—cause the floods of tears coursing down my face. The history books I collected over more than two decades are unreadable. Years of research destroyed in a moment.

My own books are ash. I can only identify them from fragments of the covers. My computer is smashed, files reduced to unusable fragments of paper. Even the police officers are stunned by the level of destruction.

I sniffle, wipe my nose on my sleeve, and then turn to Micki and Max. They stand in the doorway, speechless with shock.

"It's hopeless. Assuming the building can be saved, I might as well have someone come with a bulldozer and haul away everything as garbage. Then, I'll have it all rebuilt, redecorated, and refurnished. But I can't replace all the books, or any of the paper files." I run out of the condo, down the stairs, into the street, Micki and Max trailing behind me.

"All is not lost," Micki insists, intoning a tired cliché. "The book can still be written. Your computer files are on Dropbox. You can replace your computer and retrieve everything."

As if that is the point. "Everything that represents my life is gone."

"Just stuff. You have your friends and your memories. Your pictures are in the cloud. Stuff can be replaced. Life goes on. You will be okay."

Max's arms go around me.

"Just let it all out. Scream, cry, blame the universe for letting you down. If ever there was a time to be emotional, this is it."

I straighten and inch away so I can focus on his sharp cheekbones and kissable lips. "No helpful jokes?"

"No. I have no clever quips on this occasion." His gray eyes are stormy.

The claims adjuster arrives, and the verdict is no surprise. My condo is a complete loss.

Chapter 24

CRESS

I'm still in bed when my phone rings. I roll over, realizing Max is gone. Probably running. My eyes are gunked up. I rub them then squint at the screen. Without my glasses, I can't see the time.

"Hey, Siri. What time is it?"

"It is one PM."

Really? Max can't be running. Where is he? The phone stopped ringing while I was trying to find out the time. Now it starts again. Paul McCartney. "Michelle." Shouldn't she be at work?

"Hey." I try to sound cheerful rather than sleepy, but my early-afternoon, overslept voice is raspy.

All I hear is an eerie wail.

"Micki, what's wrong?"

Silence.

"Micki." I can't keep the alarm out of my voice.

Another wail. Burbles, gulps, sniffles are the only sounds. "Do I need to call 911?"

She rasps out one word. "Sam…"

"Dammit. What has he done now?"

"Come over." Then she starts keening. A chill runs through me at her outpouring of grief. I picture her rending her clothes.

"I can be there in half an hour, maybe forty-five minutes. Will you be okay till then?"

"I guess so." She has a catch in her throat. I hear a few whimpers of distress, then silence.

Alarmed, I hang up and call Max. He's at Trader Joe's but tells me he'll check out and be home in a few minutes. I drop the phone, take a quick shower, throw on my new sweats, and make coffee. I'm taking my first sip as I hear the front door slam.

"Cress? Cress!" I'm startled by the shouts.

"In the kitchen."

He looks me over, the expression on his face unreadable. "Are you hurt?" I shake my head no and his shoulders relax. "You gave me a hell of a scare."

"We need to go to Micki's."

"Why?"

"Something's wrong. Not sure what. Anyway, change your running pants and let's go."

"Right." He runs up the stairs. I can't help staring at his ass as the muscles flex under the tight-fitting Lycra.

My phone starts to ring. I hit answer. "Hello?"

"Cress." Paul's voice is higher than normal. "What the hell is going on?" I can hear him pacing on his squeaky hardwood floor. "I got a frantic but incoherent call from Micki. I hope you know something."

Relief floods me. "I'm not sure what happened. Something with Sam is all I could get out of her. I told her I would be there as soon as I can." I call out, "Max, I'm on the phone with Paul. Are you almost ready?"

I hear his heavy tread on the stairs then swearing and an indignant yowl. "Dammit, Dorothy."

"Meet us at Micki's?" I ignore the scrabbling, meowing, and rumbling curses.

"I'm already on my way. See you in a few."

Max looms over me, fingers flexed. "Your cats."

"What happened?"

"I narrowly avoided falling down the stairs. No thanks to Dorothy."

I put my cup in the sink and limp toward the hallway. Max grabs my shoulders.

"Are you all right?" He shakes me lightly. His eyes are so dark they look like coal fire.

I try to pull away. My head bobs madly like a runaway puppet, curls streaming over my face.

He cups my face in his hands. "Let me grab your coat and bag." Then, with a last caress, he moves away.

In the SUV, I fall back against the seat, gripping my purse as if I were strangling Sam. Max reaches over and takes my hand. I collapse like a soufflé.

In Micki's living room, we drink medicinal, slightly-too-early-in-the-day Scotch. I would have made bloody Marys, knowing Micki always has tomato juice and vodka on tap, but Paul brought a bottle of Glenfiddich with him, and the level has gone down substantially.

Paul raises his glass. "The sun is over the yardarm somewhere."

"Pretend we're in Edinburgh doing a tasting." Max's Scottish brogue is over the top.

Micki has gone from a sobbing mess to a sobbing,

drunken mess. As he has been for the last hour, Max argues that she needs to call the police. She is a victim of domestic violence, and Sam needs to be arrested.

Micki is a boulder. Not able to roll her, Max tries to chip at her resistance, but she refuses to be swayed by his arguments.

"No. He made it clear that we're done. And I'm fine... fine... with that." She gulps and looks lost.

"What happened?" I ask for maybe the tenth time.

Now she's drunk enough to come clean. "I came home and he, he was..." Micki chokes.

"Was what?" Paul has gotten louder with each new drink.

"He was fucking some girl on the couch, and he screamed at me to get out. It's my place." She looks unbelieving at the memory. "When I said that, he got off her, came over, and hit me." She touches the bruise on her forehead, winces. "Didn't even zip his pants."

"He's a jerk," Paul growls.

"But you got him to leave." I touch her shoulder.

"The girl convinced him to go. She practically dragged him out. He was still trying to pull up his pants."

I can't help the giggles that erupt. The picture of Sam, stumbling, pants around his ankles while his lover, or whatever she is, pulls at his arm, trying to steer him out the door, is too much.

Paul is aghast. "How can you laugh about this, Cress?"

"Call the police." Max is insistent.

"No." Micki folds her arms, glares at him. "Do you know what this would do to my reputation if my colleagues find out?"

"Who bloody cares?"

I put my hand on his arm. "Please, Max. I know you mean

well." I rub my thumb against his. "Micki has to make this decision herself."

"But—"

Paul shakes his head. "I agree with you, Max, but we can't force Micki to do what we think she should do."

Micki has been staring at her couch with a mournful expression. "Fuck. I can't look at this fucking piece of furniture for another minute. Can you move this piece of crap out of here?" Her voice rises. "I need it out of here, now."

"I know some guys with a truck. Let me give them a call." Paul pulls out his phone.

Micki slumps to the floor and breaks into hysterical laughter, rocking back and forth. "Oh my God, my new couch. I can't believe it. I haven't had it a week. My gorgeous purple couch. I ordered it over a year ago. It just arrived— from Italy. I loved this fucking couch."

She giggles. "Then Sam literally turned it into a fucking couch, and now I can't look at it."

We all stare at the outrageous, tufted purple velvet couch.

Micki swallows, her voice dangerously calm. "It's called Belle Epoch. It was designed by *Calia Italia*. They're hand-made in Italy and I had to order it specially. It cost a bomb."

She swipes at her face, wipes away tears. "And now I have to have it hauled away." She scrambles to her feet, shaking her fist at the violated piece of furniture.

"Can't you have it cleaned?" I can see Max is confused.

"Noooo. I can't stand looking at it. I'll never see it without visualizing them doing it." She collapses on the floor and bangs her head on the hardwood.

"I know Sam's been living here, but does he have a place?" Paul frowns at the violated couch.

Looking over at Micki, I can tell she isn't going to be able to answer. She's still on the floor, rocking back and forth, wailing. Her arms are like branches in the wind, fingers shivering like twigs. "My couch...my beautiful couch..."

She's going to recover from Sam's betrayal much more easily than the loss of her furniture.

"He has a studio over on Ravenswood." I pull up the contact information and share it with him.

"I have guys with a truck who will dump it off there. Maybe you two can take Micki to pick out a new couch."

"After we take you to the emergency room, do you want to pick out a couch? It's still pretty early." Max has been wandering the room, impatient to do something.

Micki glares. "Emergency room?"

"You need to have your bruises looked at and documented, even if you don't report it to the police. If you ever need corroboration, something should be on file. You'd advise that to any client in your position." I fold my arms.

Paul grabs her wrist and pulls her off the floor. She and I decamp to the bathroom. Ten minutes later, a calmer Micki is ready to go.

"I'm doing this under protest. And I'm not sure about buying a new couch. I may need time to recover."

We all laugh.

"So, you're happy to mourn on the floor?" Paul throws her a pointed look.

"Well, maybe we can look. In fact, clear out all the furniture, Paul. I need to cleanse the room."

"Don't worry. All traces of the crime will be gone by the time you get back."

∼

MAX

SPENDING the afternoon with Micki is surreal. Paul had to practically carry her to the car while I helped Cress. She still has trouble managing the cane. For a top-notch lawyer, Micki is being a stubborn bitch. She refuses everything she would advise her clients to do. The emergency room is a nightmare.

Paul shows up after the first hour. "You now have an empty living room."

"Best news I've had today." Micki slurs from the five shots of whisky she drank during the impromptu wake.

We're an hour and a half in, and she threatens to leave every ten minutes. Paul and I do a cafeteria run, mostly to escape.

We return juggling coffee, bottles of water, and pastries. I hand Cress coffee and a danish. Her hand trembles as she puts it on the empty seat next to her and cups the coffee with both hands.

"Thanks." She inspects the gray tile floor. The corners of her mouth droop.

I pick up the pastry then sit next to her. "Tired?"

"Eventful couple of days."

I lean back, plate balanced on my lap, and put an arm around her shoulders. "One damn thing after another."

"I just want to go to bed for a week or so. Build a pillow fort, order Chinese food, and hide out, binge on Britcoms."

"I'll see what I can do."

JL has come in. He and Micki pace around the room. Her face is red. He waves his arms.

"Who called you?"

"I called him." Cress' voice crackles like tiny ice pellets on dry autumn leaves.

"Cress thinks Micki might need protection. *Femme têtu.*"

"What the hell does that mean?" Micki is in JL's face, hands on his chest, pushing to no effect. Paul starts laughing, the coffee in his hands splashing everywhere.

"Stubborn."

"Yeah, I am." She gives up pushing and pokes him instead. "And I don't need protection."

"Ms. Press?"

Micki growls as a nurse pops up at her elbow. She glares at the short, stocky man. "What?"

"We've called your name several times. Please come back with me."

She scowls then walks off reluctantly with her unwanted attendant.

We collapse into chairs, exhausted by the drama. Cress gulps down her coffee, crams a cheese danish into her mouth, and starts to wash it down with water.

"Hungry?" JL looks awed at Cress' voraciousness.

"No breakfast," she mumbles and tries to swallow at the same time.

Coughing and choking are the result of this misguided attempt at multitasking. Paul is the closest, so he starts pounding on her back.

"Stop."

Sheepishly, Paul backs up. He throws up his hands in apology.

Micki storms out to waiting room, yelling at the nurse who was following her.

"I am not making a statement to the police. My friends insisted I get checked out. No signs of concussion, broken bones, or an uncontrolled bleed, so I'm done. Thank you for your care." She marches past us, heads for the door.

"You can't go yet. We have to release you."

Micki turns back, glares at him. "This is not the Hotel

California. I can leave any time I like." She pushes through the revolving door while we run to catch up with her.

Sofa shopping is no less strenuous. We must spend five or six hours traipsing from store to store, sitting on sofas, loveseats, chaise longues, and settees.

Cress has limped on her sprained ankle for hours, collapsing into a chair at each furniture store until Micki calls her over to look at something. I let her use me as a support as much as possible, but I can see the pain in her eyes and the whiteness around her mouth.

Paul goes home to his querulous wife, who has been calling every thirty minutes. He always has speakerphone on so we hear more and more ill-tempered grousing as the day wanes. We plan to have dinner out after the marathon shopping session and Paul tries to cajole Ellie with promises of a nice meal, but in the end, he gives in to the offer of spaghetti and salad.

He calls over his shoulder as he walks out of the millionth furniture store. "I like a peaceful life."

Micki is happier after buying a royal blue sofa, a lime green loveseat, a cream chaise longue, and a very Victorian-looking tufted settee with an ebony frame and red-velvet upholstery. I'm appalled, but Cress pinches me in warning. I press my lips together and suggest we repair to Sayat Nova for Armenian food. We're seated in a cozy alcove. Cress collapses on a chair with a groan.

"I'm so sorry, Cress." Micki's voice is tight. "I wasn't thinking about your ankle."

"You had other things on your mind. It's okay. I had Max to make sure I could manage."

"I was tempted to carry you everywhere." Cress and Micki giggle.

"A fairytale romance." JL rolls his eyes.

After a large selection of meze and some kebabs, we're stuffed. A bottle of wine and post-prandial Ararat brandy smooth the rough spots. JL regales us with stories about growing up French Canadian in Vancouver, and Cress gives us snippets of life in the court of Ivan the Terrible. Her set piece on a feast in the Kremlin is hilarious.

When we walk out into light snow, I put my arm around her. The powdering of snow on her silvery brown curls turns her into a fairy princess.

"Go home, JL." Micki turns away as he reaches out to take her arm.

"*Certainement pas.*" He crosses his arms.

"I'm going home, alone."

"What if Sam is there?

Micki makes a scoffing sound.

He grabs her wrist. "Just get into the car."

She grimaces but doesn't resist. The threat of Sam seems to deflate her pugnaciousness.

We arrive back at Micki's place. No surprise that a furious Sam paces in front of her building.

After a good deal of shouting and threats to call the police, Sam finally slinks off, still uttering verbal threats.

"Sure you don't need any protection?"

Micki turns to JL. "Maybe I do." Then she watches Sam's retreating back.

"I'll arrange it. By the way, here's your new key." She goggles at him. "How do you think I kept Sam out of your place? I arranged it while we were out. Now, go inside and try for a good night's sleep. I'll stop by in the morning with the contract." He leans forward as if to give her a light kiss. She turns her head. He takes a step back, scratches his cheek.

Micki mumbles something that might be thank you before she slams into the building.

"Well, that went well." JL seems complacent.

"Let's go." We wave at JL, who is walking to his car, mumbling in French.

Cress' hands are freezing, so I settle her on the sofa with a handy tartan throw. When I bought the house, *Mamushka* sent me a dozen in the Grant tartan. Then I turn on the fireplace, pour a couple of fingers of whisky into two tumblers, and sit next to her. Cress takes a sip and hands me her glass to put on the table. When I lean back, she grabs me, her breath hot against my neck as she curls into me.

"Are you comfortable on my tasteful sofa?" I brush my fingers into her hair. Her eyes gleam in the firelight.

"Micki is not into tasteful. She loves putting together outrageous combinations." Cress stretches and tries to smother a yawn. "Are you going to work in the morning?"

"No, I've leave until my parents decamp." I pull her into a kiss. She falls asleep. I sigh and pull the throw over both of us so we can spoon. We can sleep here all night if necessary. Dorothy and Thorfinn burrow in, and I luxuriate in the comfort of our small family. *Maybe the vandal did me a favor*, I think as I drift into sleep.

Chapter 25

CRESS

Cosmetics litter the built-in dressing table in the master bath. I tap my foot against the rail on the swivel chair.

"Oh my God, Micki. Three fucking hours in this chair. My ass is killing me."

"Hold on. This is totally worth it. You won't believe how gorgeous you are."

I slip into my new dress. Micki zips me up and smooths the back. Then she turns me toward the full-length mirror on the door of the master bath. "Well?"

I stare into the mirror. My breath catches and I put my hand over my chest. The woman looking back is me, but not me. Smoky eyes, thicker lashes. Foundation with a tiny bit of gold highlight makes my skin translucent. The barest hint of blush. My lips are stained dark rose with lip pencil. I hate the feel of lipstick.

The front door slams.

"Damn. I wanted to pose you in the living room before Max got back."

Pose? Like a model in a photo shoot? The idea is ridiculous. "No big deal."

"Let me get him out of the way. His first view should knock his socks off." Micki clatters down the stairs. "Max, get into the kitchen. I don't want you to see Cress yet." Then she bounces back into the bedroom. "Come on. He's cowering in the kitchen."

Once she has me seated, my dress pooled around my feet with my shoes peeking out, she fans herself and tells me not to move. To Max, "Go take a shower, put on your fancy duds, whatever."

I hear him call down from the top of the landing, "Fifteen minutes, tops."

Micki comes back in, studies me, then makes an adjustment to my hair. Stands back, her forefinger tapping her lips. "I wish you would let me use lipstick. So much more dramatic."

"I'll just chew it off. It feels icky. Lip pencil stays on all night."

She reaches into her pocket and pulls out some lip gloss. "Just use this every once in a while. It will give your lips a shine." My evening bag sits on the console table near the doorway. Instead of giving the gloss to me, she drops it into the purse.

"Can I come down now?"

Micki scurries out of the room. "You clean up well, Max. Very hot." She pops back in, gives me another once-over. She looks back through the archway. "Step forward, Max. You have to be presented." She bows him into the room.

Fuck. He does look hot in his bespoke black tux and bright white pleated shirt. Shirt studs, cufflinks, bow tie. Cummerbund in the Grant tartan. He shoots his cuffs. His eyes are closed.

"Open your eyes, Max. You are in the presence of royalty."

He stops dead. His jaw drops. Kettle drums pound in my chest when I see the heat in his eyes. An invisible Janissary band has taken over my body.

"God, Cress." He moistens his lips. "I have never seen a more beautiful woman. No one. Ever."

The room fades away, and all I see is Max. My lungs lock.

"Come on, Max. You can do better than that." Micki shakes a finger in his face.

"Adorable, exquisite, divine. I'd ditch this reception if Ian didn't expect us. I'd throw Micki out and ravish you on the couch."

I stand up. One hand is pressed against the fireplace bricks for balance. My body heats when I notice the bulge behind his zipper. My bottom lip catches between my teeth.

He follows my gaze toward his crotch. Spots of color stain his cheeks, a self-conscious expression spreading over his face as he tries to adjust himself.

Micki throws me an amused look. "Tongue-tied? Nothing else to say, Max? I'm disappointed in you."

He swallows. "Athena come to life."

I reach up and touch my hair. My fingers brush a gold clip in the shape of a branch that holds my updo. The tendrils of curls that frame my face tickle. David Yurman drop earrings Max bought me sway against my neck.

Beads wink on the black lace overlay of my dress. Underneath is a flesh-colored sheath than makes me look bare. Micki convinced me it's stunning, not embarrassing, but as I look at Max's expression, doubts creep in. A scooped neckline highlights my collarbones. The sweep of the hem hides the ankle brace.

"Bloody hell, Cress. I hope to God that's an underlay. Otherwise, we're staying home, no matter what Ian thinks." He rubs the back of his hand against his lips. Is he drooling?

"Don't worry, when you're up close, you can see the pattern. Pretty good, eh?" Micki chuckles.

"Micki did such a fantastic job. Hair, makeup, dress. I never believed I could look like this." I gesture down my body.

"I'm-I'm-I'm—"

That's when I lose my balance. "Dammit."

He lunges forward, grabs me around the waist. "I've got you."

I sit down with a groan. "Guess the wheelchair is a good idea after all."

"I forgot to make my obeisance, my lady." He moves back and bows. "I am honored that you have deigned to accompany me this evening."

The vein in my throat pulses in rhythm with my heartbeat.

Micki claps her hands. "Hey guys, get the fuck out of here."

Max levers his phone out, and his thumbs move rapidly across the screen.

"Dirk is just pulling up." He helps me with the new scarlet Maxmara camel hair coat I couldn't resist. My heart flutters when he swings me into his arms and carries me down the steps. "Nervous?"

"Kind of. I'm a little worried about the dress. I feel like I'm baring everything, even though I'm not."

"You're adorable." He pecks my lips. "And you smell incredible. That blend of orange and ginger turns me on."

If I wasn't in his arms, I'd melt into a little pool on the floor.

"La mia stellina, you are stunning. When we make our entrance, everyone's eyes will be on you."

MAX

CRESS HOLDS her breath as we enter the Empire Room at the Palmer House. The setting is magnificent. I've been to a lot of receptions in many elegant places, even a few royal palaces, and I would rank the Palmer House right up with the best. The pervasive gold decoration makes everything gleam, and massive mirrors magnify the size of the already grand expanse. It has the air of a room in Versailles. If you want to persuade rich people to open their wallets, surrounding them with luxury is the way to go.

"Donating the cost of the event would probably provide the foundation with years' worth of funding."

Ian stands next to Cress' wheelchair. "Doesn't work that way." He shuffles from one foot to the other, constantly scanning the room. "Even small donors expect appreciation gifts."

Cress flashes him a dirty look then shifts restlessly. She has fussed about the wheelchair ever since I suggested it, but I can see that she's relieved not to have to stand.

"I hope you're all right."

"I'm fine, Ian. Max convinced me this was the best way to deal with my sprained ankle. Being pushed around in this chair is much easier than limping around or looking for the practically non-existent seats."

"Right. See you in line." He rushes off to round up the earl and countess.

"Have you been here before?" I ask her.

"To the Palmer House, yes. I even took an architecture tour where we came in to see the Tiffany decorations. But never to this ballroom." She fans herself with the tiny bag she has nestled into the side of the chair. "The decor overwhelms, which I think is the intention. Maybe my next book should be about Gilded Age Chicago. This would certainly make a great setting for a scene, although this building wasn't here then."

I give her a questioning look.

"There have been several Palmer House hotels. The first one, built in 1871, opened thirteen days before the Great Chicago Fire."

"Bad timing."

"It was a wedding present from Potter Palmer to his wife, Bertha."

"Not an auspicious start."

"I guess they didn't believe in bad luck. Potter fell in love with her when she was thirteen and adored her. Bertha became a force in the city. Her involvement in the 1893 World's Fair sealed the deal." She shifts in the chair, drums her feet on the footrest. "Anyway, they rebuilt the hotel and it opened again in 1875. In the 1920s they rebuilt because downtown needed bigger hotels. So, this hotel post-dates the Gilded Age."

"How about a book set in the roaring twenties?"

"The Green Mill, Al Capone, the St. Valentine's Day Massacre—it would be a departure, but...well, I'll keep it in mind."

"Your next project?"

"I'm still caught up in the current one. I don't think I'll be abandoning sixteenth-century Russia for quite some time. And then I have an idea that revolves around one of the computer innovators at Bletchley Park."

"Popular subject these days. I know a bit about Bletchley."

"I might write a novel with Munro Innes as the protagonist. He's been overlooked."

"Munro Innes? Really?"

"You've heard of him?"

I run a finger around my collar. "He was my great uncle."

"I don't believe you."

"Ask Ian. Ask my parents when you meet them." I smirk.

"Ask me what?"

"Never mind," she says quickly.

My brother gives a formal bow. "Lord and Lady Kendal, may I present Dr. Cressida Taylor and my brother, the Honorable Maxim Grant."

Cress startles at my title. "Totally meaningless," I insist, glowering at Ian.

He lifts a shoulder. "Alastair, Lord Marshton, and Lady Margaret Dennys."

Lady Margaret's eyes are eating me up, and I shift from foot to foot. "What an unusual first name for a Scot. I would have thought Maxwell. Is it French for the Auld Alliance?"

"My mother's family is Russian, Lady Margaret."

"How interesting."

"Margaret." Lady Kendal gives a little warning shake of her head. "That is unpardonable. Apologize to Mr. Grant for your rudeness."

Lady Margaret, twenty-five and a bit rebellious, struggles not to make a face at her mother. Fails.

"No need for an apology. I'm asked that quite often." A

harmless lie that smooths over any unpleasantness. Few people even know my name is Maxim.

Time to mingle. I wander around, shaking hands and having desultory conversations. Cress is more limited, but she is fizzing with energy as various guests come over to speak to her.

I've just fetched a flute of champagne, and I scan the room. I spot her in a corner, away from the bustle of guests. My brother leans over her, and their conversation looks a bit heated. I sidle closer, trying to hear over the cacophony.

Popping a dainty sandwich into his mouth, Ian holds up a finger. "We've heard about you ever since Max was at Oxford."

Cress opens her mouth in surprise. "You mean the mysterious girl on the bike?" She smiles wryly.

Ian adopts a humorous tone. "Exactly. Knocked him on the head, so to speak. Instant attraction. He's been besotted ever since." His tone changes to what sounds like slight menace. "I am just not sure you are as besotted as he is."

He looks at her as if she is a mouse and he is the cat, crouched, muscles bunched, ready to pounce. "I'm not questioning your motives, but Max is part of a wealthy and ancient family. That might seem attractive. I would hate to see my little brother hurt."

"Excuse me. You still think of Max as a little boy? I don't think your 40-year-old brother would appreciate the sentiment." Point to her.

"Bloody hell. He is my little brother. I am ten years older, ten years more experienced—more than that. After all, in matters of the heart, Max is a bit of an innocent. If you are just amusing yourself with him, let him go now. I know he is well-off and almost as good-looking as me"—Ian leers—

"but he is much more emotionally fragile than his stoic exterior might suggest."

Cress pokes the tip of her tongue out just beyond her lower lip. Her words are clipped. "First, I make my own money. Second, I couldn't care less how ancient and important your family is in Britain. Third, none of this is your business."

She flushes with anger and looks like she might get out of the chair and give him a smack. "If this is a family plan to try to intimidate me…" Her fierce riposte makes my heart pound.

"No, no. This is me." Ian's tone has turned emollient. "I've seen him fall apart, and I never want to see it again."

Cress flinches, her hands pushing against the arms of the chair. "I'm not going to go into my emotional issues with you, but I love Max, even if I don't show it much in public."

Ian hangs his head as I retreat into the crowd, but stay close enough to hear. "Sorry, I didn't mean to imply…"

"Yes, you did." The red starts to fade from her cheeks. "So, what you're saying is that you are an overprotective jerk."

"Exactly." Ian beams, not bothered by the pejorative label. "That is exactly what we are establishing now. My dad hates to interfere, so as the oldest son and heir, I am taking on his role in vetting you."

He runs a hand through his hair, ruining the immaculate barbering. "After all, Max has been carrying around this idealized picture of a woman who attracted him twenty years ago. He knew nothing about you then, and he meets you, fortuitously, and falls all over again, still not knowing you. It's my job to make sure he doesn't make an arse of himself over you."

Cress smiles thinly. "You're the ass. I love Max, not his money or his posh family. And if you can't support that, you can go to hell." She starts to roll her wheelchair away. I duck behind a boisterous group, not wanting her to know I've been eavesdropping.

Ian stands there, open-mouthed at her response. Finally, before she gets too far, he runs after her. "Wait, please. Perhaps I was too brusque. I am sorry." He makes a small bowing motion and bestows a charming smile. "Please, please come back and we can begin again."

I stroll over, hand her a flute, and rest my arm on the back of her chair. Then I drop my head to brush my lips against the back of her neck. "Everything okay? Are you having a good time?"

She hands my hovering brother her glass then stands up and leans against the chair. Her liquid gaze turns me to jelly. Her face glows with delight, her eyes sparkling. "Brilliant. I'm gob-smacked that people want to talk about my books."

"Being with you has made me the luckiest guy in the room." I brush my hand over her already unraveling French twist, twisting an errant curl around my finger.

Ian hands Cress her glass, skin stretched tight over his face as he glances down the long line of impatient guests. He bows, just a slight bend at the waist. "I'll catch up with you later."

And we're done. I push Cress along the buffet line so she can point out what she likes. After parking her next to a small table, I fill our plates. The assortment is fabulous.

On our first pass, we both plump for the lobster salad with avocado, cucumber, and tarragon in a vol-au-vent, the pan-seared scallop rondo with Meyer lemon and dill butter on a Chinese spoon, seared duck breast with fig and Vidalia onion jam served on crispy crostini, and Maine lobster with garlic butter and herbs de Provence.

We are sipping a very good French champagne as we

nibble when Lord and Lady Kendal approach. They avoid looking at the wheelchair, perhaps thinking Cress might be self-conscious.

She puts them at their ease. "I'm sorry I can't curtesy, but I sprained my ankle and Max has forced me into this wheelchair for the duration of the reception."

"Curtsies aren't required, my dear. Now, if I were the queen—"

"Thank God you're not." Lord Kendal gives an exaggerated shudder.

She opens her handbag and fishes out a copy of Cress' book on Scott and Shackleton. "When dear Ian told us you were going to be here, I couldn't resist asking for an autograph."

Cress looks bemused. "Of course." She reaches for the book. I hand her the fountain pen I keep in my breast pocket.

"You carry a pen when you're wearing a tux?"

"Why not?"

With a smile, she focuses on the countess. "Do you want an inscription or just a signature?"

"An inscription would be lovely."

I look over her shoulder as she writes.

I hope you enjoy reading this book as much as I enjoyed writing it.
Thank you for all your efforts in supporting good causes.
Cressida Taylor, December 2013

BY THIS TIME, the earl has found a chair and brings it over for his wife. "Sit down, Patricia. You and Dr. Taylor can have a natter about polar exploration, and I can drag this young man off and grill him about bank security." Presumably he's been briefed on all the guests and is familiar with my CV. I had forgotten he was on the board of governors for one of the largest private banks in Britain.

After more chat and not only a second but a third round of food, Cress and I are ready to escape. Our one hour has become almost four and Cress is drooping, but I have one more thing to do before we can leave.

I grab Ian. "Thanks so much for the invite."

He waves away the thank you.

"We had a brilliant time after you finished your little rant. But I need you to do one thing for me." I point to the string quartet that has been playing softly all evening. "Can they do a string version of 'At Last'?"

"That's one of Mum and Dad's favorites." He gazes at me, a question in his eyes, and I dip my head and glance over at Cress. "Let me ask."

He grabs his assistant and whispers. Then he runs over to the string players. His mouth moves. He points at me. The quartet members wave their bows. Ian makes a little gesture with his fingers, and the ballroom lights dim.

The first strains of the music send a chill up my spine. A vision of my parents, Dad in formal kilt, Mum in a Grant tartan ballgown on Hogmanay. Everything is prepared for the *ceilidh*. Five children stand against the wall, bystanders in a private family moment.

Before the guests arrive, Brian and Viktoria Grant sweep across the floor in the Great Hall at Grant House to an old recording by Etta James. "At Last"—their song.

I turn to Cress, regal on her wheeled throne. I hold out my hand and bow. "Milady, will you dance with me."

She looks up from under her lashes and reaches for my

outstretched hand. "Oh yes, milord. I would love to dance with you."

I sweep her into my arms, bury my face in her messy bun. The quartet plays the song several times, and for eight minutes and fifteen seconds, our bodies sway as I hold her close. Ginger and orange waft from her hair. No one is in the room but us.

When the music finally fades away, I kiss her deeply. The world comes back, and the company applauds.

"I never knew you had that much romance in your soul." Ian claps a hand on my shoulder.

"I'll take Cinderella home now." I lower her back into the wheelchair and stroke her cheek.

"Thank you for the dance. This has been the most magical night of my life."

I gently run a finger under her lower lashes. "Why are you crying, *la mia stellina*?"

She sniffs. "Not crying. It's just my joy running over."

I kiss her hand. "Be back in a flash. Coats."

"She's quite the trooper." Ian walks me over to the coat check, and I fish in my pocket for the tokens. "Have breakfast with me tomorrow. I need to chat."

"What about?" Ian doesn't usually want my advice.

"Things." His vagueness prickles like gorse.

Probably to do with the family. "Come to my place about nine?"

"Easier for me if we meet up at The Drake."

"All right." I give Ian a farewell wave. Cress is chatting with Lord Alastair and Lady Margaret. I help her with her lovely red coat and slip on my Harris Tweed Balmacaan, text Dirk, and we wait by the hotel entrance for the Escalade. As I see him pull up, I signal the doorman to open the door so the wheelchair can get through.

We hear two loud, sharp cracks. Breaking glass. Screams. My training kicks in and I drop to the ground, knocking the wheelchair out of the way to get Cress out of the line of fire, just as a third shot rings out. The world goes silent. I pick myself up. The wheelchair is tipped on its side, Cress motionless on the pavement.

I drop to my knees and look for damage. No blood that I can see, thank God. My hand brushes her coat. Wetness on my fingers. Red. Blood. The color of her coat hid the fluid leaking through.

No. A howl rips from my throat. I pound my fists on the pavement, welcome the pain.

The hubbub of the crowd swirls around us.

"She's been shot. Call 911."

"What happened?"

"Hoodlums."

"No place safe these days."

"Ban guns."

"Lock 'em all up."

"I saw that woman push through the crowd with her gun out."

"Three guys, shot into the crowd, ran off."

I raise my head to check for Dirk. He holds Tina Monroe, her arms behind her. Her big hat is crushed on the ground, the gun at her feet. Her lips twist into a snarl. "Go to hell, bitch."

I want to kill her. Turn her into a smear on the pavement. Crush her like an insect.

Instead, I cradle Cress in my arms, feel her chest rise and fall. She's unresponsive, but not dead. Can't tell how badly she's hurt. My lips are against her check as senseless babble pours out of me.

"Cress, darling, you'll be fine, *la mia stellina.* I promise, everything will be okay. Open your beautiful eyes. Please." I rub my cheek against hers. Kiss her lips. Feel her shallow breaths caress me. Brush my tears from her face.

Minutes ago, we were dancing. We thought we had our fairytale ending, but the evil queen still had a part to play.

The continual braying of the sirens, Tina screaming obscenities at Cress, the stink from the gunfire, and the flashing lights from the ambulance and the police cars pummel me. The assault on my senses makes time flip back and forth. Cress morphs into Zehra and back again. I shudder and hold her like a lifeline.

EMTs take her out of my arms and place her on a stretcher.

I stop shaking and scramble to my feet, push my way to the ambulance. "I need to go with her."

"No room. Just go to the hospital."

"Which one?"

They slam the door without answering, only a screech of tires in their wake.

I stand on the pavement with Dirk, clenching and unclenching my fists as I watch the police push Tina into a squad car. Blood pounds so hard in my ears that I barely hear the cops telling me where to go to make a statement.

Dirk touches my arm. "She'll be at Northwestern Memorial Hospital."

I grab Dirk by his collar, and he rocks back and forth like a tree in a high wind while I scream at him. "We fucked up. We're supposed to protect her, and now she's bleeding in a hospital. We're fuckups."

He shakes loose, then grabs my arm. "Calm down, Max. I talked to the EMTs, and they are pretty hopeful that the wounds aren't life threatening. Let's drive to the station and give our statements. By the time we're finished, Cress will probably be out of emergency. We'll know more then."

He puts his hand on my back, propels me to the open door of the SUV.

"Get in. I called JL. He'll meet you at the hospital." His voice is rough with suppressed emotion. "Damn, I'm so sorry, Max. She's such a nice lady."

Chapter 26

MAX

After we make our statements at the District 1 station, Dirk drives me to the hospital. JL texted me that Cress is at the Feinberg Pavilion. I lean on the info desk counter.

"Hi, mate." Chummy. Maybe that will get me entrée. "I'm here to visit Cressida Taylor."

"Let me check the computer." The desk guy fiddles around with the keyboard. "Looks like she's out of surgery. When she's released from the recovery room, an orderly will take her to room 321. You can sit in the waiting area up there if you want."

"Can I see her in the recovery room?" My throat is raw from suppressed screams.

He shakes his head no. I clench my hands in frustration, force out words to thank him as I take off for the elevator. JL is leaning against the wall in the corridor when I arrive.

"Let's sit down while we wait for Cress to be transferred."

He hands me a plastic bag containing her purse, jewelry, and watch. "Somehow her bag managed to avoid the splatter, but they told me her shoes are ruined. I called Micki, and she'll stop at Target in the morning and get her something to wear when she leaves the hospital that will fit over the bandages."

I turn the bag over and over in my hands. "Did the doctors tell you anything?" I drop into a chair, take off my glasses. Scrub my eyes, surprised my fingers are wet.

"Not much. She's lucky. The bullet just missed nicking an artery. The doctors got the bullet out of her shoulder, and the other wounds were superficial, mostly from falling out of the wheelchair."

"Turns out Tina has lousy aim." We jump as Dirk's voice penetrates the ether. "She shot wildly, kind of in Cress' direction. The one that hit was a lucky shot."

"Not so lucky for Cress," I snarl.

JL is soothing. "She's lost a lot of blood, but they gave her a transfusion and she's stable. The doctor will be back in about an hour with an update, so let's sit in the lounge and you can tell me what's going on."

"Tina must have found out Cress was going to be at the reception. When we came out of the hotel, she ambushed us. There were lots of people on the sidewalk, so she could blend in. It was fast and unexpected. And Cress…" My voice hitches. "God damn it. She was a sitting duck in that fucking wheelchair."

JL touches my arm. "With her ankle the way it is, she would have been an easy target with or without the wheelchair. Don't beat yourself up. There was nothing you could do."

"I could have blocked her but instead I knocked the wheelchair out of the way, and that actually caused some of her injuries." Another monumental fail.

He wags his head in negation. "You were behind her. No way you could have blocked her." As I start to expostulate, he holds up a hand. "Dirk restrained the bitch, the police have her, and Cress will recover."

Resignation floods through me. I slump in the marginally comfortable chair, my legs stretched out, my eyes squeezed shut. "I can't figure out how Tina knew about the reception. It was a private affair with a select guest list. The consulate didn't promote it in advance."

"Maybe she had your house staked out, followed us down."

"I don't think so, Dirk." Hours of surveillance tape revealed nothing.

"Did Cress have anything in her condo about the event?" JL smooths an eyebrow.

"There was an invitation. I remember giving it to her, and she left it on a small table in the living room." I run my fingers through my hair in frustration. "If Cress' suspicions are right and Tina vandalized the condo, she might have found it."

"That's probably the answer. Who would even notice it was missing? With so much destroyed, you'd assume the card was ripped up and burned."

A tall, thin man in a white coat comes up to us, and JL introduces him. "Dr. Cranmer, this is Max Grant, Cress Taylor's fiancé."

I look at JL in surprise.

Cranmer looks me over, taking in my disheveled fancy dress. "Sorry to meet you under these circumstances. Just checked on Dr. Taylor in the recovery room. She designated you as her nearest relative, Mr. Grant. She had a mild reaction to the antibiotic we gave her, but she's stable now and everything looks good. She'll be in the room shortly. I can arrange for you to stay over if you want."

"Stay, Max. I'll go to your place and pick up some comfortable clothes for you and check on Cress' cats." JL has moved onto the balls of his feet and looks poised for flight.

I think of Cress and how spectacular she was in her sexy dress. "I guess her dress is history. The coat too."

"Yeah, bad news about her clothes. The bullet ripped right through the coat, and the blood soaked into the lining and covered a lot of the dress."

"Clothes can be replaced." My voice is harsh. The doctor touches my arm then walks off to make arrangements.

The gurney comes off the elevator. Cress. I can tell by the curly hair spilling out over the rails. The orderly rolls her into the room, but a nurse stops me at the door.

"Go sit down. Let us get her set up and comfortable. Someone will bring you back in a few minutes."

Swearing under my breath, I sit down and call Micki and Paul. They promise to come to the hospital. When I'm finally allowed to see Cress, the lights are dim, and I stand, blinking, trying to force my eyes to adjust.

I move closer to the bed and see her heavily bandaged shoulder and tubes and wires running to machines and drips. Any other damage is hidden by the hospital gown and blankets. When the wheelchair fell over, she hit her head, and I wince at the developing black eyes. From the lowered lighting, I assume she has some level of concussion.

She looks like she is out for the count. With no idea when she might wake up, I might as well be comfortable. I look around the room. There is a short sofa against one wall. Might work for an average guy, but a normal-sized piece of furniture is never big enough for me.

I can envision my head on the arm, my legs dangling off the end. I rub the back of my neck and roll my shoulders.

A nurse walks in, glances at me, and checks Cress' vitals. After she makes some notations on a chart, she looks at me. "The doctor told me you want to stay over. These chairs recline so you can sleep in them, more or less."

She looks me up and down. "Since you're so tall, if you want to use the couch, pull it out of the corner. You can put a chair at the end without an arm. I'll bring you a blanket."

I thank her and pull a non-reclining visitor's chair as close to the bed as possible. It's a bit low to the ground for my long legs, but comfort is the least of my concerns. I take Cress' hand, to soothe myself more than anything.

She moans softly so I try to drop it, but she tightens her hold. I lean over and kiss her cheek. Even though unconscious, she smiles. She wants me. I gain a measure of peace.

After an hour, I move to a recliner and pull out the laptop JL dropped off with the clothes. I log on with a VPN. Might as well do some work. Two hours later, I pull myself out of the chair, shake out my stiff muscles, and shut down for the night.

My phone is secure, so I turn it on to see I have been barraged with messages, mostly from Clay. I shoot him a text to tell him to check Dropbox for the report he wants.

One from JL tells me he is still in the waiting room, along with Micki, Paul, and Ellie. I shove the laptop under my arm and I walk down there. That way, if Micki and Paul want to go down to the room, it won't be too crowded.

CRESS

DISORIENTED. Nauseated. A tilt-a-whirl spins in my stomach. I open my eyes, blink to bring things into focus. A giant gong beats in my head. I'm not sure where I am. *Shit, shit, shit.* I can't reach my glasses.

The pain as I try to move my shoulder is sharp and unexpected. A shadow flickers in the corner of my eye, and I wonder if someone is in the room with me. I hear footsteps.

"Max?" I rasp, wincing at how raw my voice sounds.

"Hullo, Cress. I'm so sorry." Carefully he puts my glasses on for me. I squint, trying to bring him into focus. All I can see is a dim, wavering shape. "I'm so sorry. I failed you."

I sigh. "I don't remember anything."

"Nothing?" He sounds panicked. "You don't remember anything from last night?"

"I remember the reception."

"Good. And after the reception?"

I cast my mind back to the last thing I remember then try to move forward in time. Things slowly start to come back. We're leaving the Palmer House. Dirk has the SUV at the curb. Max is pushing the wheelchair. Then everything is jumbled. I remember a popping sound like a cherry bomb, screams, flashing lights, and searing pain. "I was shot."

"Yes, and now you're in hospital. The doctor says you'll be fine, but I'm not sure how long you will have to stay."

"Who shot me?"

Max leans down and touches his lips to my ear. "Tina."

"Oh my God...she really has gone off the rails."

"Apparently so." His voice is like grit filtering down from falling bricks. "Dirk restrained her until the police could take over, and JL is at the booking. She'll be arraigned in the next couple of days. I hope she's locked up for a long time."

I try to shift, but that small movement makes me gasp in pain.

A nurse walks into the room and looks at Max. Obviously, she was not expecting me to have visitors in the middle of the night, or is it early morning? No matter. "Are you a relative?"

Max shakes his head. "I, uh…"

I break in, "He's my fiancé." Surprise flashes as he glances at me.

"The doctor arranged for me to stay the night."

"Fine." She takes my wrist, checks my pulse. "The doctor will be here soon. He can tell you what's going on."

"Good." I try to smile. "I'm hoping he'll tell me I can go home." I try to sit up and wince at the pain. "Why does my head hurt so much?"

"Concussion. It's from hitting your head on the pavement when the wheelchair tipped over." I notice Max's wince. That's You have quite the lump. And black eyes." She adjusts the angle of the bed for me then sticks a thermometer in my mouth and a blood pressure cuff on my bicep. "Try not to move your arm."

"Go home?" The doctor has obviously heard me, even though I can barely project. "I'm afraid you'll have to be here for a day or two. You have a stage-three concussion, and we want to do some tests. We patched up your shoulder, but I want to be able to keep an eye on how the wound is healing. Even when you leave the hospital, you'll need to have someone check on you. Do you live with anyone?"

"She's staying with me." Max's assertion makes my skin prickle.

A tray arrives with clear soup in a cup since I can't manipulate a spoon. I've never had soup through a straw before, and I hope I never have to again.

Max helps, holding the cup, wiping my mouth when

liquid dribbles out. He also cuts the accompanying toast into small squares and feeds them to me between sips of soup. If he can love me now, maybe that means we're meant to be together.

"If Tina had to shoot me, I wish she could have hit my left shoulder instead of the right."

"Just be glad she's a lousy shot or you'd be dead. She wasn't aiming to wound you. She was trying to kill you."

The morphine makes my stomach queasy, so I don't have much of an appetite. Max urges me to eat, telling me food will help, but that seems counterintuitive. I'm so tired. Everything is fuzzy. The doctor tells me I had a reaction to the antibiotic combined with the trauma from the gunshot wound and the concussion.

If bad things come in threes, I've had mine. I'm a grumpy camper. I've been told I will be off the morphine by this evening. When Percocet is suggested, I let them know I don't react well to it, or to other prescription opioids like Oxycontin. We agree to try to just use ibuprofen for the time being.

Micki, Paul, and Ellie come in as I'm finishing the small piece of bread that came with the soup.

"Wow, Tina really did a job on you." Micki holds a bouquet of balloons.

"All she did was shoot me. The rest was the damned wheelchair falling over."

"My fault," Max mutters. I squeeze his hand to tell him everything is all right,

Ellie grimaces. "You look so bad."

Micki glares at her.

"Be nice." Paul, always the peacemaker.

"What? Why can Micki say something, and I can't?"

"I was expressing sympathy as an old friend." Micki turns her back on Ellie.

"I was expressing sympathy, too," Ellie whines.

Everyone rolls their eyes except me. That would hurt way too much.

Paul gives her a peck on the cheek. "I know, babe."

JL walks in. "Hail, hail."

"What news on the Rialto?" It's the Max and JL Shakespeare show.

"I went to the arraignment this morning. It was pretty interesting."

"Really? I thought those kinds of things are cut and dried." My energy drains quickly. I'm ready for a nap.

"Not today. Tina's defense attorney explained that she had no criminal record and gave some of Tina's history with Cress—from Tina's point of view, of course. Just as he was explaining that Tina posed no flight risk, she started ranting. Neither her lawyer nor the judge could shut her up."

He shakes his head. "She bragged about how clever she was to see the invitation, boasted about burning out your condo, and lamented that she hadn't managed to kill you. Then she whined that everything is your fault and she's the real victim. She insisted that you had to be in court and that without your presence, the proceedings were illegal. What a nutcase."

We are all open-mouthed, hardly able to credit what happened.

"Wow, I wish I could have seen that." Ellie's glee grates.

Paul frowns.

JL goes on. "Her lawyer quit and the judge had her forcibly removed. She was kicking and screaming as they carried her out. I'm surprised she didn't start foaming at the mouth. She's been sent for psychiatric evaluation. If she comes to trial, you'll be notified. You'll probably be interviewed by the police in the next day or so, but don't worry about anything else. I don't think she'll be released any time soon."

I CHECK MY WATCH, again. The last time I checked, it was 11:03 AM, and it's still 11:03 AM. How could it still be the same time? Not even a minute different. Maybe my watch stopped. I check my phone. No, still 11:03 AM. I try to scratch the itch under my sling. *Dammit.* The universe laughs at me.

I'm like a prisoner finally sprung, back in civilian clothes, waiting. Endless waiting. Where the hell is Max? I check my watch again. Half an hour to go.

My bag is packed. Three passes around the room ensures that no trace of my presence will linger. The physical therapist pops his head around the door.

"See you're ready go." He walks in, rolled papers in one hand. He smacks them against his palm. "Final instructions: shoulder exercises, ankle exercises, therapy schedule. Remember, no lifting anything heavier than silverware for the first couple of days but do the range-of-motion stuff. Take it slow."

"When will I be back to normal?"

"What's normal?"

"I'm not asking for philosophy, just a reasonable estimate of when I can start writing, knitting, all that stuff."

"Check with the doctor." He hands me the papers, gives a little wave, and he's out the door.

I look at my watch. That ate up a couple of minutes. I'm too restless to read, so I start pacing.

A nurse arrives with an envelope and a brown carrier bag. "Your instructions, prescriptions."

"What's in the bag?"

"Dressings with instructions, stuff to put on the wound, little ice packs."

"Can I take showers?"

"Just remove the dressing first. If you can have someone close by for the first few days, that would be good, especially to help with the bandaging." And she's gone. I slip the paperwork into the outside pocket on the back of my case and balance the bag on top. That killed a couple more minutes.

The harp sounds on my phone. Goody, a text message. Maybe Max is early. I picture him walking into the lobby, thumbing the keyboard. But no—it's a message from my father. *What the...*

Not going to read it. Why would he text me anyway? Certainly not out of fatherly concern. I glance down. The opening of the text catches my eye.

AARON TAYLOR: Thanks for the cash.

What? I open the message.

AARON TAYLOR: Thanks for the cash. Sorry about you getting shot.

Sorry. Like I believe that. But what is this about cash? I didn't give him any cash.

Should I text back? Call? The flutter in my chest makes me breathless. I rub the phone against it. In the bathroom, I turn on the cold water, fill a cup, rinse the bad taste out of my mouth.

I pull up my contacts. Touch my father's name. His info comes up, and my finger wavers over the number.

"*Ah, la mia stellina. Ma come sei bella.*"

The flutters in my chest continue, but now they are from desire, not anxiety. My phone drops into my lap.

"Thank God. I was starting to wonder if I would be stranded forever."

"No chance. I can't do without you. You'll be amazed at the house. JL, Micki, and I spent the whole morning bringing Christmas to Grant Manor." He glances at my lap. "Were you planning to make a call? Go ahead."

"I got a strange text—from my dad."

His lips twist into a scowl. "Really? I can't believe it."

I bring up the text message, hold the phone out.

His mouth forms an O when he sees it.

"I don't know what he means about cash. I didn't send him any cash."

"That bast…" Max drops to the bed.

I stare at him. My eyes narrow. "You know something about this." No flutters now. My heart is pounding. Heat rushes to my face and neck.

"Uh, yeah." He speaks so softly I can barely hear him. Max rubs a hand through his hair. He flushes. I am sure our red faces match.

"Okay, tell me."

Just then JL bounces into the room with Micki. "*Tu est libre, ma chère Cress. Félicitations.*" He waves a fist.

Micki looks at me, then at Max. Puts her hands on her hips. Glares. "What's going on?"

Max sits on the edge of his bed, elbows on knees, head in his hands.

I hand Micki the phone. Her eyes widen as she reads the screen. "What the hell?"

JL reads over her shoulder. "So, the bird's come home to roost." I wonder at his smug expression.

Max raises his head, his gray eyes stormy, glaring at his friend. "Shut your gob."

JL, hands on hips, growls, "Tell her, Max."

"Tell us." Micki's not about to be left out.

"I paid him off, Cress."

I want to slap him. "You what?"

"I paid him off."

"You. Paid. Him. Off. Who the fuck do you think you are?"

"I wanted him to leave you alone. I called and told him you were planning legal proceedings against him but, if he would sign an agreement not to contact you, you would pay him $100,000. He agreed. I planned to give you the agreement as one of your Christmas presents."

By the time he finishes, I am fuming. The air has been sucked out of the room. Tears gather at the corners of my eyes, but I clench my fist. *No crying, Cress.* The muscles in my right arm, immobile against my chest, twitch. "Asshole."

"That's all you have to say?" He slumps with a sigh of relief.

That will be short-lived. I am so fucking angry. If we weren't in a hospital room, I'd really let fly. "I don't even know what to say to you, you fucking jerk. Calling my father is the stupidest thing I can imagine you doing."

I'm getting into my stride now, although I keep my voice under control. I don't want nurses and doctors swarming in. "Who the hell do you think you are? You don't get to decide what's best for me. You don't even ask. You just call up my father, make up a stupid story, AND PAY HIM OFF. You reward him for bad behavior. You make me seem like an easy mark. You treat me like a child."

He opens his mouth. "No, I, please—"

I turn away. "Don't want to hear your apologies or your justifications. I. Don't. Want. To. Hear. Anything."

JL and Micki gape.

I gesture to my bag. "Can I go home with you, Micki?"

"Cress, no." Max's anguished cry tears into me, but I harden my heart. I am so done.

"Uh, sure."

I turn to JL. "Maybe you could bring Dorothy and Thorfinn over later?"

"Bien sûr."

Max's gaze focuses on the linoleum. "Of course you will, traitor." His bitterness shines out of every word.

"I told you this would bite you in the ass. You always think you know best." JL's taunt hangs in the air.

"Put a sock in it, JL." Max turns to me, his beautiful gray eyes clouded. "Cress, I love you. I did this because I love you."

I will not let myself get sucked in. "Maybe you need to learn more about how to treat someone you 'love.' You see yourself as my white knight—gallant, protective, caring. You don't see me as a strong woman who can fight her own battles. I want a partner, not a savior. If this is your idea of love, think again."

My eyes burn. My skin is hot. My stomach churns. If I wasn't sitting in a bed, I'd fall to the floor from the pain. Instead, I'm doubled over, hugging my knees. T. S. Eliot was wrong. My world ends with a bang, not a whimper.

"Cress." Micki holds up a hand. "Don't you think—"

I straighten and give her the stink eye. "Shut up, Micki."

She gasps. "Cress, I'm just—"

"Just get me to your place. I don't need your advice right now. I'm done being treated like a frail flower. I'm done being seen as someone who can't protect herself. I'm done. Period." Just then, an orderly rolls a wheelchair into the room. "Perfect timing."

I flop down into the seat. He puts the case and bag on my lap.

"All set?"

"You bet." I don't look back. I don't even say goodbye.

Chapter 27

MAX

The third time Clay passes my open door, he walks in. "At Last" is on a loop while I hunch in front of my screen and swipe through pictures.

"Go home, Max."

I shake my head and focus on the photo of Cress and me, dressed in our finery, my arm around her waist. She gazes up at me as I lower my head to give her a kiss. I wish I had one of us dancing. That was the most magical moment of my life.

Clay stands behind me. "Such a beautiful portrait of love. You should get that enlarged and framed."

"Maybe I should, as a reminder of what a screwup I am."

He frowns at my grumpy response. "You belong together. Find a way, Max. Now go home. You're useless." He turns at the doorway. "Merry Christmas."

At Union Station, my family swarms me. Ian has shown

up to help manage the wave. After kissing me, the first words out of Mum's mouth chill me. "Where's Cress?"

I look over to Ian. He's the only one who knows. With a shrug, he lets me know I'm on my own.

"She's so sorry, but she had to go out of town. Something to do with her research."

"What a shame. Your mother and I were looking forward to meeting her."

I can't tell if they buy the excuse, but no one calls me on it.

AFTER THE CHAOS at Union Station, I need a breather. Mum has asked me three times when Cress will be back from her research trip, and Ian throws me pitying looks every time I give some vague reply. If I don't tell them she's gone, I can pretend none of this is real. Porky is my middle name.

The onslaught of thirteen people, five of them under fifteen, equipped with forty pieces of luggage, is a tsunami. Getting everyone settled has been a comedy of errors. Even with six bedrooms, trying to figure out who sleeps where is tricky. I give my parents the master suite. I don't want to sleep there without Cress. I've been sleeping in the small guest room ever since she left.

Frank and Liz have a big bedroom on the second floor, as do Diana and Les. The five kids squealed with joy when they saw the converted attic designated as their lair. There's space for Ian if he wants to stay over on Christmas Eve.

With so many people and no time to cook, I had last night's dinner catered. In addition to the family, I invited JL, Jarvis and his partner, and Clay and his wife to join us as well as Micki, Paul, and Ellie.

From the scallops to the prime rib to the sticky toffee pudding, everyone was delighted, even the kids. My parents brought us up to enjoy food, and my siblings are no different with their offspring.

After only one day, I'm tired of all Christmas and all family all the time. I need to escape. Ian has work commitments, and Frank and Les are taking the kids to the Shedd Aquarium and the Field Museum. Later, Ian will pick up Pequod's Pizza for a casual family meal.

My dad is as eager to decamp as I am. Tempting him with a ride in one of the sports cars is embellishing the frame, so to speak.

"A drive sounds just the ticket. Which car?" He sounds eager to go.

"I was thinking the Lamborghini or the Bugatti, unless you want the Mercury."

"I don't need a classic car, especially a convertible, in the winter. Let's try the Bugatti."

"Right. I'll call the garage and have them get it ready."

We drive northwest toward Rockford, picking up the Stagecoach Trail in Lena. The road between Lena and Galena is narrow with twists and turns that give me a chance to show Dad some of great features of the car, although sadly I don't need the amazing track acceleration. Speeds over 250 mph aren't in the cards for this trip.

As we cruise the main drag in Galena, I look for a place to park and treat Dad to a late lunch at One Eleven Main. He enthuses at length about the quality of the fish and chips. Then he looks at me shrewdly.

"I'm so happy you've found love, Max."

Startled, I start coughing. "Yeah, well…"

"It's written all over you."

"I've screwed everything up." I pick up a chip.

"Is that why we haven't met her yet?"

I'm not ready for this conversation. "How did you know Mum was the one?"

"She was standing on a private runway at the airport in Inverness swaying in stiletto heels. Red shoes. I couldn't understand why this woman, in an evening dress, dripping with diamonds, huddled in a fur coat, was at the airfield. She was standing next to my Bristol Type 22, staring at the cockpit."

"Funny, Cress was wearing red shoes when her bag crashed into my arm at Everest. The first time I'd seen her in twenty years. Not that I realized it that night."

"Meant to be then." He looks off as if into the past. "Your mother was the most beautiful woman I had ever seen, like the Ice Queen in *The Nutcracker*. She shimmered like a piece of Venetian glass." He clears his throat. "A few hairline cracks now, but still breathtaking."

"And?"

"I thought, who the hell are you? 'I need a ride,' she said. 'Someone told me about a daredevil pilot with a World War I vintage plane who might accommodate me.' I flew her to Paris and back. We walked by the Seine, had coffee in little cafes, ate in famous bistros. Two days in Paris…she stole my heart."

He studies me. "And Cress, she's the one?"

I nod. "I think I knew the day she knocked me down in Oxford, but I wasn't ready. It's only taken twenty years to penetrate. When she was shot, I knew living without her would be impossible."

He claps me on the back. "So how did you screw up?"

I tell him about paying off Aaron Taylor.

"You know, Max, trying to be the hero is a bit of a thing

for Grant men, and you're a chip off the old block." He gives me a long look. "Never ends well, though."

"Great."

"And you want her back?"

"More than anything in the world."

"Well, I think it's time for a grand gesture."

I try to wrap my mind around that. "Like what? I tried to explain, to apologize. But she wouldn't listen."

"And how long has it been since the blowup?"

"A week."

"You're muttering, boy. Speak up."

"A week." People look around. Guess I was too loud.

"She's probably cooled down a bit by now. If she loves you as much as you love her, I think she might accept an apology now. Is there anything she wants from you?"

Hmmm. Is there? Then it strikes me. There is something she wants. No more secrets. "She wants to know about about what happened in Istanbul."

"Then tell her."

I balk, but he's right. If she can't love me despite my past, we have no future. The time for secrets is over.

As we drive back to meet the family for dinner, my heart is lighter. I have a plan.

"Thanks, Dad. I have Grannie's opal as a promise ring if she accepts my apology."

"That's perfect." He whistles a bit of "Stand Fast, Craigel-lachie!" I join in. We pull into the garage, and I hand the keys over to the attendant.

Dad punches my shoulder. "Thanks for a grand day out. The car ran like a dream."

～

CRESS

ALL WEEK MICKI has hammered me. During the day, she's at work. That gives me a little reprieve. If I didn't have the cats, I would have decamped to a hotel days ago.

The more she pushes, the more stubborn I am. Even now, when I know I've made a horrible mistake, I can't admit it to her.

"Cress, you really overreacted. Max did something stupid—"

"Stupid. That's putting it mildly."

"He loves you. He did it out of love."

"I don't need a knight in shining armor. I need a man who…hell, I don't need a man at all."

I miss Max. His warmth. His kisses. The way he wants to take care of me. Even, if I'm honest, his bad jokes. He is careful, solicitous. He has even given me some of his secret hurts. I'm devastated, not by his actions but by mine. After one day without him, I knew I'd made a colossal mistake. How do I fix this? I want him back.

I stare down at my knitting basket, and a plan starts to develop. The first piece is to find out what size socks Max wears. I contact Ian. He approves my plan. Then I need to go shopping. Unwilling to let Micki in on my scheme, I enlist JL for this task but swear him to secrecy.

"A wool shop? Why are we here, Cress?"

"I need some yarn, for socks."

"Socks? I don't understand."

"I knit socks." He gives me side-eye. "They're for Max, to show him I made a mistake."

"Why not just call him and say so?"

"Words aren't enough." Sadness sweeps over me. I contemplate the bleakness of a life without him if he doesn't accept my gift and my apology.

I explain my project to the store owner. We find cashmere blend sock yarn in black, red, forest green, navy, and sky blue. She helps me chart out a mosaic knit design for the cuff that includes a bicycle and the Grant motto, *Stand Fast, Craigellachie!* The rest of the sock will be an argyle pattern in the clan colors.

"What's the bicycle for?" She's busy caking the skeins.

JL has stopped prowling the shop and straddles a chair, his crossed arms resting on the back. "A cute story." He laughs.

"My first encounter with Max was when we were students at Oxford University. I was riding a borrowed bicycle and lost control."

"You fell and he picked you up." She sighs and puts a palm against her chest. Her eyes are starry. "So romantic."

"Not exactly. I ran into him and knocked him down."

"Still, love at first sight, just like the romances I devour. I know lots of readers don't like instalove, but I'm a huge fan."

Well, how about that. A new reader? I'll see if I can find a card to give her when we leave. "Might have been for him." I grin. "I just ran away, embarrassed."

"But you're together now, right?"

"We just had our dark moment." Might as well use romance reader jargon. I sweep my uninjured arm toward the yarn. "This is my grand gesture."

"Oh my God." She gives me a concerned look, disappointment clouding her eyes. "How are you going to knit?"

"I can take the sling off when I'm at home. The physical therapist tells me I have enough range of motion if I'm careful." My statement is airy, unconcerned, but I wonder if I can manage.

"So romantic." She hands JL the bag with the yarn and sock needles. I find a card in the pocket of the vest I am using instead of a purse.

"I write historical romances. If you read ebooks, my medieval romance is free right now." I write the title on the back of the card and hand it to her.

"Oh wow. Thank you so much. Good luck with your socks. Take a picture and post it on our website when it's done."

~

THE SOCKS ARE FINISHED. They're laid out on my lap, and I stroke the soft fabric. I hold one up and admire the design and the even stitches. These are the most complicated socks I've ever made. I've had to take frequent breaks to ice my shoulder and let it rest.

Micki walks into the room. "Socks? You've been knitting socks?"

"I'm ready to apologize to Max. Will you help me wrap them and drive me over to his house?"

~

MAX

I PULL at the bottom of my waistcoat. My dad, Frank, Les, and Ian, all kilted, walk around me. Each casts a critical eye. I am in full regalia—kilt, sporran, jacket, pleated shirt, Grant tartan tie. Even the *sgian-dubh* is in my sock, and there are a couple of additions. I hold a plumed knight's helm in one hand and a sword in the other.

"What do you think, boys? Does he pass muster?"

"I still think the helm is a bit over the top." Frank gestures to the silver bucket resting on my forearm.

"He needs to make this over the top." Ian's suggestions over the past few days have been more and more outrageous. A band of pipers for God's sake.

"I think he's fine." My brother-in-law, Les, never likes to rock the boat.

"Right." Ian checks his phone. "I have the music loaded. It's showtime."

Micki knows the plan. She'll let me in then go join Dad and the rest of the gang at a coffee shop down the street. Once Cress has forgiven me, if she forgives me, I'll text her and they will come in for the grand finale to the grand gesture.

As soon as the lock clicks open, I'm running up the stairs to Micki's fourth floor flat. She opens the door just as I raise my arm to knock. Cress sits on the sofa. When she sees me, her mouth opens. I can't tell if it's in welcome or just shock.

I'm transfixed. Her hair is tumbled, curls cascading down her shoulders. The oversized sweater hides the bandages. I check for her sling. It has been tossed on a table. When I gaze into her eyes, they glint green and gold.

"Did Micki tell you I was coming?" My voice is muffled by the helm.

"No. I didn't tell her anything."

I turn. Micki has slipped on her parka. "I'm leaving now. See you later." The door slams as she walks out.

"Is that a helmet?" Cress' eyes are wide.

I remove it. "Yes, milady." I go down on one knee and

proffer my sword, hilt first. "I am your white knight. I seek your forgiveness for my stupidity and disregard for your feelings. I implore you to accept my fealty and my devotion."

"Oh, Max." Cress' voice is low, unsteady.

She reaches forward and puts her hand on the hilt, winces. I move closer.

"Welcome, sir knight. I grant you forgiveness and accept your fealty and devotion. Please discard your helm and sword and sit with me."

I breathe a sigh of relief as I put my accoutrements on the floor and perch on the sofa, close but not too close.

Cress hands me a bundle, swaddled in colorful paper, that was resting on her lap. "I also seek forgiveness. I was hasty and said things in anger that I have repented since. In return for your devotion, I give you a token of my love."

I tear off the wrapping. Her gift is staggering. Kilt socks. But not just any kilt socks. I finger the cuff, decorated with the Grant family motto and a bicycle. The leg is in an argyle pattern that reflects the tartan I'm wearing. I stroke the soft fabric, slip off my shoes, and swap out the socks. "Did you make these?"

She nods.

"They're amazing. I will wear them with pride."

Mindful of her shoulder, I put my arms around her waist and draw her in for a kiss. I nibble her lips then slip my tongue between them. I can taste the bitter coffee softened with a hint of cream and chocolate she had for breakfast. We can't get enough of each other. My phone beeps, reminding me that time is moving on.

"Cress, I have something to tell you."

"Can't it wait?" She's plaintive.

"No. I need to tell you now, before I bottle it. No more secrets. You deserve to know what happened in Istanbul."

She presses her hand against my chest. "Thank you."

"In November 2003, Al-Qaeda orchestrated several terrorist incidents in Istanbul. One was the bombing of two synagogues during Saturday services. Five days later, the HSBC building and the British Consulate were the targets." I jump up and start pacing. "MI6 had been working with Turkish security services since 9-11, and they heard chatter that the British counsel, Roger Short, might be a target."

"Wasn't he killed in the consulate blast?"

I stop and face her. "Yes." My lips twist in a frown. "He went out to get his shoes polished shortly before the van blew up. After an extensive search, his body was found in the rubble of a shop selling dental chairs."

I'm circling the room. I can't look at her. "I'd been living in Istanbul for about a month when everything went to shit. After the bombings, I was tasked to help the Turks, rounding up the instigators and planners. One was a well-known Al-Qaeda operative named Nasim Faez. He and his brother Ahmet were Yemeni terrorists who had been in Turkey for months, creating an Islamic fundamentalist cell."

When I manage to look at Cress, she's watching me as if she knows this is not the important part of the story. "And?"

I pull off my glasses and run my hands over my face. I can barely get the next words out. "I arrived in Istanbul in early October and met my teammates. Something happened." I look over at her.

Cress stares back. "It must have been momentous."

"Unprecedented." I sit down and scrub a hand over my face. "One of the team members was a woman named Zehra Arslan." A memory of her hits me and I jump back up. More pacing. "Long red hair, wide blue eyes, milky skin. She was gorgeous, but her looks weren't the main attraction. She was smart, fearless, outspoken, went after what she wanted. And she wanted me. She made that clear in the first few minutes after we met."

My legs shake as I see her face redden. My knees give out, and I collapse to the floor. *Fuck.* Maybe she won't be able to forgive me after all. Thorfinn plops down into my lap, rubs his head against my chest. My hand strokes restlessly up and down his smoky gray fur.

"You won't be surprised that relationships were not my thing. I'd managed to avoid anything more than very occasional one-night stands. No entanglements."

I hazard another glance. Cress, her chin resting on a fist, studies me, intent. She gives a thin smile of encouragement.

"Anyway, I was felled like I'd been shot by a cannon. At the end of the week, I'd moved out of my anonymous hotel and into her flat. It was bliss, and I thought it was love."

"You don't think that now?" Cress' voice is hoarse. "Why?"

Acid bubbles into my throat. "E-eh-eh-ahem." Clearing my throat takes a minute. "You taught me what being in love means. Believe me, while my feelings for Zehra were more than lust, they definitely were not the deep commitment I feel for you."

Thorfinn seems to sense my distress and touches a paw against my cheek.

I clear my throat again, desperate to get the rest of it out. "Just before the November 15 bombings, I received a message that Guy was close to death. Frantic, I asked for leave, even if it was just a few days."

My fingers twist together. "I was denied. Things were at a critical point. I didn't take it well. I was resentful, moody. Zehra tried to lift my spirits. Her brother, Yavuz, argued with her, trying to get her to throw me out. He had hated it when I moved in, told her it was a bad idea to get involved with a foreign agent and I wouldn't be around long." My chest heaves, my breath ragged.

Cress' eyes are wet. I want to go to her, put my arms around her. But I resist the pull.

"Guy died on November 18." I bang my fist against the sofa frame. Cress starts to get up, but I wave her back as I struggle to get my voice under control. "Soon after the second bombings, intel came in that seemed to pinpoint where the Faez brothers were holed up, and we quickly put together an operation to catch them."

A paroxysm of coughing stops me. Cress jumps up and gets me a glass of water. I've moved off the floor and onto the sofa. My feet shuffle back and forth against the hardwood. I swallow half the water in a gulp then put it on the side table, not bothering with a mat.

"I had a bad feeling about the operation, and I tried to convince Zehra not to go. We had enough personnel without her. It was the one time Yavuz and I agreed on anything." My hands open and close.

"We had a big fight. The more I tried to convince her not to go, the more she pushed back, insisting it was her choice. I moved back into the hotel. We weren't speaking by the time the operation started.

"Turned out, we had a traitor in our group. The operation was a setup, and the trap was cleverly sprung. Our little convoy turned into an alley. There was a vehicle at the other end, and it exploded. Normally Zehra would have been my driver, but she pointedly chose to drive Mehmet in the second Jeep. Mine was at the end of the line and hadn't made it into the alley when the IED went off. My driver and I were the only two survivors."

Cress gasps.

"I watched her turn into a fireball."

Her hands are over her mouth as she tries not to scream. I hear her gurgling in distress.

"Oh no." Tears pour down her face for a woman she never knew.

I don't bother to tell her about the gunfight, how I killed Ahmet Faez, how Nasim Faez was arrested, shouting about revenge. How Yavuz, who managed to get assigned to drive some Turkish VIP around that day, forgave me for Zehra's death.

Forgiveness…everybody forgave me, but I haven't been able to forgive myself.

"If we hadn't fought, she would have been my driver. She would have survived."

A tissue brushes against my cheek. Cress is on her knees beside me, wiping at the moisture. "It's okay." She holds me, crooning over and over. "You hate that you survived, but you need to forgive yourself. Not for Zehra, not for Guy. For you. Zehra made the choice to go. She made the choice to be in a different vehicle."

I hold up my hand, but she barrels on.

"Even if you had disobeyed and flown home, there is no guarantee Guy would have been alive when you arrived. There was a reason you lived. If you had died, we couldn't be together."

"I might have made it. And if I hadn't pushed so hard, Zehra might have been safe."

"Maybe, might have. There's no guarantee that if you had made different choices, the outcome would have been different. Be grateful that you're still here. I certainly am."

"You don't hate me?"

"I love you. Now you need to love yourself."

I pull my grandmother's Victorian opal and emerald ring

out of my pocket and slip it on her finger. "This is a promise ring. I promise my everlasting love."

Cress' eyes shine. She fingers the ring. "I accept your promise. And I give you mine."

I take a deep breath and pull my phone out of my sporran then tap in *Come now*.

We are entangled on the sofa when the troops arrive.

"What's going on?" Cress pulls away, mouth agape at the sight of four large, kilted men.

My dad steps forward. "Nice to meet you, Cress. I'm Brian Grant, and these are my other sons, Ian and Frank, and my son-in-law, Les." He makes a sweeping gesture. Then he looks me in the eyes, nods his head. "Stand up, Max."

Ian pulls out his phone. The opening rhythms of The Proclaimers' "I'm Gonna Be (500 Miles)" bang out, and the Grant men sing.

Chapter 28

MAX

"Deck the halls." I wince as two off-key voices rend the air.

Ian and Frank bang so hard on the bedroom door that it pops open. My older and younger brothers are much too cheerful for this early hour.

"What time is it?" I groaned.

"Late," Frank carols, off-key.

"About six, you lazy bastard." Ian glories in annoying me.

Cress and I didn't go to bed until after two. Four hours of sleep is pathetic.

"What are you, infants? Are your kids even up yet, Frank?"

"No, they sleep surprisingly late. Must be Liz's influence. Get up, we need to prepare everything before they know Santa's been. Plug in the tree, light the fire, start breakfast. Seriously, Max, where's your Christmas spirit?"

"Too early for it." As Cress stirs, I curse. "Shit, now

you've done it." My brothers look confused. "You've woken Cress. Get out of my bedroom and shut the door behind you. I'll be out in a minute." As I hear the click of my brothers' retreat, I turn to my beautiful partner, who is struggling to sit up.

"What's all the noise? Is it time to get up? It's so dark." Her voice is heavy with sleep.

I lean over and rub her back. "It's too early for anyone but clowns. My brothers are arses. Even the kids aren't up yet. You try to rest a bit more. This day is going to be mad."

Cress looks at me, her eyes looking heavy and bruised with exhaustion. "I thought you said today would be quiet, restful."

I run a finger under the delicate skin of one eye then lean in and kiss each eyelid. She settles her back against the pillows, and I run my tongue along her lips, ending in a passionate, open-mouthed snog. "Between opening gifts and endless meals as well my family's love to talk, it won't be quiet." I have her lying down now, and I caress her hair. "I'll wake you in a little while. Love you."

When Cress makes her appearance around eight AM, we've finished breakfast, and everyone is heading into the living room to open presents. I have spent my entire morning trying to remind everyone to keep the noise level down so she can sleep. My sisters think this is adorable. Mum is annoyed. She hasn't quite forgiven Cress for dumping me. Dad reads the paper and ignores my futile attempts to keep my brothers, nieces, and nephews quiet.

Cress carefully negotiates her way down the stairs. I restrain my urge to run over and help her down. Instead, I move toward the dining room, calling out, "Cress, everything is in here. Come grab something."

Mum is still at table, nibbling a last piece of toast thickly spread with cherry jam, sipping coffee. As Cress shuffles in, she gets up and refills her cup. She pours one for Cress as well—a sign that she is coming around.

"No rush, darling. Have your coffee and something to eat." She gestures at the table, which is littered with pastries, a dish of scrambled eggs, a plate of bacon, and cold toast. "Watching the kids open gifts isn't necessarily exciting—they aren't yours after all. The adult gifts are after."

Cress puts some toast and bacon on a plate and heaps marmalade on the side. Then she adds a few drops of cream to her coffee and puts the cup on the edge of the plate. Everything wobbles, so I grab the plate with one hand and her coffee with the other, and we follow Mum out to join the family.

Cress' voice is still thick with sleep. "I want to see the kids open their gifts. It's nice to see the joy."

I steer her to the oversized armchair and settle her in my lap. She snuggles against me, and I luxuriate in her warmth. The children run around, plunder their stockings, tear the wrapping off their gifts, steal each other's booty while their fathers and uncles grab them for tickles, try to hide already opened presents, and generally mess about. The cats lie at the top of the cat tree, curious but cautious.

Dad pulls over a stool and proceeds to tell Cress about Christmas in Scotland when he was a boy. "I didn't grow up with a huge Christmas celebration. We had a small tree and a few gifts. Scotland is all about Hogmanay, so the family threw a *ceilidh*. But Viktoria, being from an old White Russian family, is all about Christmas. Even they celebrated on the Orthodox calendar, so here we are, full of English and Russian traditions. Except, of course, the stockings are usually hung in the bedrooms. Our concession to being in

America." He gestures vaguely in the direction of the fireplace.

Mum turns to me. "Max, why aren't you playing with the kids?"

I nuzzle Cress' neck before answering. "Happy right here, *Mamushka*. Frank, Les, and Ian should be sufficient." Now that I have Cress back, I'm not letting her go.

My eye is drawn to the tree glowing in the corner. My parents brought other ornaments that are glinting at me. There is a mini St. Basil's, a tiny icon, a silvery salmon, the Grant crest, and a couple of pipers. These representations of my heritage make my breath catch in my throat.

Cress observes Mum, looking for signs that she doesn't approve.

"Hey. Stop thinking about why my family shouldn't like you."

"How do you know what I'm thinking?"

"You are transparent."

"Cress." Meggy motions for her to come over. "We're ready to open the adult gifts. Detach yourself from Max and help me pass them out." She pulls down the stockings. "Once everyone has their pile, we'll keep going round in a circle. Takes an age."

"Seriously Meggy, you're asking Cress to help? You didn't notice the sling?" I frown.

"Put my foot in it again. Just stay where you are, Cress, and soak up my brother's uxoriousness."

"It's fine, Meggy. I still have one working arm."

With reluctance I release Cress so she can join the fun. Meggy starts handing stockings to Cress, telling her who each one is for. Each stocking was specially made. Mine has an Aston Martin, a spyglass, and a rugby ball.

Meggy hands her the next to last. "Cress, this one is for you."

Cress takes the stocking my parents had made for her, holds it up, and turns it back and forth, admiring the design. Then she puts her hand to her heart. Her stocking is decorated with books and cats. An outline of the Chicago skyline runs up the middle on each side.

I pull her back down and, despite her spirited protests, start pulling out the contents—a packet of tea, several mandarins, some walnuts, a tea scoop with Oxford engraved on the bowl, and a clever tea towel with parody books on it. I fish out the square lump in the toe and hand her the small jewelry box.

Her hand shakes as she tries to pry the box open. Grannie's opal winks on her finger, and she squeals with delight when she finds a pair of gold earrings with dangling book charms and small opal beads. "Oh Max, how beautiful. Thank you."

"Why are you thanking me? The stocking gifts are all from Santa. How could you not know that? I'm sorry you were so badly brought up."

"Max, be nice to your girlfriend." Dad's tone is sharp, but laughter lines crease the corners of his eyes.

"Santa must have been consulting with someone close to me to pick such a perfect gift." She slips them into her earlobes.

"Do you have an October birthday?"

Cress shakes her head when Mum mutters sotto voce, "Bad luck."

"December. Turquoise is traditional, but I love opals and don't believe in the old wives' tales. My lucky charm is a beautiful opal." She strokes the gem embedded in a gold Victorian setting.

Meggy halloos.

Frank sends her a sharp look as his children take up the cry. "For God's sake, Meggy, you're not at a hunt. Set a bad example why don't you?"

She ignores him. "Ready for the real gifts now." The kids, who have been trying to entice Dorothy and Thorfinn from their perches, give up and rush over to join the gift-opening scrum.

My family have given me the most amazing assortment of gifts that includes a house sign for the lawn that proclaims I live in Grant Manor, a silk tie with race cars on it, and a cuff-link case with a pair of race-car cufflinks.

"The cufflinks are handmade. I chose the racing-green enamel, but if you prefer red, they can be exchanged." Dad grins.

"They're perfect." I ease Cress off my lap to give hugs to Mum and Dad.

Cress' gift is the piece de resistance. When I open the Bremont box, I am gob-smacked. The Codebreaker is their newest special edition, with historic artifacts from Bletchley Park incorporated into the case. "I can't believe this."

"It's numbered on the back, and yours is the tenth one made. Bletchley Park Trust gets part of the proceeds."

So convenient that she is sitting in my lap as I give her a squeeze. "So, you had already forgiven me?"

A sigh escapes her beautiful lips. "Once I cooled down, I knew I'd overreacted."

I wipe my eyes. "Thank you so much." I can't manage any other words.

Cress is admiring the charm bracelet that matches the earrings in her stocking. There's also a pearl necklace with a Grant family crest pendant, a gift card to Nordstrom's, tickets to three shows at Broadway in Chicago, and gift certificates for brunch at Gather and The Publican.

My family gives her bookstore gift cards and surprisingly sexy lingerie. Then, we blindfold her and lead her into my game room to unveil an air hockey table from Mum and Dad. They asked me to order it before they left London. Cress gurgles but is unable to speak.

Mum raps on the table. "Your dad and I have one more gift for everyone."

We all groan, knowing what is to come, and Cress grabs my arm. "What is it, Max? Everyone else knows. Should I be scared?"

I shake my head no, biting my lip as I try not to laugh.

"Max, Ian, give me a hand." Dad heads up the stairs. We stagger down with piles of wrapped rectangular boxes. The paper is the Grant tartan. Each is carefully labeled, and Mum starts handing them out. Cress gasps as all is revealed— matching reindeer Christmas jumpers for everyone. Stitched round the neck is a Grant tartan ribbon. Cress regards hers with a mixture of horror and delight.

"It's a family tradition. I can't tell you how many Christmas pullovers I have. Mum kept all the kiddy ones, and I have all my adult ones. I have a storage chest just for them."

She's speechless, eyes wide.

"Go get changed." A martinet command from Dad, a reminder of his RAF command.

I lean over to Cress. "We have to wear them until dinner."

"What happens at dinner?"

"Formal dress." I didn't think her eyes could grow any wider. I squeeze her hand. "We'll all be wearing tartan. Kilts for the men, long gowns for the women. Sashes."

"What should I wear?" She sounds panicky.

"I have a Grant tartan sash you can wear with your black

dress. After the holiday, we need to go shopping. You have hardly any clothes."

Five-year-old Vanessa takes her finger out of her mouth. "Where are your jumpers, Mumma and Pop-Pop?"

"In our room, lovey. Let's all change. Then we'll clean up from breakfast and start lunch." Mum starts to round up the brood.

Meggy ambles over to Cress as everyone starts to move, jumpers in hand. I strain to hear. "I was so excited to see that Max got me your book. I want to talk to you about it later."

I could kiss my sister.

~

CRESS

I SCOPE out the dining room while everyone else naps. The table glitters with beautiful china, crystal, and silver, all hired for the occasion. Max told me earlier that the table can seat 24. Such an enormous table struck me as more than over the top, but we are a group of fifteen, so maybe not so unrealistic in Max's world.

An elegant Christmas cracker is positioned at each setting, and caterers toil away in the kitchen to produce the traditional holiday meal. I'm sorry for the two cooks and their helpers who cook, decorate, serve, and clean up.

The main cook has a different view. "I need a breather from my family. Holidays are so intense. They'll be happier to see me if we've all had a few hours apart."

We have drinks in the living room. The men look magnificent in their red and green Grant tartan kilts, even Les, who adopted it when he married into the family. An Englishman, he didn't have a family tartan, so there was no difficulty about competing clans. Max is wearing the kilt socks I made, and the ooohs and aaahs give me goose bumps.

The little girls have cute tartan dresses with nipped-in waists and flared, pleated skirts. They twirl to make the skirts billow. The boys sport white shirts, green vests, and tartan slacks.

The women, including me, wear plain dark green dresses with the clan sash. I was touched when Viktoria handed me a dress and sash. Diana did my hair in a French twist with curls framing my face. The hairpins all have tiny replicas of the Grant crest.

When Max suggested I wear my black dress, he was being sneaky. He told his mother my size and she ordered the dress as they were leaving for the ship. It was waiting at their New York hotel. The ingenuity and generosity of the family is overwhelming. I have had several teary episodes, but I've been able to escape undetected each time. At least I think I have since no one has mentioned anything.

With all the elaborate arrangements, I worry Brian hired a piper as well. However, even he doesn't go that far over the top. Instead, we have a recorded version of the pipes playing the anthem of the Grants as the family processes into the dining room in strict order. First Brian and Viktoria, then Ian with Meggy, Max and me, Diana and Les, and finally Frank and Liz, the couples arm in arm with the kids trailing behind.

I turn to Les, who is seated beside me. "Max didn't tell me what to expect, or anything about the family history."

Viktoria briefly squeezes her eyes closed as Brian clears his throat. Before he can start, Ian puts on his comic Scots accent. "The Grants have a long history of playing both sides in various famous Scottish conflicts, frequently siding with the English. We weren't very popular with other clans, and it didn't help that we're Protestant when many Highlanders stayed Catholic. We weren't affected by the clearances, so there wasn't a lot of emigration. Queen Victoria visited Grantown, home of Clan Grant, and commented on the food."

Brian glowers as Ian goes for the big finish.

He throws out his arms. "And. There. Are. Still. Lots. Of. Grants. Everywhere. THE END."

Everyone laughs.

As he wipes tears of laughter from his eyes, Frank calls to me across the table. "If you want the long history, I've no doubt Dad will be happy to sit with you later and give you the blow-by-blow."

Meggy, on my other side, leans into me and whispers, "It's not that we're not proud of our past, but we've all heard it before, and we'd rather eat."

The kids yell "Hear, hear" and clink their knives and forks against their plates. Bored by adult conversation, they fiddle with the silver and red crackers. I'm so not used to children, but they grow on you, I guess. I can almost imagine being an aunt.

Several treble voices call out in unison. "Dad, can we pull the crackers now?"

Frank grabs his off the plate. "Crackers first, then we eat."

Cheers break out.

Les holds out his cracker. "Don't be nervous."

"Careful, Cress. Watch for the sparks." At that, I glare at Max. Even I know how crackers work.

Les smirks. "The worst that can happen is that it won't pop. These are nice ones, so we should get a good crack. Just take hold of the end. Right, now pull."

The cracker makes a satisfying popgun sound. Les pulls out what turns out to be a paper dunce hat, a charm in the shape of a Labrador, a mini-Maglite, and a slip of paper. Silly though it seems, he puts the dunce cap on.

"Now, let's pull yours." A tiny kaleidoscope, a compass rose charm, and a slip of paper fall out. My hat turns out to be a crown. Max also gets a crown, so we are proclaimed the Christmas King and Queen.

"Thank God." Max blows me a kiss. "I was afraid I'd end up with Meggy or Diana as my queen."

"Were you that sure you would be king?"

"Of course. There's no one kinglier in the room."

"Max, you and Cress should exchange your crowns with your dad and me. We are the obvious king and queen in this family."

Brian nods vigorously. "Hand them over, son."

I take my crown off to give to Viktoria, and Les touches my arm. "They're joking. Put your crown back on and resume your regal expression."

When Max catches my eye, he winks.

To my chagrin, the slips of paper are bad jokes. I discover the Grant family delights in reading stupid jokes like the one Meggy reads out. "Children: This turkey tastes like an old sofa! Mum: Well, you asked for something with plenty of stuffing!"

Guffaws ring out with each new howler. Max comes by his love for bad jokes honestly. They are all done, except for mine.

"Come on, Cress." The calls escalate. I guess I don't have a choice.

"What do you call a bunch of chess players bragging about their games in a hotel lobby? Chess nuts boasting in an open foyer!"

Delighted shouts of laughter greet my less-than-enthusiastic recital. Then silence descends when a fantastic mushroom soup is served. I love mushrooms in any form. The unctuous, creamy liquid, brimful of mushroom pieces, tickles my tongue. I'd ask for another bowl if I didn't know what was coming next.

Replete after goose, prime rib, potatoes, bread stuffing, gravy, sprouts, cabbage, marzipan-stuffed apples, and salad followed by flaming plum pudding with a choice of hard sauce, cream, or custard, we decamp to the living room. The gas fire casts an eerie glow in the darkened room. The children fall asleep on the floor as we sip whisky and Ian, Frank, and Brian tell ghost stories.

In that moment, curled in Max's arms, I watch the firelight and shadows flicker across his gorgeous face. Love fills my heart. I have never had a more perfect Christmas.

Chapter 29

CRESS

Christmas rolls into Boxing Day. We don't follow the British or American tradition of lining up at stores to return unwanted gifts or to shop the sales. Instead, Max arranges for us to volunteer at a soup kitchen.

Having fifteen people show up, ages two to seventy-seven, appears to be a shock for the organizers, but they soon put us to work. We help in the kitchen and dish out food. The guests love watching Felicity, the toddler, bowl around the room. She wheedles for bits of bread and sits on laps. Warmed with love, we go back to Max's place for an early dinner of leftovers.

I'm exhausted, even though I was able to sit in a chair and hand out napkin-wrapped silverware. Max ends his conversation with his dad, picks me up, and carries me off to bed. I barely have time to call out good night as he whisks me away.

I curl up, safe in his arms. We kiss for what seems like

hours, until our lips are so swollen and sore that we have to stop. Max tastes of whisky and brandy, cream and sugar. I slip my hand in his and slide into sleep.

Leave-taking is bittersweet. A large van takes the luggage, now a massive fifty pieces, to Union Station. As a final treat, we descend on Lou Mitchell's for an all-American brunch. Everyone is given a doughnut hole as we walk in, and all the women get mini boxes of Milk Duds.

Stretched out at the long tables that fill the aisles between the fixed booths, we stuff ourselves with three-egg, double-yolked omelets, buttermilk pancakes, and French toast. His family is off on the overnight train to New York.

They will spend one night in the city then take the Queen Mary 2 back to Southampton. I'm huddled against Max as Brian steers the family to the waiting room. The only one missing is Ian. He moved back to his apartment yesterday, complaining about having to work.

The kids run around the Great Hall. Their high-pitched shrieks carry all the way back to the waiting room. Liz and Diana herded them to a more public space in the hope that their yells would be absorbed by the bustle of travelers dragging wheel luggage.

"I guess being older is a good thing. We won't have to worry about children." Max claps his hands over his ears in mock horror, and I give him a sharp look. He pecks my cheek. "Sorry, moving ahead too fast."

I sag against him, relieved. I'm not ready to think of marriage.

His thumb caresses my palm. "Just a matter of time. And I have lots of time."

Brian and Viktoria come over as the call for boarding sounds over the loudspeaker.

"Darling Max, it was so good to see you." Viktoria hugs

him tightly then shakes her finger. "Don't leave it so long next time." She turns to me. "Take good care of my boy. He worries so much about others that he forgets to take care of himself." She air-kisses me on both cheeks.

Brian has already given me a kiss. Now he slaps Max on the back. "When are you coming over? And don't say you don't know or that it will be a year or two. We expect you in the next few months."

I bite my lip. "I have a trip coming up to Paris and Venice in April. Perhaps we can see you then."

Max gives me a stupid stare. I haven't told him about the trip and just committed us to a visit with his family.

"Perfect. Right around my birthday. We'll have a grand party. Send the details soon." Brian emits a loud whistle to gather the family together and points to the gate. The ragtag gang follows down the track to their assigned train car.

A hollow place builds in my chest as they disappear into the maw of the train.

"They were so nice to me."

"Of course they were." He turns and cups my face. "We're going to Venice? Why didn't you say?"

"You're okay with this?"

He grabs me for a long, voluptuous kiss. Wolf whistles and cries of "Get a room" echo through the boarding area.

As we break apart, I take a deep breath. "The conference is a few days after the awards dinner in Paris. I got the confirmation yesterday, but there wasn't a good time to discuss it. I thought I'd wait until they left. I hope you want to go."

"Of course I do, whether or not it interferes with work." His eyes are misty. "What made you decide to tell them?"

"Just tumbled out of my mouth."

My feet leave the ground and Max spins me around like a

top. My legs fly out with wild abandon. When he sets me down, I'm dizzy and grab his arm for support.

He lets out a breath and gazes down the track, where the train pulls out. "We'll see them soon in Scotland. I love them, but I'm not sorry to see them go."

MAX

AFTER SEEING OFF THE FAMILY, Cress and I decide we aren't quite ready to go home. After almost two weeks of nonstop chaos, the idea of returning to an empty house is less appealing than we anticipated. She's healing well enough that we decide to make the twenty-minute walk. I carefully tuck her uninjured arm through mine so I can keep her balanced on the slippery pavement.

Warm air cradles our reddened skin as we push through the door of The Publican. I scan the crowd. Not as many as usual so we don't have to sit long to get one of the few booths. I crave privacy. I want to lose myself in Cress' hazel orbs. Drink in her scent. Caress her skin. I shift as I feel myself harden. Blast. All I want to do is cradle Cress on the sofa and kiss for an hour or two. We should pull up our socks and go home.

"Hey mate." I wave down a server and order a beer flight. Cress gets a glass of red wine. Captivated by the ever-changeable colors, I get lost in the feral glow of her eyes, almost orange. They reflect the burnt amber of her polo-neck sweater.

"Tell me about this trip to Venice."

"A major writer's conference is being held there in April, and I proposed a paper on doing historical research for one of the panels. When I didn't hear anything, I assumed the furor over the plagiarism accusation meant I wasn't selected."

"But you said you only just found out. Does that mean they changed their minds?"

Cress gives a slight cough. "No, I was accepted early on, but the original notification got lost in the mail." Lacing her fingers, she goes on, "They wondered why I didn't respond and called me yesterday. All straightened out. The bonus is that it is a week after the awards dinner in Paris, so we can have a couple of weeks in Europe."

I stroke her palm and wrist with one finger. Her eyes blink rapidly. *Stupid move, Max*, I tell myself. "We could make it a proper holiday. Go to Scotland and spend a bit of time with my parents, then move on to Paris, and cap it off by taking the Orient Express to Venice for your conference."

Cress closes her eyes. Her lips move.

My chest constricts. I'll beg if I have to. I'm at the besotted stage where the idea of being away from her is insupportable. I pull my hair into spikes. "I want to be with you every minute of every day."

She explodes in laughter. "Another week or so of my constant presence will knock that right out of you."

I cough as I gulp down the last dregs of my beer. "I'm up for it."

She sips some water. Her eyes have turned green. Soft, misty like a forest in a drizzle. "I'd love it."

We make our way through the heavy wooden doors that turn each booth into a secret hideaway. After all the huge meals we've eaten, neither of us is hungry. A selection of oysters, charcuterie plate, and salad fits the bill. We manage most of it and have the rest packed up. Cress yawns.

Bundled up in our heavy coats, I use my shoulder against the wind to get the door open. Cress blows out a breath. "Such a relief not to worry about someone out there gunning for me." We push out into the cold, glad our ride has already arrived.

I squeeze her hand. "We shouldn't have to worry about tripping on LEGOs, being ambushed by my mum, or spending hours reminiscing about my childhood peccadillos either."

She silently snuggles into my side, drowsing during the short ride to what I now think of as our home.

When we get out of the car, I sweep Cress into my arms, careful to avoid jarring her still bandaged shoulder.

I carry her up the front steps. "Do you want to stay up for a while? Or are you too tired?"

"What time is it?" she mumbles into my shoulder.

I tighten my arm around her so I can check my watch. "Just past ten."

"Think I want to go to bed. I can hardly keep my eyes open."

I set her down so I can pull out my keys and open the door. Voice-controlled entry goes on my mental to-do list.

Once Cress is in bed, I retreat to the bedroom armchair and watch her sleep.

Cress wakes up about an hour later. "Bathroom." She rolls out, barely getting upright, and hobbles toward the nightlight outlining the open doorway, urgent squeaks sounding in her wake. "Wine and coffee just before bed is a bad idea."

I pull off my shirt and drop my trousers and pants. I'm in bed by the time she comes back, and she snuggles into my arms. My lips caress her neck. I stroke her arm with one hand. She quivers. My other hand cups her chin as I kiss her. I want more than a cuddle.

She stretches. "I'm kind of awake." Her legs rub against mine.

I prop myself up against the headboard, turn on the lamp, and pull her against me, trying to run my fingers through her hair, but the attempt to untangle the curls is a lost cause.

"Oww." She squawks as I pull.

"Sorry." I stroke her back gently and bury my nose into the silky strands. "Guess hair pulling won't be a thing."

"You better believe it. I'm not into pain." She pokes my chest, and I cup the back of her head so she has to look at me. I kiss her neck, just below her ear.

"Got it. No pain." I stroke her cheek, move my fingers down her throat. Caress her breast. "I just want you, Cress. I always want you."

"I want you too. I've wanted you since the first time I saw you."

"In Oxford? The entitled jerk you despised?"

She kisses my chin then puts a finger against my lips.

"I thought you were hot—until you opened your mouth." She giggles. "I would see you punting on the Cher. I could hardly tear my eyes away. You looked like you stepped out of *Brideshead Revisited*, with Sebastian Flyte in a white suit, reclining on the cushions while you poled."

I start laughing at the scene she conjures up. "Was I wearing a boater and striped blazer?"

"What else."

"Your convenient Sebastian was my cousin Guy."

"I didn't know that at the time, and I thought you were lovers."

I bite my tongue in surprise. "O-kay. Did that bother you?"

"It made me sad. Although there was always the hope you'd be bi." She carefully lowers herself and props her uninjured shoulder against the pillows. "Then I met Kev. He was aggressively hetero."

"You preferred that?"

She shrugs. "I had no preference. But he pursued me, and I'd never had anyone show an interest before. There are powerful feelings that rise up when you suddenly wanted for the first time in your life."

I lie down so we are facing each other on the lightly patterned sheets, the duvet pushed to the floor. The minutes stretch interminably.

"When did you decide you wanted me?"

"When we were at Hopleaf." She licks her lips and runs her fingers down my throat. "The way you sucked mussels off the shells. The way they slid down, how your Adam's apple bobbed."

I clamp my jaw at the ludicrous vision. What sounds silly to me turns her on. Who knew?

"So sexy. Like the eating scene in *Tom Jones*." She sucks her fingers as if they were coated with melted butter.

"Did you still think I was gay?"

"I didn't think about it. You seemed to be interested in me, and that was all I noticed." She pushes her hair back behind her ears. "I hate hair in my face."

I reach out, wrap her hair around my fist, and run my tongue over her lips, chapped from the cold. Her mouth opens just enough for me to push inside and stroke her tongue with mine.

Her body vibrates against me. Her voice, when she can eventually speak, is thready. "Max, I'm scared."

"What are you afraid of?" I try to keep the surprise out of my voice as I rub her back. A Jag XJR thrums in my chest. Her gaze locks with mine.

"It's been so long, and my few experiences weren't very

good." Her voice catches in a sob. Her skin is white marble, the veins a delicate blue. I trace one finger up her arm from the wrist to the elbow as pinkness suffuses her chest above the scoop of her tank top.

I caress her cheek, silent for a moment. "How long?"

Her face turns bright red as she shifts away from my touch, folding her arms. "Since Oxford. Kev has been the only one. He told me I was terrible in bed. He made it clear that was why he was leaving me. After that, well, I wasn't interested." Her voice is flint, hard and sharp.

I'm stunned. "After three years? He was with you for three years and that's his excuse at the end? Bastard." I pull back, catch her gaze with mine. "Not bloody likely. One night or one week, maybe, if he was a prick. Three years..." My fingers blanch as I clench my fists. "An inadequate prick, blaming you for his own shortcomings. You were inexperienced. If he had been a caring lover..."

I sit quiet, watching as she mops up and blows her nose. I put my hands on my head, scratching at my scalp, trying to figure out where to go next. When she throws the tissue on the night table, I drop my hands to her shoulders.

"We don't have to do anything tonight." I know she hears the longing I can't suppress. My body is primed, and I squirm, trying to get comfortable. She glances down and sees the bulge in my sleep pants, bites her lip.

"I can't put it off forever." She sounds like she's steeling herself for a session in a torture chamber.

"Best wait until you want sex. I want to give you joy, not help you cross a chore off your list." I try to make my voice sound light. "If sex is going to be an ordeal, we can just cuddle until we fall back asleep."

She gives a little shake. Terror and desire war in her expression, her eyes orange pools, her lips almost burgundy.

After a few seconds, her shoulders drop, and her muscles soften. Her arms come around my neck.

"Not an ordeal." Her kiss burns my lips. "I want you, Max. I want you more than my fear."

"Don't worry. It's like riding a bicycle. We'll be good together."

She twitches then laughs. "And we know how good I am at riding a bike."

"You can knock me down any time."

I can hear what she isn't asking. What if penetration is painful? What if we have a bad experience? What if, what if? She vibrates with the fears.

"What if I'm so bad you leave me in disgust?" It comes out on a sob.

"Hey, there's nothing about you that would disgust me." I smooth her hair. "We'll take things slowly. My only goal is to make you melt with desire. We can stop whenever you like."

I wonder if, at a certain point, I won't be able to stop, even if she begs. No, that can't happen. I've never been that lover, even if my experiences have mostly been one-night stands.

I push on. "However far we get, if you feel good, we'll have had a successful evening. Just relax and let me cherish you." I pull her in close, kissing her over and over as I caress her everywhere. Her body relaxes, melts, opens to me. "We'll keep at it until we're perfect, and then we'll keep at it because nothing is ever perfect."

She smiles, and I hear her hum against my throat, like bees on a hot summer day. I'm not sure what the music is, and now is not the time to ask. I lie on my back, position her on top of me, and tell her I love her, over and over and over.

Chapter 30

CRESS

I'm curled up on the chaise longue in a gray t-shirt and my cat-face flannel pajama bottoms, meditating on the last week. Sex gets better and better. Practice makes perfect after all. I've been able to come to terms with feelings I've repressed for almost twenty years. I'm a little sore, but I don't mind.

After the catharsis of Max's revelations, my fears of abandonment evaporated. We can work through our roadblocks now. There's open and honest communication and trust. Max's feelings of guilt haven't magically disappeared. He hasn't finished mourning. Maybe he never will, but the corrosion of guilt has lessened. He hasn't had a nightmare since he told me about Istanbul.

Episodes of insecurity may still blindside me, but my ice walls have melted. Max's protective armor has been blown to smithereens.

I reach down to pick up the book that is face down

on the floor. Dorothy, snuggled up against me, raises her head and glares at the movement. Thorfinn stands a little way off, meowing loudly. He wants a share of the action.

The front door clicks open, and a loud "Fuck" rings out. "Bloody nuisance." Shoes bang against a wall. "Bugger." The voice is louder. As Max walks, his gait sounds uneven.

I look over into the glowering eyes of the man who is my whole world. He limps. Pain twists his mouth as he continues to mutter curses. I push off an indignant Dorothy as Thorfinn scampers out of the way. Max puts out a hand and lowers himself to the couch.

"Twisted my bloody ankle. Slipped on the ice."

"You were running on ice?"

"No, I slipped when I got out of the car. I thought I'd park in front to make it easier when we go out later."

"I'll get you a cold pack." I move toward the kitchen, tripping slightly over the toes of my socks, but I manage to recover my balance. Two gimps, what a pair.

I hear him laugh at the irony. "Fuck it, Cress. Be careful. We don't need two bloody invalids, and your ankle has just healed."

I drop to my knees, wrap his ankle, and pull the Velcro tight. Then I push over an ottoman to elevate his leg.

"Do you think you'll be able to go?" Max and I are meeting Micki for brunch at Big Jones in a few hours. I've ignored my grumbling stomach in anticipation of shrimp and grits. "We can cancel. I'll make you waffles. We still have back bacon in the freezer."

"I'll be fine." Max grits his teeth. "There are crepe bandages under the sink in the lav. I'll wrap it after the ice treatment."

I climb the stairs, rummage through the small cabinet

where all the medical supplies are kept, and triumphantly emerge with two ACE bandages of different lengths.

I walk down humming Dan Fogelberg's "To the Morning," which is playing on my iPad. I can remember waking up to it every morning at six AM when I was a teenager. Thank you, Jim Unrath, for introducing me to Fogelberg's music. A peaceful wave flows through me.

I hear the downstairs bathroom door slam as I negotiate the steps. I still favor my ankle, and the shoulder brace makes me awkward. Typing with one hand is awkward, and the dictation software isn't great.

Thankfully, my editor is being understanding about deadlines. I can't believe it will be another month before it can come off. All the knitting I did for Max's socks set me back. Totally worth it.

Max limps out of the bathroom. He's balling up paper towels as he hobbles back toward the living room. With his sleeves rolled up to the elbows, I can admire the fine dusting of hair on his lightly muscled forearms.

His magnetic field pulls me like a heap of iron filings. He hugs me, and the wad of paper scratches against my skin. With a shamefaced grin, he looks down at the mess in his hand then tosses it toward a waste basket in the corner.

"Been thinking…even though your condo fits you to a T, I could never be comfortable there, even after the rebuild is complete. It would be like living in a doll's house. Once the renovations are done, please sell it or rent it out or something and stay in my spacious abode forever."

He gestures around the room like a realtor doing a showing.

Then he pauses, looking puzzled. "This is unfamiliar music. Not classical."

"No. It's Dan Fogelberg."

"Who?"

"He was a Chicago folk-rock singer. Went to U of I for a couple of years."

"Your alma mater." Max winces as he refastens the ice pack.

"He died of prostate cancer a few years ago." The stricken look in Max's eyes tears at my heart. "I've always loved this song. The promise of a new day is so—"

"Hopeful." Max's shoulders relax.

"If we're still going, would you be willing to retrieve one of your fancy cars?"

"Sorry, *la mia stellina*. Too slick. And I don't want to chance the clutch with a wonky ankle. We'll have to take the SUV."

I glance at said ankle. "I have to go to Anderson's after brunch. Is that too much of a drive?"

"We'll be in Andersonville already." He looks puzzled.

"Not Andersonville, Anderson's."

"Anderson, Indiana? What for?"

"No, Anderson's Bookstore."

"That's all the way out in Naperville. Won't something closer, like City Lit or the Book Cellar or Women and Children First, have what you want? Why drive all that way when the roads are still icy?"

"I don't need a book." I grin. "I have a meet and greet there this afternoon. I thought we'd take Micki along. I'm in great demand now that I've been shortlisted for the new Sigrid Undstet Prize for Women's Historical Fiction. If it's too much of a drive, I'll Uber out."

I got the word yesterday, along with the last-minute invitation to do the pop-up signing. After all the brouhaha over Tina's plagiarism accusation, the nomination for another prize is sweet.

"Should be okay. Thank God I rucked my left ankle."

Max reaches out with his long arm, grabs my wrist, and pulls me down. "Congratulations." He kisses my hand. "You deserve it." He strokes my cheek. "You need an award a day." He licks my ear. "Perhaps one every hour."

By now I'm dissolving with laughter.

"You've already congratulated me." I wriggle out of his embrace. "I thought we could celebrate it on New Year's Day with a party."

"Sounds like fun." He looks at his phone. "Well, I'll be damned." The skin around his eyes crinkles as he scans the screen. "Micki will meet us at Big Jones."

"Why is she texting you?" I can't repress my miffed tone. She's my friend, dammit.

"She didn't. That was JL. He's coming to brunch, too."

That makes more sense. I'm so glad Micki and JL are exploring the possibilities. She needs someone fun to hang with.

"I thought something might be going on there." Then my gaze shifts and I point to the wad of paper towels lying in the basket. "What's with the paper towels?"

He looks down. "Oh yeah. I noticed soap in the sink when I went to put on the crepe bandage. Lots of soap."

One of his puerile jokes. I turn away, trying not to laugh.

"It dripped all over from that automatic dispenser Paul and Ellie gave you."

Okay, not a joke. Thorfinn reappears, paws at my leg, chirrups. I look down. His wet feet soak through my pajama pants. I wrench my attention to Max.

"The soap was all over when I went in. It was a mess." He retrieves the balled-up paper. "I cleared it up, hence the towels. Not sure why I carried them in here, though. I'll take them out to the kitchen."

I jump up, almost tripping over the door sill as I rush into the bathroom. My attention is on Dorothy, who stands in the deep, rectangular, stainless-steel sink. With every wave of her tail, soap oozes out of the all-too-handy automatic dispenser, globs covering the bottom of the sink. I turn, cracking up, right into Max's arms.

"Hah. You're falling about."

"It's the cats." My stomach starts to ache I'm laughing so hard.

Max leans against the wall to take the strain off his ankle, pulls me close, and tips my face up, kissing me hard. As my laughter turns to passion, my breathing becomes labored. Eventually, slowly, I pull away, flushing.

Then I tell him the joke I've managed to memorize. "I tried to say, 'I'm a functional adult,' but my phone changed it to 'fictional adult,' and I feel like that's more accurate."

"A joke—I don't believe it. You will be a proud addition to the clan one of these days." Max grabs my hand, pulls me in again. "Come on, help me up the stairs so we can get dolled up for brunch."

I look at our entwined hands then gaze into his serene gray eyes. My heart cracks open. I may not have fallen in love at first sight, but I'm all the way there now.

I look up at his smiling face. *Mine*, I think. *Max is mine.*

Peek behind the scenes with Max and Cress

Sign up for my newsletter, "Sharin' the (Micha)love" for your FREE copy of *At First Sight Outtakes*

AFTERWORD

Guy's letter to Max is based on a journal entry written by my late husband, Peter Michalove. From the time he retired from the University of Illinois at Urbana-Champaign in 2006 until his death in December 2013, Peter devoted much of his time and energy to teaching about and composing music. When he realized that he was dying of very aggressive prostate cancer, he decided that one way to cope was to write a record of his feelings while he was ill.

This particular piece was written about how he felt when he found that he was no longer able to compose a piece of music he had promised to a friend. Fortunately, another composer who was a friend of both Peter and the performer, was willing to take up the task and the piece, for viola and clarinet, was played at his memorial concert in February 2014. I would like to thank composer Elaine Fine for the composition "Three Character Pieces (and one Transcription) for Clarinet and Viola," and Lydia Tang for her performance . I just wish that Peter had been able to hear it.

I modified his essay very slightly for clarity and length, but all the words are his.

ACKNOWLEDGMENTS

Thanks to all the people who have helped along the way—early readers, cheerleaders, betas, writing groups, critique partners, and fellow writers. I couldn't have done it without you. If it takes a village, mine is large.

As a person who has never had much interest in cars, I was stunned when Max insisted that cars were a major part of his life. I would like to acknowledge three people who were very generous with the details that helped me write about Max's passion. Thank you so much to race car driver and knitter extraordinaire Merritt Scott Collins, my brother Mark Grodsky, and my nephew Benjamin Grodsky. That said, any errors are mine.

ABOUT THE AUTHOR

I was born in Chicago and grew up in the suburbs. I moved back to Chicago in 2017. Besides watching hockey, travel is my passion. I love history, reading, cooking, writing, and various less elevated activities like eating pastry and sampling gins and single malts.

My goal is to create stories full of romance, suspense, and mystery. Seasoned romance where love has no age limit. Stories that prove second chances can happen, enemies can become friends, and friends can become lovers. Stories that show no two happy endings are the same. And at the core of every story is love.

If you liked this book, please think about leaving a review on Goodreads or Amazon. Thanks.

To be in the loop for new releases and giveaways, you can subscribe to my newsletter at sharonmichalove.com.

ALSO BY SHARON MICHALOVE

AT THE CROSSROADS

COMING IN 2022

Max Grant finally has the girl of his dreams but his past roars back with a vengeance when he is targeted by a Turkish terrorist seeking revenge for an event ten years ago.

Made in the USA
Middletown, DE
25 September 2021